THE MYSTERIOUS LOST CHILD

THE MYSTERIOUS LOST CHILD

THE INSCRUTABLE PARIS BEAUFONT™ BOOK 2

SARAH NOFFKE
MICHAEL ANDERLE

DISRUPTIVE IMAGINATION®

LMBPN Publishing
PMB 196, 2540 South Maryland Pkwy
Las Vegas, NV 89109

First Edition, April 2021
eBook ISBN: 978-1-64971-689-7
Print ISBN: 978-1-64971-690-3

THE MYSTERIOUS LOST CHILD TEAM

Thanks to the JIT Readers

Misty Roa
Dave Hicks
Dorothy Lloyd
Deb Mader
Debi Sateren
Zacc Pelter
Veronica Stephan-Miller
Jackey Hankard-Brodie
Diane L. Smith
Angel LaVey

If I've missed anyone, please let me know!

Editor
The Skyhunter Editing Team

To the ladies who are responsible for keeping me sane, Jess and Cry. Some would say you're doing a lousy job, but those dummies have no idea how crazy I'd be without you.

— Sarah

To Family, Friends and
Those Who Love
to Read.
May We All Enjoy Grace
to Live the Life We Are
Called.

— Michael

CHAPTER ONE

Not quite alive and definitely not dead, the Deathly Shadow soared through Roya Lane, slipping around corners and haunting the mostly deserted streets. The entity hadn't been a man for a long, long time. It had been even longer since it lost its soul.

Well, one didn't really lose that which they gave away...

When the Deathly Shadow encountered a person on the cobbled lane, they didn't notice the smoky presence that passed through them like a ghost. However, they felt the pain and haunting anguish that the evil source left with them.

Most never knew when the Deathly Shadow had been around them. A person might feel a chill, think a draft had swept through the space, or get a strange foreboding feeling that they couldn't place. It was also common to suddenly feel utter despair as if all hope in the world was lost. That, at its core, was the Deathly Shadow and what had made the monster what it was. The lack of hope invited in a host of misery, and it spread like a disease making the monster supremely evil.

"Finally," the Deathly Shadow growled, slowing and circling in the misty fog settling around Roya Lane. The black creature went unnoticed most of the time, only registering to others as a plume of smoke. However, in the dark of the cobbled streets and with the thick fog it was even harder to make out the form that twisted and turned in the air, snaking its way until it centered itself in front of the Fairy Law Enforcement Agency.

"I have waited a very long time for this," the Deathly Shadow hissed to the cold night air in a haunting voice as it lurked outside the office, watching a dark figure moving behind the agency's large windows.

For two decades, the Deathly Shadow had searched for the girl who was both a fairy and a magician with unique blood—having learned the prophecy that she'd be born to Warriors for the House of Fourteen. For too many long years before that, the demon had searched for the key. Guinevere Paris Beaufont was it—she was the key to bringing back his body. Only her blood would work. Not simply because she was a halfling, but partly because of that.

Her parents had learned of the prophecy too and took action. Until now, the Deathly Shadow hadn't known where to find the missing girl. However, someone had revealed the truth the night before, and word spread fast. Now the dark entity knew where the halfling was.

The problem was the Deathly Shadow couldn't reach the fairy who was also a magician. Not presently. Not while she was at fairy godmother college. Still, as the monster lurked outside the Fairy Law Enforcement Agency, it grew more confident that its plight was drawing to an end.

The Deathly Shadow watched as someone moved behind the building's windows. This had been where they'd hidden the girl—on Roya Lane, behind the disguise of a new identity. The person inside had to be the one who had protected the halfling all these years, keeping her hidden from the Deathly Shadow.

That time was over. It was finally the end of being disembodied for the Deathly Shadow. Of being a cloud of smoke and energy and evil thoughts. It was time to track down Guinevere Beaufont and take her life force, giving the Deathly Shadow back that which had been stolen—his body.

With a building rage that shook the stone streets of Roya Lane, the black smoke darkened, nearly solid for a moment. The windows of the Fairy Law Enforcement Agency vibrated violently until they all shattered. The person on the other side screamed, glass exploding all over them. Then the monster swept into the office to strangle the fairy, putting him one step closer to Guinevere Beaufont.

Now that the Deathly Shadow knew where to look, he wouldn't stop until he had blocked every escape route for the halfling, leading her straight into his waiting grasp.

CHAPTER TWO

"What do you think the chances are that last night's whole fiasco was a dream?" Paris asked Faraday, the talking squirrel, as she sat on the edge of her pink canopy bed and tugged on her boots.

"Do you want the news that you're a halfling born to Warriors for the House of Fourteen, who changed your identity for no known reason and mysteriously disappeared to be a dream?" His matter-of-fact response floated over from where he sat on the windowsill and eyed the grassy lawn of the Enchanted Grounds.

Paris tied her shoes and blew out a breath. "No, actually, I don't."

For some reason, Paris slept better the night before than she'd remembered in a long time. She would've thought the shocking news of her true identity would leave her mind reeling with possibilities. However, it was the opposite.

Before, Paris always wrestled with a quiet sense of longing that she never quite understood. For some strange reason, she never questioned that her parents were absent. Now it seemed obvious to her that she should have wondered about them. Wanted to see pictures of their faces. Asked her Uncle John questions...and yet, she had never been curious about it.

Still, the longing—well, that was always there when she awoke, went about her day, and especially at night when everything got quiet. However, last night she fell into a dreamless sleep as if something suddenly lifted off her.

"It's just that it's a lot, and I realize now that the sun has risen that I'm not the only one who knows my little secret," Paris confessed and stretched to a standing position.

Faraday poked his head out the open window and peered around. "According to my calculations, the entire college knows that you're a halfling with an assorted past."

"What are these calculations based on?" Paris leaned down and rested her elbows on the windowsill, looking out and hoping to catch a refreshing breeze on her face. Instead, she saw something that confirmed the nervous feeling in the pit of her stomach.

Faraday nodded in the direction of the various groups huddled on the Enchanted Grounds. "My calculations are based on observation."

Paris shoved the squirrel more behind the curtain, hoping that the students pointing toward her open window hadn't seen him. She was already the center of attention at Happily Ever After College. The last thing she needed was for everyone to know she talked to a squirrel.

She slid her back against the opposite wall and glared at the squirrel. "I hope no one saw you."

"I don't think they did." He checked his tiny arms as if her abrupt action might have harmed them. "But if you wanted to get their attention, assaulting an animal would do that."

Paris rolled her eyes. "I didn't hurt you."

"Only on the inside." He sniffed. "Yes, I think that everyone at Happily Ever After College knows the news and they all appear very interested in it."

Sighing, Paris nodded. "Maybe it's not too late to go to jail instead of serving my sentence here at the college."

"I fear your problems will follow you there," Faraday stated. "Isn't that where they're likely to send Shannon Butcher?"

Paris gulped, realizing he was right. "Yeah, and the witch would probably tell everyone who I was."

"I'm guessing that most of the criminals in jail were put there by your parents, Liv Beaufont and Stefan Ludwig. From what I've heard of those Warriors, they were quite effective at enforcing magical laws and putting those who broke them away."

"I don't know anything about them," Paris admitted, the idea still so foreign that her parents were these people—who were important, apparently. Or that she never cared to think about who her parents were...not until then, as if a spell had lifted that kept her from wondering.

Faraday leaned forward and peered out the window again. "I get the impression that others here might know about the Warriors for the House of Fourteen based on the excited chatter."

"Yeah, and all that interest is what I was worried about. I mean, I get that I was outed in front of a ton of people so I should expect many to know the news."

"Something like this, that's of supreme interest and a rarity will definitely spread," Faraday observed. "According to what I'm aware of, there has never been a godmother who wasn't a fairy, so Headmistress Starr allowing such a thing is unprecedented."

Glancing up at the ceiling, Paris pretended to talk to the heavens. "Dear angels above, please stop with the hallucinations. I'll be good, I promise. Or at least I'll try."

"Why is it that you believe you're hallucinating?" Faraday asked. "Is this like earlier when you thought it possible that you dreamed last night's news?"

She shook her head. "No, it's because I'm talking to a squirrel about my problems, which he refers to as unprecedented after making 'calculations' and 'observations.'"

"I don't see what's so weird about that," he huffed.

"Well, I do," she chimed. "Now that it's all starting to sink in and I realize how much investigating I'll need to do, I wish I got to deal with all this without everyone being in my business."

"Will it help if I assist with the investigation?" Excitement buzzed in Faraday's large brown eyes. "Research is my very favorite thing."

"Whereas all other squirrels' favorite thing is to jump from branch to branch," Paris teased.

He grimaced. "Those squirrels are so very uncivilized. There are so many better ways to spend one's time. Well, unless they were testing and studying the laws of gravity. Then I'd approve of such activities."

Paris couldn't help but laugh. "One of these days, I'm going to figure out what's wrong with you."

"Or what's right with me," he countered. "Until then, you want my help with researching?"

Paris shrugged. "I guess it wouldn't hurt. Meet me in the study area during lunch. We'll see what we can dig up."

"It's not the Great Library, but I guess it will do." He exhaled a disappointed sigh.

"Great Library?" she questioned.

His eyes widened. "It's the best place on Earth with every volume that's ever been written, although I'm not allowed there."

"Because you're a squirrel?" she guessed.

"Yeah, sure," he chirped. "But you will be allowed entry as a fairy godmother, so maybe you'll smuggle me in at some point."

"Maybe," she sang while heading for the door and waving over her shoulder. "See you later and stay out of trouble."

"You too, although I realize that's a lot to ask and highly improbable."

She rolled her eyes at him. "You're highly improbable."

CHAPTER THREE

A hush fell over the crowded dining hall as soon as Paris entered. She tensed, looking at the many faces that were studying her. Whispers started to spread throughout the line of students and fairy godmothers standing in the buffet line or seated at the long table.

"That's her," she heard someone say in a hush.

"Magician," someone else hissed.

That was all followed by more terse inaudible whispering that immediately made Paris want to spin on her heels and head back to her room. Maybe she didn't need to eat—ever again. Or perhaps jail was the right place for her. She could convince the inmates that she wasn't like her parents...or her uncle, who was also probably responsible for many being locked up in prison.

Time seemed to freeze as Paris remained stock still and everyone in the large dining hall continued to regard her like she was a caged monkey.

"Oh, would you all stop staring at me!" Christine exclaimed, arriving in the room and standing next to Paris, her hands in the air. "I get that I performed a pretty awesome binding spell on

Professor Butcher, but can we all move on from those events? There are better things to do with our time." Her gaze landed on the pile of bacon on the buffet. "Like eat that maple bacon."

That broke the tension, and all at once, everyone went back to what they were doing, filling their plates, eating, or talking.

Christine breezed by Paris, making for the buffet line.

Letting out a sigh of relief, Paris took the spot behind Christine, picking up a warm plate from the buffet's start. "Thanks for that."

The fairy turned about, glancing at her with mock surprise. "For what? Calling out these gossipers for not having their own life and gawking?"

Paris offered her a tame smile as she loaded up on eggs, country potatoes, and of course, maple bacon. "Thanks for breaking the tension. I was about to hightail it out of here."

Christine shook her head of bluish-gray, straight hair. "Don't let them get to you. Nothing ever happens here so you've given these busybodies the first real thing to talk about in ages."

Paris still received curious glances and heard whispers from the crowd, but it was a lot less noticeable than before. "You were pretty good with the binding spell."

The fairy beamed and turned to search for a spot at the crowded dining room table. "Why, thank you. I only knew the spell because of you, which means you must teach me more. All I know at this point to get me out of dangerous situations is how to turn caterpillars into butterflies and make flowers intoxicate people. If I get mugged, I'm screwed."

Paris laughed. "Why would you need those spells anyway?"

"Apparently butterflies and drunkenness help people fall in love." Christine pointed at a set of empty seats. "You want to sit over there?"

Paris nodded, grateful that her new friend was still that—her friend. She expected that she'd experience a good deal of prejudice now that everyone knew she was also a magician.

The two races didn't always get along since they were so different, with unique skill sets that didn't always complement one another. Fairies, as a race, were all about love and harmony. Magicians, on the other hand, were all about logic and intellect. They often insulted each other by stating that the other race was missing what was important. Still, what if they were supposed to be complementary? Paris had often wondered, and now she knew why.

Chef Ash and Hemingway sat opposite the pair when they took seats. They both wore unquestionably curious expressions, but thankfully they were both directed at Christine.

"That was quite the display you made just now," Chef Ash teased with a broad grin. He was in his chef's uniform, his trademark pencil behind his ear.

"Well," Christine drew out the word as she held up a strip of thick bacon. "Everyone was staring at me, and you know how I don't like the attention."

Hemingway laughed. The dimple in his right cheek surfaced, and the glint in his blue eyes twinkled. He wore his usual button-up flannel shirt, and his dark brown hair was windswept from being outside. "I don't think they were staring at you."

"Since when do you not like the attention?" Chef Ash asked.

Christine craned her head around to look at a group of girls who weren't even hiding their pointing in their direction. Becky Montgomery was at the center of the group. "It's weird. It's almost like you all have never seen a magician before."

"We've seen them," Becky fired back. "It's just that we're not used to them bending the rules to get into our college and creating so much drama."

"Coming from the drama queen, that's funny," Chef Ash said under his breath.

"Well, you did fail cotillion a few times didn't you, Becky," Christine quipped. "So I get that manners aren't really your thing. Most well-behaved people know that you're not supposed to stare and point, especially at people who can probably blow you up with magic if they chose."

Red flared across the bridge of Becky's nose as her friends all sat back in an embarrassed hush. She glanced around at the girls. "Mother says that word about the halfling invading our school is already spreading in the magical world. Saint Valentine is probably going to intervene. Otherwise, this could be bad for the college's reputation."

Paris wanted to point out that Headmistress Starr had endorsed her staying at the college. However, to her disappointment, Willow wasn't anywhere to be seen. Nor was Mae Ling. Without them there, it would only be her word, and currently, that didn't seem like a very credible source.

Penny Pullman took the seat on the other side of Paris, giving her a nervous glance before glancing down the table at Becky and her bully friends.

"Didn't your mother fail the entrance exam to Happily Ever After College three times?" Christine asked Becky, appearing quite serious in her reply before turning her attention to Paris. "After that, the money to fund the observatory magically appeared, and Margo Montgomery was allowed entry to the college."

Becky's nose shot straight into the air. "My mother got in here of her own accord, and my family has often donated to the college. Regardless, we get into the college through honorable means. Not because of who our uncle is or because we're trying to stay out of jail."

Christine nodded as if she couldn't care less and glanced at Paris. "Why did you almost go to jail?"

Although the question felt threatening, the curious and excited expression on Christine's face melted away any tension surrounding it, putting Paris more at ease. "A series of supposed criminal offenses, mostly where I was at the scene of a crime that I wasn't guilty of."

"That's what all criminals say," Becky retorted.

"How would you know what criminals say?" Hemingway asked, taking a bite of a breakfast sandwich.

"I don't have to answer that." Becky sounded flustered. "You all socializing with a reject halfling will undoubtedly reflect on you."

Christine nodded understandingly. "Undoubtedly. Good thing we aren't hobnobbing with rich snobs. Imagine how that would make us look."

"Like real losers," Penny related and flushed red, suddenly embarrassed.

Becky and her friends all shot them angry expressions before turning their narrowed gazes toward each other to huddle up and probably gossip.

Chef Ash leaned forward, tapping the table between them. "Well, on the long list of good things you've done, Paris, you've made the good fairy godmother students speak up for themselves and the not-so-good ones, well, do what they've always done." He directed his thoughtful gaze to Penny, who flushed even pinker.

"I don't know why I said it...it's just that—"

Christine cut her off with a laugh. "That you finally don't feel like being the butt of Becky's jokes since you realize that you don't have to be. You helped pin down the worst of the bullies, Professor Butcher, with me and you finally have some confidence?"

Penny nodded, although she still looked ashamed.

"I'm not here to create trouble," Paris admitted when things went silent.

"No, you stirred everything up and questioned the status quo." Hemingway laughed. "I think we needed a little trouble in our midst. Otherwise, when was real change going to happen?"

Chef Ash nodded. "I agree. People like Becky Montgomery and her family have been running things for too long. I bet that Saint Valentine does hear about this and investigates, then realizes that his problems are because of deeper structural problems at Matters of the Heart and FGM Agency." He pulled the pencil from behind his ear and pointed it at Paris. "I've said for the longest time that this place needed some diversity. Good on Headmistress Starr for finally implementing it, which reminds me, there's a five-layer cake I've wanted to experiment with." He magicked some paper and went straight to sketching.

As if his spell had sparked something, an envelope appeared beside Paris' plate. She looked up at the others, silently asking for their input on the sudden appearance of the note.

"It's a new class schedule," Hemingway answered without her having to ask.

"I'm guessing with Professor Butcher gone, you'll be reassigned something," Penny stated.

"Well, and she tested out of that dumb class," Christine stated. "I bet the headmistress replaced it with something more helpful. I hope so. Maybe combat magic."

Excited to see what she would be learning instead of table manners and napkin folding, Paris tore into the envelope and ran her eyes over what was definitely her new class schedule. Then her hope disappeared. A new class replaced Cotillion, but it wasn't something that interested Paris much at all, and she had zero hopes that she'd be good at it.

Her class schedule was the same as it had been with ballroom dancing, astrology, magical gardening, then cooking and baking. However, added to the list was one that didn't at all pique her interests, but she admitted it was probably necessary for fairy godmothers. It was called Art of Love.

CHAPTER FOUR

Paris had said farewell and parted with her friends before asking them where she could find her first class—Art of Love. It still felt so strange to call real people "friends." She almost thought she was going to jinx herself. Still, they had stuck up for her when Becky the Bully had tried to insult her, calling her a criminal magician halfling. In truth, that's what Paris was, and she realized she should probably own it rather than try and defend herself.

Finding the hallways empty since most were still eating breakfast, Paris decided to call on the one person always eager to help her.

"Wilfred, I need your help," she said aloud to the deserted corridor.

A moment later, the polished butler appeared out of seemingly nowhere wearing a three-piece pinstriped suit with tails as usual and a restrained expression. "Yes, Ms. Beaufont?"

Paris started at the name, not used to being called that yet. It was hers, although it didn't feel right. She desperately wanted to talk to Uncle John and ask him so many questions. Of all the times for him to be on a stakeout and unreachable, this was the absolute worst. It was almost as if someone had planned it all, but who could coordinate such a thing? Only someone very powerful and all-knowing like Father Time, if such a person existed, although Paris doubted it.

Sensing her tension, Wilfred offered her a thoughtful expression. "Do you not prefer to go by that name? I can call you Ms. Westbridge if you prefer."

She forced a smile. "It's fine. It is my name after all."

"And a very good one," he remarked proudly.

"Oh, you would know about the Beaufonts, wouldn't you?" Paris realized with surprise. "You know about everything, right?"

"Anything I can find on the World Wide Web," he stated.

"So pretty much everything then," she joked, but this didn't produce a laugh from the AI magitech butler.

Clearing his throat, Wilfred Bitmore recited, "The Beaufont family are one of three founder families for the House of Fourteen. They are magicians of Royal blood and are tasked with protecting magic from an unknown source. Would you like me to continue?"

Indeed Paris did. The little bit of information on her real family was instantly like an addictive drug, and she desperately wanted more. However, she would be late for her first class if she wasn't careful. "I do, but not right now. I'll page you when I have a break."

"I will be happy to help when you call on me." He bowed. "Now, is there anything else that you need?"

She nodded. "Yes, I don't know where my first class is, Art of Love. Can you please direct me?"

He held out his hand. "I'll do one better and take you to your professor's office. She is still there and probably will want to see you beforehand."

"Oh," Paris said with surprise, wondering who this professor would be that wanted to see her.

CHAPTER FIVE

Paris was surprised when the butler led her to the headmistress' office.

"Headmistress Starr is my professor for Art of Love?" she asked as Wilfred lifted his white-gloved hand to knock on the closed door.

"Naturally." He rapped three times and waited for the okay to enter.

"Come in, Wilfred," Willow said, probably used to the butler's trademark knock.

He opened the door and stepped through. "Ms. Paris Beaufont to see you, madam. I thought you might want to see her before your first class."

Sitting behind her desk in her fairy godmother blue gown with the pink sash, the headmistress nodded her head of bouncing bluish-gray hair. "You're right, as usual. I did want to see how she was doing after last night's excitement."

He bowed and stepped to the side to allow Paris to enter. "I thought as much. Will there be anything else?"

"Not at the moment." Willow suddenly sounded stressed.

Paris stepped around Wilfred into the large and wholesome office that, like many parts of the manor, reminded her of a grandmother's house. She was surprised to find Mae Ling sitting in one of the armchairs opposite Willow's desk, a calm expression on her face.

"How are you feeling, Paris?" Willow asked as Wilfred pulled the door shut behind her.

"I'm fine," Paris lied.

What was she supposed to say? Her world had suddenly turned upside down, and she didn't feel like herself anymore, but in truth, she didn't really know who she was anymore. That was her first goal—to find out what she didn't know and go from there.

However, Mae Ling had warned her that it would take time and that leaving the college now would be dangerous so Paris wasn't in a hurry to create more problems for herself. There would be time for that later. Paris hadn't allowed herself to think about her parents or what had happened to them but she would when given the time to process.

Headmistress Starr's sensitive expression made Paris think that she didn't believe she was "fine."

"I'm sure you're going through a lot of emotions right now," Willow offered.

"Is Saint Valentine not going to want me at Happily Ever After?" The question spilled from Paris' lips before she could stop it.

Willow's gaze shot to Mae Ling suddenly, worry on her face. "Saint Valentine's authority on such things only extends so far. Also, he's not the closed-minded man that most think him to be. I think it will simply take him time to adjust to the idea."

"Is he worried that by allowing me into the college, you'll have to allow others who aren't fairy-blood?" Paris rocked forward on her boots and back again, suddenly feeling nervous.

"You are fairy-blooded," Mae Ling stated.

"That's right," Willow stated. "I have no plans of allowing those who aren't fairies entry to our college. There are some things that should remain the same, although we're looking at all facets that we might need to renovate for better outcomes."

"So if someone is a fairy and something else, they could attend Happily Ever After?" Paris asked.

"There aren't any others who are half-fairy and another race," Mae Ling offered.

"How do you know?" Paris questioned.

In reply, Mae Ling simply gave her a confident expression that seemed to say, "I know."

The fairy godmother who didn't wear the standard blue gown and seemed so unassuming was an enigma. Paris sensed that she was much more powerful and all-knowing than most, but why, she didn't know.

"You're my professor for Art of Love?" Paris asked the head-mistress.

She nodded with a polite smile. "Yes, and although it's a second-year class, I think after the success of last night's Valentine's event that you should try it out. You have some good ideas that could help the college, but having a foundation of how love works can help."

"So that's what we learn about in the class? Love and how it works?" Paris didn't think anyone could teach this since it was so varied. Two people didn't love the same way. To her, love was like a fingerprint and was unique to each person, but what did she know about the subject, she reasoned.

"We study it from multiple angles, using many different sources," Willow answered. "We can get to that in class. I'll bring you up to speed, don't worry."

The headmistress' words were ironic because that's exactly what she sounded like—worried.

Paris' gaze drifted to the love meter on the wall, the curtain that covered it pulled back. Her mouth popped open, and her heart sank. "What's happened to love?"

CHAPTER SIX

The love meter that hung on Willow's office wall was much lower than the night before. It had ticked up on Valentine's and was at thirty percent. Currently, it was half that.

"I thought that the Valentine's Day event had helped to spread love." Paris remembered that Willow had explained that usually the meter went down on that day because people were forced to be loving.

"It had," Willow replied heavily. "However, there's another event that's having far-reaching and very damaging effects on love."

Paris had been surprised that an event of one hundred couples had made a difference with the love meter at all, but Willow had explained that when love was created, it had a ripple effect. People were better in all aspects of their life, radiating more love that circulated, spreading fast.

As if reading her thoughts, the headmistress said, "Remember that I told you last night that love was infectious and multiplied?"

Paris simply nodded in reply.

"Well, unfortunately, the same thing happens with hate,"

Willow explained. "Feuds, jealousy, resentment, competition, and the like all perpetuates itself, and that has a hugely negative effect on the love meter."

"So there's an event that caused this suddenly?" Paris asked. "Like a war or something?"

Willow shook her head. "Although wars are horrible and usually always wrong, they often make the love meter increase."

Paris' brow registered her confusion. "So Valentine's Day makes the meter go down, and wars make it go up? I'm not sure I understand how this works."

"Wars make people realize how much they love one another," Mae Ling explained, entering the conversation. "It puts people's commitments to the test, and they exemplify sacrifice and passion. Valentine's Day often makes lovers feel obligated to do something nice for each other, which has the opposite effect on the love meter as war."

"Wow, that makes sense," Paris mused. "So it wasn't a war that made the love meter go down. Was it Valentine's Day yesterday? The aftermath, like a lot of women woke up unhappy that their guy got them generic chocolates when they heard that their friend got some heartfelt gift."

Willow offered Mae Ling a proud look before turning her attention back to Paris. "That's a very astute observation and usually exactly what happens after Valentine's Day. The men are resentful too for other reasons because people really shouldn't be forced to love each other more on a particular day. It should be natural and an everyday thing. However, after seeing a bit of an uptick after last night, it's rare to see it decline this much the next day."

"We think that this particular decline is due to a recent situation where a Cinderella and Prince Charming failed to match," Mae Ling imparted.

The headmistress nodded in agreement. "Yes, unfortunately, a few weeks ago we had a veteran fairy godmother make a mistake, and she botched a match with a Ms. Amelia Rose and Mr. Grayson McGregor, who by all of our findings are true lovers."

"That made the love meter go down by half?" Paris asked.

"Well, remember what I said about the domino effect," Willow stated. "Ms. Rose, frustrated by her failed encounter with Mr. McGregor finally accepted a proposal with her long-time on-and-off-again boyfriend, Bryce Tyler."

"Who she's not at all in love with," Paris guessed.

Mae Ling nodded. "Making the love meter decline because she's forcing herself into something and missing her opportunity for true love, which someone only finds once."

Willow let out a soft breath. "I'm certain that Ms. Rose felt the spark when she met Mr. McGregor and now feels the loss of things not going well."

"That's a big effect on the love meter for two people not matching up who are true lovers," Paris observed, looking at the instrument on the wall.

"Well, Mr. McGregor also forced himself into a relationship that's unfulfilling and toxic," Mae Ling explained.

"And to make matters much worse," Willow continued. "Ms. Rose, with the funding of her fiancé, started her competing corporation across the river from Mr. McGregor's and the two have wasted little time trying to ruin each other. Their employees are feuding, their customers getting involved in sabotaging, and the whole rivalry has created some very hostile feelings."

"That's spreading hate instead of love," Paris guessed.

"Yes, so as you can see, a fairy godmother's job is very important and also very delicate," Willow said. "One mistake can have far-reaching effects."

Mae Ling sighed. "The longer this goes on, the worse it will get, I fear."

The headmistress nodded in agreement. "And the harder it will be to get these two lovers together, which I'm starting to believe is a crucial match."

"It sounds like when we miss the chance to get two people together that it becomes exponentially harder," Paris observed.

"Correct," Willow chirped. "Which is why match-making is a fine art form and one that we must perfect to avoid situations like this."

She stood, eyeing the love meter briefly before shaking her head with disappointment. "Well, we will have to hope that we can get this situation under control soon before it gets any worse. For now, we should focus on your education." Willow held her arm out to the door. "Shall I lead the way to Art of Love?"

Paris nodded, looking forward to the class now, knowing how important it was to study love to create successful matches.

CHAPTER SEVEN

"You're in the wrong class," Becky jabbed when Paris entered the classroom that Headmistress Starr had indicated. She'd hung back momentarily in the hallway to speak with another fairy godmother.

Paris had a motto that wasn't like the phrase, "Keep your friends close and your enemies closer." It was more like, "When someone is annoyed by you, really take advantage of this."

She took the seat right next to Becky and scooted it closer to the girl. "So I shouldn't sit here then?"

Becky grimaced and slid away as though repulsed by Paris. That only made her inch closer.

"Headmistress Starr," Becky fired as soon as the fairy godmother swept into the large classroom set up with typical desks and chairs, a chalkboard at the front, and electronic equipment. "Will you please tell Paris that she doesn't belong in this class since it's for second-years?"

Willow blinked at the girl before offering a polite smile. "Oh, but she does. I think she's ready for this, especially after testing out of Cotillion early."

That brought a sour expression to Becky's face. "I didn't think we could test out of classes."

"Well," the headmistress began cheerfully. "It hasn't happened before, but I don't see any reason that it can't. If someone shows they've mastered the curriculum, there's no point in holding them back." She eyed how close Paris was to Becky and tilted her head, momentarily confused. Seeming to dismiss the confusion, Willow glanced out at the rest of the class. "Your last assignment was to study the film *Sabrina* and do a full analysis on it regarding why the main character falls for Linus Larrabee. Who wants to share their report first?"

Paris' eyes widened. "We study romantic comedies in this class?"

Apparently, most didn't speak out of turn in the headmistress' class, according to the many gasps around the room. However, Willow simply smiled thoughtfully.

"We study romantic movies, love ballads, and poetry," the fairy godmother explained. "It's all about understanding the art of love and how it's created. For instance, it helps us as matchmakers to understand how two people must grow to fall in love."

Paris didn't make a habit of watching romantic comedies. She preferred music that she could bang her head to. Poetry was what girls named Fern wrote on their palms while lying in the grass and dreamily watching the football team practice in the distance. However, she'd watched *Sabrina* a time or two because it was her Uncle John's favorite movie. It was also because of him that she knew the words to every single Beatle's song and how to fix a toaster and replace a spark plug.

Glancing around the room, Willow said, "Now, reports. Who wants to offer theirs first?"

"It was all about timing," Paris blurted, surprising herself more than anyone else, although she did get some pretty shocked glances from around the room. She stared back at all the gawkers and shrugged. "What? I've seen the movie, and none of you were piping up."

"I'd love to hear what you have to say about the movie," Willow stated. "You said it was about timing."

"Yeah, Sabrina needed to leave and go to Paris to evolve as a person and a woman," Paris began slowly at first, her confidence growing as the headmistress encouraged her with a continuous nod of her head. "It wasn't really about becoming a woman or getting refined or a new haircut. I think that Sabrina needed to expand her world and realize there was a land outside the Larrabee estate. When she returned, the Larrabee's weren't her whole world anymore. She wasn't a girl watching the parties from the tree but rather someone they wanted to attend because she had something to offer. Paris unlocks the magic inside her."

When Paris finished talking, she couldn't believe all those words came out of her mouth.

Willow smiled broadly at Paris, an appreciative look on her face. "That's an accurate assessment. Confidence was key to Sabrina finding love and attracting the right person for her."

"She also still has a beautiful vulnerability," Paris continued, that bit just occurring to her. "She's still the young girl who pined for the wealthy and worldly Linus Larrabee, but she's unashamed of who she is and not afraid of showing it. What does she say…" Paris thought for a moment, feeling all eyes on her as the line from her uncle's favorite movie came back to her. "She says, 'I have learned how to live, how to be *in* the world and *of* the world, and not just to stand aside and watch. And I will never, never again run away from life. Or from love, either.'"

A hush fell over the classroom and Paris thought for a moment that she'd answered the question wrong. Willow's clapping made her flinch. "That was perfect. Have you watched the movie recently?"

Paris shook her head, her face turning red. "No, I've seen it a few times and have a knack for good lines."

"How very romantic of you," Willow observed.

"What I don't understand," a girl at the back began. "Is why Linus falls for Sabrina. I mean, he can have anyone in the world. She's the chauffeur's daughter. It's disgraceful to his family."

Paris glanced back at the girl, giving her an incredulous expression. "Spoken like the real privileged and ignorant. I think it's obvious why the millionaire fell for her."

The girl shot Paris an annoyed look.

"I'd like to hear your reasoning," Willow stated, interrupting the heated stares between the two. "Go on, Paris."

She turned and faced the headmistress. "Well, Linus can have it all. He's had it all. Sabrina is something different. She's not all pretenses and glitz and glamour. What you see is what you get with her, and it's refreshing. Against his attempts, the rich tycoon falls for her because she's pure. I think he says, 'I don't deserve her. I know that. But I need her, and I don't need anything.'"

"That's perfectly put," Willow commended as many students bent and scribbled notes all of a sudden. "Your assessment is correct. Sabrina evolves, becoming a whole person who is genuine. And Linus, well, it took trying to deceive the chauffeur's daughter to realize what he'd been missing all along. She was what made him realize he hadn't been living, which is exactly something that our Cinderellas can do for their Prince Charmings, and vice-versa."

"Exactly," Paris found herself speaking again without her permission. "It's highlighted in the poem that's Sabrina's namesake. It's about a sprite who saves a virgin from a fate worse than death."

Beside her, so unassuming that Paris didn't even realize she was there, Penny popped up to attention. "That's right! Linus asked if Sabrina was the virgin."

Paris nodded. "And she informs him that she's the savior."

"The unlikely savior," Penny added. "Because no one would expect for the chauffeur's daughter to save the millionaire, but as he says to her, he's been following in others' footsteps all his life. He even asks her to save him, saying, you're the only one who can."

Pressing her hands in front of her chest, Willow beamed as the two went back and forth, and many started to exchange comments excitedly. "Well, I'd say this is one of the more energetic discussions we've had. Why don't you all divide up into pairs to share your analysis of the movie?"

Turning to face Penny, Paris gave her a questioning look, and she nodded adamantly, silently agreeing to be her partner.

When the ruckus from chairs moving had died down, and the groups were talking, Willow breezed over to where Paris was with Penny. "Thanks for your participation in today's discussion. I didn't think you'd have much to contribute since it was your first class, but I was wrong. The whole thing reminds me of my favorite quote from the movie *Sabrina*."

Paris thought for a moment. "They say you're the world's only living heart donor?" she guessed, thinking of the line that Sabrina said to the supposed heartless tycoon, Linus.

Willow shook her head. "No, at the end of the movie when Linus surprises Sabrina, repeating her words from before, 'Paris is always a good idea.'"

CHAPTER EIGHT

P aris might have been able to find usefulness in the art of love, magical gardening, and baking classes, but she was still struggling with the purpose of ballroom dancing.

Wilfred, sensing her hesitation when told to practice the waltz, offered her a pursed expression. "Ballroom dancing is a discipline and an art form. When we master new skills, we create all sorts of new potentials for ourselves."

"Cool." Paris crossed her arms as she regarded the other students practicing in the ballroom. "So once I master this dancing business, I get to move on? Like, onto calligraphy in the twenty-first century or something equally as useless like yo-yoing or parkouring?"

"We don't offer those courses here at the college," Wilfred said in a very dignified voice.

"Yes, I get that." Paris batted her eyelashes at the butler, also her ballroom dancing instructor. "That was one of those jokes. How about if I allow you to teach me how to ballroom dance and in return, I teach you how to laugh?"

He gave her a measured glare. "I don't think that laughing is something one can teach."

"Look at monkeys," Paris countered. "And giants and gnomes. Those guys at one point couldn't laugh to save their mines of gemstones and coal. You get a few dozen beers in them, and they'll laugh as hard at a dad joke as a fairy."

"Are you suggesting that I get inebriated to accomplish this laughing?" Wilfred asked, quite seriously.

Paris threw her hands into the air, exasperated. "No, but I might need to get sauced to deal with you. I can't do this ballroom dancing business unless I get to make jokes and my comedy routine is useless unless there's someone to laugh in response. I don't tell these jokes for my benefit…well, I do, but it's best with an audience."

"I'll laugh at your jokes," Hemingway said at her shoulder. "But they must be funny, perfectly timed, and both witty and crude."

"Deal," Paris said with a grin.

Wilfred sighed. "Oh, good, Mr. Nobel, would you be so kind as to be Ms. Beaufont's dance partner for the next several minutes? I have other things to attend to."

"What he's saying is that I'm giving him a headache with my antics," Paris teased.

"I am physically incapable of experiencing a headache," Wilfred replied.

"Or in discerning sarcasm," Paris quipped. "That's fine. I'll teach the class on the Art of Comedy, and you can teach me how to wave from a train and drink tea with my pinky in the air."

"Those are not formal disciplines," Wilfred began, then nodded. "That was one of those jokes again, wasn't it?"

"Not a very good one, apparently." Paris eyed the tame grin on Hemingway's face.

"Yes, I'll be happy to lead Paris in a waltz," Hemingway informed the butler. "I'm certain she's not as bad at it as she thinks."

She glanced down at his boots. "I hope those are sturdy shoes you're wearing."

He chuckled and offered her his hand. "That laugh I gave away. The others you must earn."

She took his hand, finding it warm in hers, and allowed herself to be pulled into his grasp as he led them in a waltz.

Hemingway was surprisingly a good dancer, making it a little easier for Paris since he led her in the dance. However, Paris still stepped on his shoes a few times and made the wrong moves continuously. "I find that it's better to busy your mind when dancing. Otherwise, you'll overthink the steps."

"Should we do word problems then?" Paris teased. "Math keeps my mind busy with confusion and frustration."

He gave her a sideways smile but no laugh. "I think simple conversation usually does the trick. Last night was exciting…"

Paris nearly tripped on her feet, but thankfully Hemingway kept her upright, leading her around the dance floor. "Yeah, you mean the part where killer doves attacked our Valentine's Day event or when we all took a giant shower together?"

A glint flashed in his blue eyes. "Although that was a rarity for any fairy godmother event that I've attended, I was referring to your new situation and having the whole school learn it at once. You handled the attention well."

Paris shook her head. "I'm pretty certain I went into shock and still haven't come out of it yet."

"Understandably so," he offered, spinning her around. "I'm sure you have lots of questions."

She knew he was trying to be sensitive and supportive, but Paris didn't know what to do with that kind of question, so she did what she did best and deflected. "I do. Like, Headmistress Starr says that enrollment is down at the college. What was it before?"

He toggled his head back and forth, blowing out a breath. "It's been slowly dwindling. I think there were only a handful of first-years this term and there are none lined up for the next year."

Hemingway glanced out at the dance floor where several students were practicing. "Whereas being a fairy godmother used to be seen as an honor, now it doesn't have the same appeal to the younger generation. I think it was our parents and their parents who romanticized the idea of creating true love around the globe."

The mention of parents made Paris tense suddenly, nearly sweeping Hemingway off his feet from her blunder. He recovered easily, pausing them in the middle of the dance floor. "Are you all right?"

She nodded, swallowed, and diverted her gaze from his scrutiny. "Yeah, and I can understand. Why would any modern-day fairy want to make herself look prematurely old by putting on that blue gown and getting gray hair?"

Hemingway nodded. "It's believed that fairy godmothers have to look trustworthy, and no one trusts anyone more than a grandmother type."

"I guess." Paris shrugged, never having met her grandmothers. She never thought to ask Uncle John about them—or any other relatives. For some strange reason, she'd always accepted that he was her only living relative without question. Another weird piece of the puzzle she was putting together.

"The students who are here now are usually from old families who wanted them to follow in their ancestors' footsteps," Hemingway explained while leading them back in the waltz. "Even those loyal followers are few and far between. At this rate, the school really won't churn out very many fairy godmothers for the agencies to employ."

"Yeah, it seems that things are reverting in a way," Paris observed.

They were silent for a moment, only listening to the music overhead and the sounds of their footsteps. Paris immediately began to overthink each step, and before too long she'd nearly fallen again, taking Hemingway with her.

He tugged her straight, correcting her mistake, and gripped her tighter, holding her in closer. "So you're a one-of-a-kind halfling..."

She sighed, not meeting his gaze. "That's the rumor around town."

"We don't have to talk about it," he said at once. "Just trying to keep your mind occupied, and that's the obvious elephant in the room."

Paris couldn't help but laugh. Who was she trying to fool anyway? It wasn't like she could pretend that this all wasn't her reality. "It's fine. I'm trying to wrap my brain around it. Imagine if you woke up to find out that you weren't a fairy anymore."

"Or not only a fairy," he corrected, turning them gracefully in a circle. "I think that would turn my world upside down and I'd have a lot of questions. How do you think you'll go about answering them?"

She thought for a moment, wondering if she wanted to talk to Hemingway about this. Something in his sturdy gaze told her not only could she rely on him with such delicate matters related to her, but she should. She shook off the feeling, trying to focus. "I've been told that I'm not safe outside Happily Ever After College now that Shannon revealed this secret, so I need to be careful not to attract too much trouble on my quest for information."

He nodded. "That was already a problem for you before. I'm not sure what kind of dangers would be out there lurking for you, although it makes good sense. You're an anomaly, and things like that in the magical world are prized."

Paris hadn't thought about it that way. Honestly, she hadn't had much time to think about it in general—having known this information for a whole twelve hours. "You should tell the elf's face who I rearranged once that I'm this prize. I bet he'd disagree."

Hemingway laughed, caught himself, and straightened his face into a mock-serious expression. "Why did you beat up this elf?"

"He kept trying to push his hippie balm on this old lady on Roya Lane," Paris explained. "The jerk simply wasn't taking no for an answer, and he was totally pressuring her to give over the last of her money, telling her she'd regret it if she didn't."

"So you stood up for the old woman," Hemingway guessed, arching an eyebrow at her.

"I don't like it when those who are more powerful take advantage of others," she replied. "That old lady had some ailment, and he was convincing her that his hippie-ass junk was the only cure. She could have gone down to Heals Pills and gotten an elixir that was guaranteed to work and was half the price, and the elf knew it. That's why he kept pushing the woman. So I intervened, and as usual, one thing led to another until it was the bad salesman who needed his balm. I told him I'd done him a favor setting him straight and that he'd see what a rip-off his cream was." Paris chuckled, remembering the incident. "He said, 'you're not the prize you think you are, fairy,' and ran off."

"Then what happened?" Hemingway twirled Paris around. To her surprise, her feet seemed to know all the moves until she was back in his arms once more.

"Well, the incident attracted the attention of the authorities—"

"Your uncle," Hemingway guessed.

Paris nodded. "I was found at the scene of the crime with the hippie balm, which apparently had illegal magical ingredients in it. The old woman had hobbled off by then, her hip bothering her or something."

"And with no witnesses, they blamed you for the whole thing," he stated.

"Yep, that's how my life goes." She sighed. "If there's trouble out there, it finds Paris West—" She cut off her sentence prematurely, remembering that wasn't her name.

"So I could go along with you to Roya Lane or wherever else you need to go to start your investigation for answers," Hemingway offered. "I know that I haven't beaten up many elves and giants, but I'm tough."

Also an excellent dancer, Paris thought, impressed by how smoothly and expertly Hemingway moved.

"Thanks, but…"

"It's only an offer," Hemingway cut in. "No pressure. If you want some company, I'm happy to help."

"You have your responsibilities here," she argued.

He nodded. "Yes, but I'm clever enough to have those covered using magic in my absence. Besides, I haven't ever been to Roya Lane. Well, I haven't really left Happily Ever After College. Going to Los Angeles for the Valentine's Day event was a first."

"It's a nice offer, it's—"

"You're new to this all," he interrupted. "And you don't really know me and probably don't know if you can trust me."

"I'm pretty good on my own." She avoided his gaze still.

"You know," he began in a low tone. "The best way to find out if you can trust somebody is to trust them."

She paused with her feet firmly on the floor and looked directly at him with a discerning expression. "Is that an Ernest Hemingway line?"

He gave her a sheepish grin. "How did you know?"

"His lines aren't like yours," she answered.

Hemingway pretended to be offended, pressing his hand to his chest. "Are you saying that I don't speak like a prolific, prize-winning novelist? How dare you?"

Paris laughed. "I know, shocking, right? Your point remains. I'll think about your offer."

He nodded, bowing slightly to her. "Also, for what it's worth, even if you don't like ballroom dancing much, I think you're a natural."

Paris smiled at him, not saying what she thought. First, that she wanted to trust him. She didn't want to investigate on her own, as she had most all of her life—being a loner. Second—and this one was harder to admit to herself, mostly—Paris quite liked ballroom dancing when she didn't overthink it and found all the moves.

CHAPTER NINE

Still full from breakfast and tired of all the gawkers, Paris skipped lunch and astrology class. She had already made arrangements with Faraday to help her with research in the study area then but hadn't forgotten to grab him a cheese sandwich from the kitchen. Chef Ash assumed it was for her since she was skipping lunch and didn't blame her after witnessing that morning's events at breakfast.

Thankfully the study area on the second floor of the fairy godmother mansion was deserted when Paris arrived with the cheese sandwich wrapped in parchment and tied with a bow— Chef Ash was ever so thoughtful, always making things extra special. Everyone would be at lunch, hopefully meaning no one saw Faraday helping her.

The squirrel hadn't shown up, which gave Paris an idea.

"Wilfred, can you please help me?"

A moment later, the AI magitech fairy popped up. "Yes, how may I be of assistance to you, Ms. Beaufont? Do you want me to continue to give you the information I've found on your parents?"

She did, but Paris also hoped that she could do it on her own with Faraday. She held up her phone. "Thanks to my brilliant uncle and his many magitech hacks, my phone works here in that it allows me to make calls, but that's it."

He arched an eyebrow at her. "Then you're the only one. That's a very impressive hack you have on your device."

She nodded. "He's brilliant, like I said. But the Wi-Fi doesn't work or messaging. Do you have the password or something?"

The butler shook his head. "I regrettably must inform you that Wi-Fi and access to the internet are strictly prohibited at Happily Ever After College."

"Because..." Paris drew out the word.

"Because it's believed these technologies serve as distractions to the creative endeavors of our faculty and students," he explained.

Paris blew out an exasperated breath. "And also keep us in the Dark Ages."

"I do, as you're aware, have access to the whole World Wide Web and can offer you any information that you desire, within reason, of course."

"Of course," Paris said in a snooty voice, her chin high in the air as she mocked the butler.

He didn't seem to mind. "What is it that you'd like me to retrieve for you, Ms. Beaufont? There is some information on the Internet about your namesake."

She sighed. "Although I'm grateful for that, I hoped that I could research on my own, like, at a computer or using my phone. No offense, but it's kind of a personal thing, and I'd like to do it by myself."

Right on the heels of her words, Paris noticed something scurry in the hallway at Wilfred's back. She tensed. Maybe he spied her tension, or he heard the squirrel's claws as he hid behind a large vase. The butler turned his head and glanced in Faraday's direction before returning his attention to Paris.

"Are we pretending that the squirrel is not here in the mansion and also your roommate?" he asked, a clever glint in his green eyes.

CHAPTER TEN

Paris groaned, realizing that she should have figured out that the all-knowing magitech AI butler knew that Faraday was in FGE. "Am I in trouble?"

"I don't have the authority for such things," Wilfred admitted.

"Have you told anyone?" Hope edged into her voice.

He shook his head. "I didn't see that it was of concern to anyone. My job is to serve the students and staff and care for the estate. As long as your friend isn't causing issues to those responsibilities, I don't see the problem in him being here, although I will admit that it is a bit unorthodox."

"Wait until you meet my talking squirrel." Paris laughed and waved in Faraday's direction. "Go ahead and come on out. We've been caught."

The squirrel poked his head out from behind the large ornately decorated vase and sniffed the air. Hesitation flickered in Faraday's gaze before he scurried down the corridor, his tail curled and flying in the air like a flag. Abruptly the squirrel halted in front of the two, looking up curiously at Wilfred.

"You are an incredible piece of technology that I'd love to study," Faraday said as his way of greeting the butler.

Paris sighed. "I told you. He's very strange and says things like that all the time."

"A talking squirrel is also a very interesting entity that many would want to study," Wilfred returned while eyeing Faraday, who had climbed up onto one of the bookcases and started to scan the selection.

"These are all books on spells, romance, and study skills," Faraday muttered, running down the shelf and reading the titles on the spines. "Do you have anything on other subjects?"

"What subjects are of interest to you?" Wilfred regarded the squirrel with mild interest.

Faraday paused. "The shorter answer is to the question, 'what subjects aren't of interest to me,'" he stated with a small chuckle. "I'm fascinated by most all things. Presently I'm studying Happily Ever After College since it's such an interesting place."

"That it is." Wilfred rocked forward on his toes and back again, his hands pinned behind his back. "I don't see why I can't answer most questions you have."

"Great!" Faraday chirped, making Paris glance around suddenly with nervousness.

"Will you keep it down?" she urged. "Just because Wilfred isn't going to rat us out doesn't mean that we can parade you about for everyone to know. Someone could overhear us, so keep it down."

Faraday nodded.

Wilfred pursed his lips. "There is no one on this floor but us presently. They are all eating lunch. I will, of course, tell you if that should change."

Paris let out a breath of relief. Maybe Wilfred would be much more helpful to have in her corner of secrets than she realized.

"So first things first," Faraday began in his squeaky voice. "Why is the Serenity Garden off-limits on Tuesdays?"

"That I can't answer," Wilfred stated at once.

THE MYSTERIOUS LOST CHILD

Paris laughed. "That's how the irony of my life works too. Someone tells me they can answer most all of my questions, but when I ask the burning one, they inform me not that one."

"How about the Bewilder Forest?" Faraday asked. "Why can't one go in there at night?"

Wilfred shook his head. "Again, I'm not at liberty to say."

Paris plopped down in one of the armchairs, laughing. "Maybe start with something that's less cloaked in mystery and restrictions."

"Fine," Faraday asked. "Where can I learn more information about Happily Ever After College?"

Wilfred cleared his throat. "The college's full history is kept in a volume entitled, *The Complete History of Fairy Godmothers.*"

"Fantastic! Where is this book?" Faraday asked.

"In the Great Library," Wilfred answered. "Which isn't accessible by first-years."

"So that means I can't portal there," Paris guessed.

"Correct, Ms. Beaufont," Wilfred stated. "There is a door directly to the Great Library on the third floor as well, but students aren't allowed on that level, as the headmistress informed you."

"Because?" she asked.

"Because it is off-limits to students," he stated matter-of-factly.

"And you're not allowed there until next year." Faraday sighed and turned back to study the row of books.

"Plus, I'm your way into the Great Library," she added.

"I'll find what I'm looking for." Faraday's voice held a hint of mischief. "But we are here because we're trying to help you find information on the Beaufonts and the Ludwigs. The key to good research when you have an AI at your disposal is to ask all the right questions."

Paris grinned at her helpful friend. "I think you're right. So what's the question we should start with?"

Faraday climbed up on the next shelf so he was higher up and looking more directly at Wilfred. "I think that should be easy, although we will have to deduce the answer based on the records that we have access to."

"What is your question?" Wilfred asked, unflustered as the squirrel flicked his tail and chirped a little—apparently thinking.

"My first question is, why is Paris regarded as a Beaufont when her father's name was Ludwig?" Faraday asked. "Why wouldn't she be considered Ludwig when this whole thing was announced?"

CHAPTER ELEVEN

That was an excellent question, Paris thought while pulling the heart-shaped locket from her pocket that she kept there full-time. Uncle John had given it to her because it had her initials on it: PW.

That had seemed like a logical reason for her uncle to give her the locket that was abandoned in an evidence locker long ago. However, there had never been any explanation for why the locket didn't open or the other inscription on the back that read, "You have to keep breaking your heart until it opens. –Rumi."

Paris was suddenly perplexed by the squirrel's question about why she wouldn't have her father's name. Also, where had the name Westbridge come from? Why had her identity been covered up? There were so many questions.

As she regarded the locket that she remembered for most of her life, a brand-new concern joined them.

Paris nearly dropped the locket from shock—as if it was red hot and burning her—as she jumped to a standing position.

Both the butler and the squirrel looked at her with sudden alarm as she stared down at the locket in her hand.

The initials had changed. Now etched across the surface of the heart-shaped locket were two letters: GB.

CHAPTER TWELVE

"**A**re you all right?" Wilfred looked Paris over, who was visibly shaking. "Your heart rate has spiked, and you're now perspiring."

Faraday scampered off the bookshelf and onto the side table next to Paris, his focus on the object in her hands. "What is it?"

"The initials on my locket..." She opened her hand to study the necklace again, thinking that maybe she'd imagined the change. She hadn't. "They've changed. They used to say 'PW.' For as long as I can remember, they said that."

"For Paris Westbridge," Wilfred offered.

She nodded. "My uncle gave this to me. He said that he found it and since it had my initials, it seemed fitting that I have it." Paris held up the chain, allowing the heart-shaped locket to dangle in the air, displaying it for both butler and squirrel to see. "But now, all of a sudden, it has..."

"GB." Faraday leaned forward and read the initials from his perch.

"For Guinevere Beaufont," Wilfred supplied.

She nodded, having no other explanation. "But how? Because I learned yesterday who I truly am?"

"That's a powerful protective identity spell," Wilfred stated matter-of-factly.

"A-a-a what?" Paris sputtered, not having expected him to say that.

"This situation, with what you've supplied, makes me think that the locket in your possession had a protective spell on it," Wilfred explained.

Paris glanced at Faraday, who nodded. "That makes sense."

"The locket was spelled?" Paris questioned. "I don't understand. It came from an abandoned evidence locker."

"Before yesterday," Wilfred began. "Did you ever question what had happened to your parents or why your uncle raised you?"

Paris shook her head. "I've not so much as asked him their names."

He nodded as if he'd expected this answer. "And now? Do you find yourself more curious about them?"

"Well, of course," she said brusquely. "I've found out that not only am I a halfling but that my parents were powerful magicians. Who wouldn't want to know more about this past that's been covered up for who knows why?"

"Now that she knows the truth," Faraday slowly said as if working it out. "The locket has changed to reveal her true initials."

"Precisely," Wilfred said with confidence.

Paris eyed the locket as it continued to sway, turning in the air to display the quote as well as the letters. "T-T-The locket was spelled..." she stuttered, still having trouble wrapping her brain around the newest surprise.

"In scenarios where protective identity spells are used," Wilfred began, "an object is employed to keep someone from asking questions about who they are, their past, the people related to them, or anything else that can unravel the truth. They only believe what others tell them, but the spell breaks the moment that someone tells them who they truly are and the object used for the spell reveals this truth."

"So when Shannon Butcher told me I was Guinevere Beaufont…"

"It broke the spell," Faraday supplied.

"Now I want to know the truth, whereas before, I wasn't curious about my parents." Paris' knees suddenly went weak. She felt for the back of the chair and sat. "I want to know who they were. I want to know why someone covered up my past. That's all…"

"That seems like it will contain a fair bit of information," Wilfred stated blandly.

Paris nodded. "It's even more complicated. I have a feeling that not just anyone can tell me. Mae Ling makes me believe there's been other spellwork done that prevents most from telling me the truth—like her, for instance."

"It appears that there has been quite a lot orchestrated to hide this information," Wilfred observed.

"From me?" Paris asked as if he knew the answer. "Why?"

"I think that while it is improbable that your truth was hidden from you," Faraday said, averting his gaze suddenly. "You might also consider that it hid your identity from others."

She turned her gaze on him sharply, suddenly paranoid. "What do you know?"

"I'm simply working out the evidence based on what's been presented," he offered. "It seems illogical to think that this information was harmful for you to know, but the knowledge of a halfling would potentially be of great interest to others."

"He's right," Wilfred added. "Halflings are extremely rare, and therefore not much is known of them. From what I've found on the Internet there is much lore surrounding the powerfulness of a halfling since it's believed they have the strengths of both their races, which often cancels out the negatives. There is a case of halflings who are both mortal and fae. Triplets according to magipedia.com."

"I've met them," Paris admitted, remembering the women she met in the bar the night that King Rudolf Sweetwater shared the odd story with her about love. "They aren't happy about the fact that they're halflings because they're so different from both of their races and can't relate to either mortals or fae."

Wilfred nodded. "That's understandable. It is assumed that they will have half of the lifespan of a normal fae, which is five times longer than a mortal's."

"Which would make it tough to find a mate," Paris muttered, the true implications of this halfling business coming to light.

"Exactly," Wilfred continued. "They have the attractiveness of a fae but the fragility of a mortal. Also, their mortal blood tempers their magic, but conversely, their intelligence is much higher than that of a fae."

Paris held the locket firmly in her fingers, finding that it still didn't open—it never had, and she had no idea what was in it or if there was anything at all. "Maybe my identity was hidden from me because of the psychological implications."

"That's a reasonable conclusion based on what we've discovered thus far," Wilfred confidently agreed.

"There are still so many questions to be answered, like how could two magicians have a halfling?" Paris mumbled, her head starting to cramp from all the overwhelming thoughts. "And Faraday is right."

"About what?" he chirped, his eyes skirting to the side and an uncertain expression on his face.

"About the strangeness that I carry my mother's maiden name instead of my father's," she answered.

The squirrel perked up. "Of course! Yes, it is a brooding question I've had since you told me."

"I think I've discovered some information that might shine a light on that," Wilfred offered.

"Go on," Paris urged.

"According to what I've found on the Beaufont family, which isn't much," he began. "There are presently only two remaining family members living. A Mr. Clark Beaufont and a Ms. Sophia Beaufont."

"So my mother is dead..." Paris slumped, the information a blow although it had always been her reality about her mother and father. However, before Uncle John had simply said her parents were missing, but them being dead had always been a possibility— although Paris never thought about it and now she knew why.

"What I've found simply says those are the only two Royals with the Beaufont family's blood," Wilfred stated. "Conversely, your father's family, the Ludwigs, have many members. From what I can gather, if the Beaufont name died out, they'd lose their place in the House of Fourteen. Your uncle, Clark Beaufont, is currently a Councilor for the House. His wife, Mrs. Alicia Beaufont, is the Warrior who replaced your mother. Sophia Beaufont is the leader of both the Dragon Elite and the Rogue Riders, making her ineligible to work for the House of Fourteen. It goes to reason that your parents decided you'd carry the Beaufont family name so that it wouldn't die and that you could one day be either a Councilor or a Warrior."

"Not to mention that it's a stronger name since it belongs to a founder family," Faraday added.

Paris shot him a skeptical look. "How do you know about that? Wilfred only told me that this morning."

The squirrel's tail flickered. "I overheard..."

The butler tilted his head to the side slightly, a discerning look in his eyes that Paris couldn't quite read.

"Why is it that you showed up when you did exactly when I was leaving for Happily Ever After College?" she asked the squirrel while folding her arms.

"I was in the neighborhood and saw you talking to yourself," he answered at once.

"Where are you from?" she asked.

"A small town in Louisiana. You haven't heard of it."

"Why don't you have a southern accent?" she instantly questioned, not missing a beat.

"I worked to get rid of it."

"Yeah, that seems like real squirrel behavior," she retorted bitterly, suddenly paranoid about everything.

"It isn't something that most would think to do as squirrels, but I'm obviously different."

"How did you get to Roya Lane? Why are you a talking squirrel who doesn't act like one? And why did you want to accompany me and help me out so much?" she demanded in rapid succession.

Wilfred's gaze slid to the squirrel as his teeth chattered as though he was chewing on air.

"I slid through a portal that an elf opened without them knowing," he stated. "That's often how I get around, regrettably."

"Yeah, like when you followed me here," she muttered.

"I understand that my ability to talk is an anomaly, but I assure you that there's nothing nefarious about it," he continued.

"The fact that you use the words 'anomaly' and 'nefarious' is exactly why I don't trust you," Paris fired at him. "Tell me something about you. Anything other than that you're a nerdy squirrel who is allergic to nuts and prefers high thread counts on your sheets."

Wilfred was watching a tennis match, his gaze directing back to Faraday.

"I was born to simple parents in the backwoods of Louisiana, who wanted me to live a simple life," Faraday explained in a shy voice. "I was never content with foraging in the forest or hunting around in the swamps."

"Squirrels don't hunt," she corrected.

"Maybe he means it in terms of 'searching' or 'seeking,'" Wilfred offered.

Paris narrowed her eyes at the AI but didn't think he was in cahoots with the strange squirrel. Turning her attention back to Faraday, she directed, "Go on."

"I escaped to the city as soon as I could," the squirrel continued. "I was always fascinated by science and magic and spent much of my time at the universities and following various scholarly magicians around."

"Is that how you learned to talk?" Wilfred asked.

Faraday's gaze slid to the left as if he'd suddenly caught something out of the corner of his vision. "I'm a talking squirrel because of a spell."

"Why are you following me around?" Paris questioned, although she was starting to lose her fire. So far everything that Faraday said made sense and didn't make him sound untrustworthy. What had Hemingway quoted to her that morning? "The best way to find out if you can trust somebody is to trust them." She sighed with resignation, wanting Faraday to check out. He was her first real friend, but it all relied on how he answered this question.

"I was in the right place at the right time," he began. "I saw you talking to yourself, and I was curious about you. Of course, from a scientific standpoint, I'd want to investigate Happily Ever After College, so when I discovered you were going there, I simply thought it was a good opportunity to research. Furthermore, you were alone and looked like you could use a friend, and I wanted to know you. Now that I know you're a halfling, I'm even more interested in learning about you."

"One last question," she said through clenched teeth, watching his every move and expression to see if he was lying. "Did you know that I was a halfling?"

"No, I did not," he asserted.

"Did you know that I was a Beaufont?" she added, the thought suddenly occurring to her.

"You did say only one last question," Wilfred cut in.

"I want to know," Paris seethed, not taking her gaze off the squirrel.

"I can honestly say that I didn't," Faraday answered. "Before meeting you on Roya Lane, I didn't know a single thing about you."

She sighed and sat back in the large armchair. "Fine. I won't have Chef Ash make you into squirrel sausage."

"According to my findings," Wilfred began. "You need approximately fifteen squirrels to make the standard squirrel sausage recipe."

Paris leveled her gaze at the butler. "It was a joke. I don't even like sausage that much."

"Can we not talk about food that I could become?" Faraday asked.

"Yes." She sighed and glanced at Wilfred. "What else have you dug up on the Beaufonts and the Ludwigs? Anything of interest?"

"The Ludwigs are a relatively new family to the magical world," Wilfred stated in a rehearsed voice. "There's much information on how they made money in magical trades and served in many noble ways. Raina Ludwig, a current Councilor for the House of Fourteen, is of Royal blood and married a Fane Popa-Ludwig from Lupei, making him a Warrior to replace your father, Stefan."

"He took her name," Faraday observed. "How very progressive."

"It's the twenty-first century," Paris replied.

"Again, I think it's to preserve the family status in the House of Fourteen," Wilfred observed. "The organization that governs magic appears to be dictated by many customs and old traditions, although there isn't much on the subject."

"And the Beaufonts?" The name still sounded strange to Paris, knowing it was hers.

"There is very little information on them, and much of what I've found appears redacted," Wilfred supplied.

"So that's where I need to investigate." Paris pulled her phone out.

"I thought you said that your data and messaging didn't work on your phone." Wilfred gave her a skeptical look.

"It doesn't." She dialed the only number she knew by heart. The only one she ever called. "But I can still make calls, and there's only one person who I want to talk to right now. Thanks for your help." A smile flicked to her face, politely dismissing the butler.

CHAPTER THIRTEEN

Paris had expected to leave a message for her uncle, which was why she was surprised when he picked up the phone after only one ring.

"Hey, Pare." Uncle John's voice was a little gruffer than usual.

Something caught in her throat, and Paris was unable to speak.

"Pare? You there?"

A cough sputtered over her lips and Paris sucked in a sudden breath. "Yeah, I'm here. I didn't expect you to answer. I thought you were on a stakeout."

"I was," he answered. "Something happened...I had to return to FLEA."

"Something happened?" Paris wanted to ask her burning questions as soon as she heard Uncle John's voice, but now, she sensed brand-new stress in his voice, and it didn't feel right. Also, she wanted to talk to him in person and not over the phone when it involved something serious and life-changing.

"It's...well, it's nothing for you to worry about," he answered. "I'll tell you the next time I see you."

"About that," Paris said tentatively. "Are you around tonight?"

"Tonight?" he questioned. "To see me? Is everything all right there?"

"It's fine," she lied, not knowing how she could tell him she was in shock without explaining to him that her whole life had turned upside down. That's what she'd do when they saw each other in person. "I thought I'd stop by tonight if you're available."

"For you, always, Pare."

"Great." Paris smiled, her unwavering fondness for her uncle warming her chest. Maybe he had lied and hidden her past, or perhaps he was in the dark. She'd find out, but at her core, Paris knew that her Uncle John would never do anything to deceive her without a good reason. "I'll see you around eight then."

"See you then," he agreed.

Paris shut off the phone and hurried out of the study area, looking forward to seeing Uncle John, although she couldn't shake the feeling that he was very upset about something. She'd find out about that tonight and hopefully much, much more.

CHAPTER FOURTEEN

Although Paris could have skipped her afternoon classes, per Headmistress Starr's permission, she found that she wanted to attend Gardening and Baking-slash-Cooking. Most of the students were gathered in the greenhouse when Paris took her seat at the back.

As if Hemingway was simply waiting for her to show up, he clapped once as soon as Paris sat.

"Welcome, welcome first through fourth years," he stated excitedly. "I have something to show you today that I don't think any of you have seen before regardless of your level. I've only just found it in the Bewilder Forest for the very first time recently."

Sitting on a high table in front of Hemingway was something draped in a small green tarp.

With enthusiasm buzzing in his eyes, Hemingway yanked the covering off to reveal a small green plant with purple flowers and little black berries.

"For one thousand points," Hemingway began. "Who can tell me what this plant is?"

Unlike usual when he asked a question, not a single hand went into the air. The students all looked at each other with confusion.

However, Hemingway nodded understandingly. "This plant isn't cataloged in any of your textbooks, so I'm not sure where you would have run across it. This is a very rare and dare I say, poisonous plant known as the Deadly Nightshade."

Gasps echoed around the room. Many covered their mouths. Whispers flew around the greenhouse rapidly.

"Ingesting only ten to twenty of these berries," Hemingway continued, "can cause death in adults. The leaves and petals in small doses will most likely lead to an impromptu nap, and waking up is a gamble depending on the person."

Many in the front row leaned back as if afraid that mere proximity to the plant was dangerous.

"If this plant is so toxic, why did you harvest it and bring it in here?" Penny Pullman pushed her glasses up on her nose.

Hemingway nodded. "Good question. I don't make a habit of playing with poisonous plants. However, education is important, and before today, I didn't have the opportunity to show you all what Deadly Nightshade looks like. Now you all know and can avoid it since even touching the plant could be dangerous."

"Why did it recently show up in the Bewilder Forest?" Paris thought the timing was a little strange.

"Well, it's more likely that I only now discovered it in the Bewilder Forest," Hemingway offered while giving her a thoughtful look. "They aren't the easiest plant to find because they grow low to the ground, and other plants covered this one. However, it is worth speculating on the reason that it was in the Bewilder Forest since although many unique magical plants grow there, the properties of Happily Ever After College discourage dangerous plants or animals from living in our bubble. Although that brings me to a relevant point, which is that even though Deadly Nightshade is extremely lethal, it does have some benefits. Does anyone know what those are?"

He was silent for a moment, staring around the room, waiting for someone to reply. When no one did, Hemingway nodded, understanding the lack of knowledge on the plant.

"Although the plant is, as its name indicated, very deadly, there are some extraordinary benefits if handled properly," he explained. "In the past, women have used it cosmetically since it can dilate pupils. In stronger doses, the plant can be administered as a mild sedative to treat colds and alleviate stomach discomfort. It also can be a pain reliever, anti-inflammatory, and muscle relaxer. Those attending Burning Man might use it as a hallucinogen. Regardless, working with this plant is very dangerous, and there's a fine line between using it for a medicinal purpose and creating a poison."

"Do you know how to make any of that stuff with the plant?" a girl toward the front of the class asked.

Hemingway shook his head. "I would only trust an experienced alchemist with such a task. Therefore, none of you should play with this bad boy. Take note of what the plant looks like and stay away from it. If you do spot one in the Bewilder Forest, let one of the faculty know. I'm not sure whether there are any more out there or if this was the only one but do keep an eye out."

Hemingway clapped again and rubbed his hands together eagerly. "Okay, now onto our more hands-on lesson for today. We're going to continue classifying different plants in the green-house, on the Enchanted Grounds, and for higher-level students, you're free to venture into the Bewilder Forest. If you have trouble identifying a plant, please come and find me. I'm going to be repotting some Unearthly Orchids." He indicated some flowers in the back corner that didn't look from this planet. They were seemingly impossible shades of neon green, blue, and bright pinks—colors that Paris had never seen on flowers.

Not needing to be ushered anymore, most students got up and started for the grounds or the forest to classify the plants they came across.

Drawn to the strange orchids, Paris strode over as Hemingway went straight to work, shoveling fluffy soil into pots. She figured she could cross the Unearthly Orchids off her list for classifications and learn about them in one go.

"These are very interesting." She indicated the delicate blooms, although she'd learned that the fragile-looking flowers could be very hardy.

Hemingway nodded. "And quite temperamental. I think I've finally figured out what they needed to grow."

Paris lifted an eyebrow. "Moon rocks?"

He laughed and shook his head. "Good guess. Legend has it that an alien race left the orchids behind from their planet and that's why it's almost impossible to get them to grow. I think the reason they're so difficult is that they don't require the things we usually think of when trying to get orchids to flourish."

"You mean it's not a specific type of dirt or fertilizer or food?" she asked.

"Yeah, if my findings are correct," Hemingway began. "I think that the Unearthly Orchid wants to form a relationship with its gardener—but a healthy one."

Paris shot him a skeptical expression. "Like, you have to court the flower? How does that work?"

"Pretty much." He chuckled. "Many plants simply want their basic needs met, but that hasn't worked with the Unearthly Orchid, I've observed. Two different plants can get the same thing, but one will do better than the others. So I started to wonder what the distinguishing factor was. That's when I started to observe my behavior around them. I realized that I might find myself singing as I tended to one of the orchids. The next day it would do better and the other beside it would have wilted and died. So I started playing around with it and realized that the ones that got positive attention flourished more than others who either got negative treatment or none at all."

"I have heard that plants like for people to talk to them," Paris said. "I thought that the logical reason was it was the carbon dioxide we breathe out that they liked."

"Spoken like a real pragmatist." He nodded. "That was my thought too, but then it would mean that regardless of whether an orchid was spoken to in a nice or mean way, that it would do fine. However, I found that only ones that had positive treatment flourished."

"Kind of like the shame plants then?" Paris guessed.

"Sort of," he answered. "Those pick up on our emotions. With the Unearthly Orchids, one really has to form a relationship with them, and like any healthy partnership, it takes constant maintenance. If one day I don't give the orchids affection, they start to deteriorate."

"Wow, that's fascinating."

He nodded while regarding the strange orchids. "Indeed. There are so many lessons we can learn from plants that surprise even me."

"I'm listening." She waited for him to continue.

"Well, this one here." Hemingway indicated the closest orchid, which was about two feet tall with several blooms. "It was really struggling yesterday. I offered it the attention that I thought would help, but it was failing, and I really thought it was a goner. All day, I kept telling the plant that we couldn't give up and did everything I could think of. Anyway, I came into the greenhouse this morning, fully expecting to find the orchid dead or close to."

"It looks healthier than the others," Paris observed.

Hemingway flashed her a smile. "That it does. I was surprised to find it doing great this morning even though my hope had dwindled. Like I said before, I think that one has to form a relationship with the Unearthly Orchids and like any relationship, they're complex. I didn't give up on the plant yesterday and offered it everything I could until I was exhausted. I was pretty demoralized this morning and the flower was robust and really lent me some inspiration that I needed when I came in this morning. It reminded me of an important relationship principle."

Paris lowered her chin, giving him a silent look that urged him to continue.

"In a relationship, two people have the best chance of making it if they both don't give up," he explained. "But we're all human so it's difficult not to lose hope. Instead, a healthy relationship is one where the two don't give up at the same time."

Paris smiled. "So you gave the Unearthly Orchid all you had and had all the hope. This morning, when you were at your lowest, it had risen to the challenge and lent you the hope."

He nodded victoriously. "That was enough to encourage me to give the orchid what it needed so it could continue to flourish. Now I think it's strong enough to be repotted."

"That's pretty amazing."

Something outside the glass walls of the greenhouse caught Hemingway's attention. "Oh, if you want to see something amazing, follow me." He grabbed her hand and pulled her to the door. "Hurry, before it's gone."

CHAPTER FIFTEEN

Hemingway didn't release Paris until they were outside on the Enchanted Grounds, the sunshine making everything sparkle. There was a palpable excitement in the college's groundskeeper.

He led her over to a set of bushes with tiny white blossoms. "Aren't they delightful?"

At first, Paris didn't see what Hemingway was referring to. Then she did and was completely in awe. Flying around the bush was a little creature that resembled a hummingbird but also a butterfly. Its wings beat extremely fast, making a drumming sound, and it had a long tongue that dipped into the flowers, gathering nectar.

"What is it?" She watched the creature, which moved so fast it was difficult to keep up with its actions.

"It's a hummingbird hawk-moth," Hemingway answered. "Isn't it fun?"

Paris nodded, noticing that the animal had a bird-like body and butterfly wings. It was like its own type of halfling, and Paris instantly liked it.

"They're fairly rare to see here on the grounds, for whatever reason," Hemingway stated. "I think it's a good omen. Some believe them to signify luck." He tilted his head back and forth. "However, some also think that they represent mystery, transformation, and moving from darkness to light. So I guess it depends on what meaning you want to endorse."

"I'll go with luck. That seems like the most straightforward option," Paris remarked, watching as the hummingbird hawk-moth gathered nectar from a flower efficiently before moving on to the next. It was an incredibly remarkable creature and moved with such grace. "Why is it that new plants are showing up here on the grounds and now a rare sighting of this moth?"

Hemingway looked at her, studying her expression for a moment. "It's hard to say. Happily Ever After is influenced by many factors, although I haven't seen this many changes at once. The people, the type of magic in use, and the level of the love meter all affect the college and its grounds."

Paris didn't want to think it was her and her unique brand of magic affecting Happily Ever After, although she might want to take credit for the hummingbird hawk-moth. Not the Deadly Nightshade though. She reasoned that the love meter was down and that could be the cause. Not to mention that they'd lost an instructor the night before who had betrayed the college in an attempt to sabotage Paris, so there were many factors at play.

"Speaking of strange new things on the grounds," Hemingway muttered, kneeling beside the bushes and inspecting the grass and dirt.

"What is it?" Paris asked.

He combed his hand over the dirt, lifting his fingers to study them afterward. Hemingway shook his head. "I've been finding strange tracks lately...well, for a few weeks."

"Strange tracks?" Paris asked. "Like, a predator? I didn't think there were any harmful animals on the grounds."

He shook his head. "I can't guarantee that, although I've never seen one. No, this isn't anything harmful. Merely curious. It's a type of rodent that I haven't seen here."

"Rodent?" Paris tensed.

Hemingway stood. "Yeah, we have chipmunks here on the grounds, and I'm used to finding their tracks. These are larger. It almost seems like a fox squirrel, but I'm not sure why we'd have one of those."

Paris worked to keep the tension off her face. Those were Faraday's tracks. She knew it. Although Wilfred knew about the talking squirrel and wasn't about to say anything, she'd prefer if others didn't know about her roommate. Paris had enough attention right then without others knowing that she'd smuggled a strange animal into Happily Ever After College. "I'm sure it's nothing," she remarked and pointed at the hummingbird hawk-moth, trying to distract him. "I'm glad you spotted this and showed me."

An uncertain expression flickered in his eyes, but Hemingway smiled. "Well, it's rare to see them, or at least it used to be. Seems when you're around, I find things of interest."

CHAPTER SIXTEEN

Paris didn't know what Hemingway meant by his statement about finding things of interest when she was around, which was why she made up an excuse and dismissed herself immediately.

Having skipped lunch, she was looking forward to magical cooking with Chef Ash more than usual. It had quickly become one of her favorite classes anyway because the carpenter cook, as she liked to call him, was so easy-going and smiled often. Also, he was very supportive of her endeavors, and his passion for cooking came through in his instructions.

"Cooking is all about instinct," he explained to the class that afternoon. "Whereas with baking, the measurements are rigid and the process usually straightforward, there are many different ways to achieve desired results with cooking. It can be a pinch of this and a dash of that until you get where you want with a dish. Baking is the precise art form of love. Cooking is the feeling version of it."

He strode up to the front of the room and picked up a whisk from the countertop. "Today, I want you all to create a recipe using some key ingredients. You can make an appetizer, a main entrée or soup or salad, but you must use all three of these magical ingredients."

Chef Ash twirled the whisk, and a large picnic basket sitting on the counter opened. Three jars of spices rose from it before settling down on the work surface.

Indicating the first jar with a bright red ground spice, he said, "We have Gaelic Smoked Paprika, which is known for affecting emotions. Too much of it, and whoever eats your dish will be as fiery and pissing mad as a Scotsman whose wife went on a shopping spree."

Many of the ladies around the room giggled, earning a satisfied expression from Chef Ash.

"Second." He pointed at the middle jar full of dark brown spice. "We have Artisan Cumin. Its main magical property is creativity. It's mostly an amplifier, so its effects will be related to whatever you pair it with. Put it in sufficient amounts with Gaelic Smoked Paprika, and you'll be well on your way to inspiring a romantic poet who cries easily and is moved by the slightest winds. However, pair it with more of our last spice and the effects are totally different."

Chef Ash indicated the third jar, which was full of a light tan spice. "Southern Coriander is known for sparking friendships. A pinch of it and people will be more responsive to making friends and bonding with others. Too much of it, and well, let's just say that too much of any magical spice is a bad thing."

He twirled the whisk again, and identical jars appeared on all the workstations in front of each student. "The idea with magical spices and cooking is not to create love potions. We all know those don't work and often backfire. Instead, the idea is to set the stage for pleasant interactions. We're simply nudging two people who have potential. Yes, they could have a glass of wine to loosen up or a bite of chocolate to release endorphins. They could also have a bite of a quiche that makes them open up and be more receptive to another's advances. The key though, is about harmonizing the spices. While this isn't baking with precise measurements, it is about balance. Too much of one spice can have the opposite effects of what you intended to make."

Chef Ash glanced around the room as if expecting the students would have questions or comments. When no one did, he smiled wide. "All right, so today's assignment is for you to invent a recipe, making anything you want. There are only two requirements." He held up one finger. "The first is that you must use all three magical spices." Then ticked off another finger. "The second is that your dish must have the effect of creating a favorable setting for two people. Maybe you make spiced mushrooms that encourage flirting. Or you could cook a grilled chicken that makes two people more open to each other. What you do is up to you, and I look forward to reviewing your concoctions."

Christine's hand shot into the air, waving slightly. "If you're judging the recipes, is that safe?"

He chuckled. "I see your concern that I might be drunk from all the spices if I was trying all your dishes. However, for my grading, I'll simply be relying on magic. My waistline and my mind really can't handle that much magical cooking."

Chef Ash studied the room, waiting for other questions. When there weren't any, he twirled the whisk again. "With that, you can get started." A timer appeared on the workstation beside him and began ticking. "You have two hours to make something from scratch. Good luck."

Paris looked at the three full spice jars in front of her and the pantry of ingredients across the room. Two hours seemed like a lot of time—if it wasn't for the fact that she had no idea what to make.

[illegible] what I intended to make.

Chef [illegible]

[illegible] "All right [illegible] making anything [illegible] [illegible] that you [illegible] all [illegible] [illegible] must [illegible] [illegible] Maybe [illegible] piece [illegible] Or you could cook [illegible] [illegible] are open to each other. What [illegible] forward to reviewing your [illegible]"

Chef [illegible] shot [illegible] judging the recipes is [illegible]

He chuckled. [illegible] you [illegible] the [illegible] I'll simply [illegible] can't handle that much [illegible]

Chef [illegible] the room [illegible] [illegible] pretty [illegible] [illegible] good [illegible]

Tess looked at the three [illegible] the [illegible] ingredients across the room. [illegible] if it wasn't for the fact that she [illegible] what to make

CHAPTER SEVENTEEN

M ost of the students were already cooking. Paris remained frozen, staring at the magical spices as if they would tele-pathically tell her what to do with them. She didn't have a lot of experience cooking, mostly grabbing things from cafés on Roya Lane.

Uncle John cooked for her when he wasn't working, and he was quite good at creating tasty meals. His favorite cuisine was Mexican, and he made a chili that just thinking about it made Paris miss him. A strong feeling of nostalgia wrapped around her suddenly and she knew she needed to try and replicate the Mexican beef chili.

Even though she didn't know what all was in it, Paris thought she could get close enough.

"It has to have the basics," she reasoned, talking to herself as she pulled out an onion, jalapeños, and garlic from the pantry.

Paris chose some lean ground beef after recalling visuals of watching Uncle John sauté the meat, waving his hand in the air to bring the steam up with the spices as he cooked, checking the aroma.

Feeling much more confident than when the assignment started, Paris filled her arms with canned beans, tomatoes, and broth before making one last trip back to her workstation. She knew that chili needed time for the flavors to "marry." That's how Uncle John always put it, but she reasoned that she could use some magic to compress the cooking time.

As the meat sautéed, Paris went to work chopping and dropping her vegetables into the pot.

"You're humming," Chef Ash observed, buzzing by her workstation to check her progress.

Paris paused, realizing that she had been humming to herself—not something she ever did. "Yeah, I guess I was. Cooking relaxes me."

He nodded proudly. "Me too. And I know why. You're creating something that nourishes people. How can that not be fulfilling? The only thing better would be creating a home for them to live in."

Paris stirred the pot of vegetables and meat, the steam rising and wreathing around her face. "If you love carpentry so much, why didn't you go into that?"

Chef Ash touched the pencil behind his ear reflexively but left it in place. "I get that question a lot. Although carpentry was my first love, I felt like the world needed me as a chef. Magical carpentry is a very tricky art form that can have disastrous ramifications if you don't construct something right. In the end, I decided on the profession that allowed me to construct and use magic in a safer way. This opportunity at the college opened, and it made sense that I pursued it. I've had zero regrets. I get to do both things I love, in a way."

"I guess that's how life goes," Paris mused. "Life usually dictates our path. That's why I'm here."

"We're glad about that detour life sent you on." Chef Ash winked.

"Thanks." Paris blushed. "There are ramifications to magical cooking, like you said."

"Oh yes," Chef Ash stated gravely. "Thankfully, it's pretty quick to mitigate them. If you get a magical carpentry spell wrong, residents might find themselves forever locked inside their house or wake up to find their rooms shrinking, about to crush them. I didn't want that kind of pressure on my shoulders."

"Yeah, I wouldn't either," Paris agreed.

"Well, not to scare you, but you're responsible for helping two people fall in love. I can't think of a more important or tougher job."

Paris blew out a breath and pinched a little Gaelic Smoked Paprika into the pot. "Believe me, I'm scared."

Chef Ash chuckled good-naturedly and indicated her pot. "Don't worry. You seem to have an instinct for cooking, which makes me think you'll have it for match-making. The skills are complementary."

When Chef Ash had moved onto supervise a different workstation, Paris added the other two magical spices and used a spell to compress the cooking time. She'd read about something similar in one of her books and figured she could adapt it for cooking. The onions instantly caramelized and the tomatoes darkened, making her think that it had worked. The spices and smell of jalapeños filled the air.

Since Paris didn't want to force relationships but rather create ideal circumstances for two people to fall in love, she decided that her Mexican beef chili would engender warm feelings. She hoped it would help endear a Cinderella and Prince Charming to one another if they were compatible. Kind of like how warm cider made someone feel comforted and a little euphoric.

Realizing that she'd forgotten to grab fresh cilantro and sharp cheddar cheese from the refrigerator, Paris went back to the pantry area. Uncle John always topped his chili with tons of cilantro and cheese, saying that it was the finishing touches that made a dish perfect.

Paris caught herself humming again when she ducked back out of the refrigerator. However, she instantly halted at the sights in the kitchen. In the short time that she'd disappeared to the back, the scene around the classroom had dramatically changed. Students were yelling at one another, throwing utensils, and holding their fists in the air. It appeared that the peaceful students of Happily Ever After College were moments from tearing each other into pieces.

CHAPTER EIGHTEEN

"I can't stand you!" Becky Montgomery yelled at the top of her lungs. She plunged her hand into a bowl of chopped cabbage and threw it at Penny Pullman, covering her long stringy hair with the shreds of vegetables.

"I'm so mad!" someone else screamed, throwing her arm wide and pushing everything off her workstation, making a racket as all the bowls and supplies tumbled to the floor.

Around the classroom, most were shouting phrases of anger and throwing things at one another. It quickly turned into a food fight and chaos.

Chef Ash, who had ducked out of the classroom for a moment, rushed back in at the commotion. His eyes were filled with urgency as he glanced around frantically. His gaze fell on Paris' pot where green smoke wafted from her chili.

"Paris!" he yelled while sprinting over and retrieving his whisk from the center workstation. He twirled it, and the lid lifted into the air and clamped down on the pot, sealing in the fumes.

Paris dropped the ingredients in her arms and rushed over, looking around and wondering what she could do.

"Hold your nose and clear the smell in the air," Chef Ash urged, picking up the boiling pot of chili and running for the door.

Paris pinched her nose and turned, briefly taking in the chaos still ensuing. Various sauces or other ingredients covered most of the students. They were yelling and barking threats at each other.

Not hesitating, Paris lifted her finger and used a siphoning spell. She didn't know where it came from, not having learned it from anywhere. Much like cooking, the spell came to her through what felt like instinct.

The green smoke in the air evaporated almost all at once, and whatever was making Paris' eyes burn and water dissipated. She kept her nose plugged and breathed through her mouth.

Around the room, the students all paused, looking around disoriented as if trying to figure out how curry had covered them or why they had chopped celery in their hair.

Some began helping others to pick themselves up from the floor while others simply shook their heads and blinked around in continued confusion.

Chef Ash rushed back into the demo kitchen, his hands empty, having gotten rid of the pot of chili somehow. He glanced around the room, relief filling his face.

Pulling the whisk from his apron, he forced a smile to his face. "Well, you all are dismissed for the remainder of the class. We will try this again tomorrow with a few more guidelines." He gave Paris an amused look. She was relieved he didn't appear to be angry at her. He twirled his whisk, and most of the mess from the food fights disappeared, making the large kitchen appear clean once more. "Go ahead and go get yourselves cleaned up for dinner. I dare say, you all have probably worked up an appetite after that."

Paris knew better than to follow the other students out. Instead, she waited until they'd all left and Chef Ash turned to face her directly, an impressed expression on his face.

"Well, if I knew that you were going to employ advanced spells on your creation, I would have supervised you a little more." He shook his head and pulled the pencil from behind his ear. "Actually, if I knew you knew advanced spells, I would have given you a whole different assignment."

CHAPTER NINETEEN

"What did I do?" Paris looked around the classroom as if she'd find evidence of the catastrophe, although Chef Ash had cleaned it all up with a flick of his wrist.

"The best I can tell, you combined a quick-cooking spell with three powerful magical spices," he explained, and his eyes bulged. "Oh, and your use of sizzling aromatic vegetables like onions and jalapeños simply magnified things, carrying the intoxicating spell throughout the classroom."

"Quick-cooking spell?" Paris asked. "I'm sorry, but I'm going to need you to back up and explain this to me like a fae who is drunk."

He chuckled and nodded. "Sure thing. I get it. This is all very new to you, and no one expected those results. Honestly, I've been doing this for a few dozen years and haven't seen students perform and get results like that in…well, ever."

Paris didn't know whether to laugh or run. She decided to do neither.

"You see," Chef Ash continued, sensing Paris' nervousness and trying to put her at ease, "your spice combination was probably good. I think using them in chili was a brilliant idea, using all of their robust strengths to the dish's advantage. However, I never would have dreamed you knew a quick-cooking spell. We don't teach it here since it has mixed results, as you've seen."

"I didn't really know it," Paris admitted. "But you said that cooking was instinct and I sort of made it up, thinking of the quick-growing spell I read about in gardening."

He nodded as if this suddenly made sense. "That's pretty impressive. Most fairies wouldn't take a lesson from one class and apply it to another. Not to mention the mechanics of the spell would have to be quite different." Chef Ash tapped the pencil on the side of his head. "This must be the magician part of your brain piecing together things we fairies don't see."

She shrugged, her ears suddenly hot. "I don't know. I wasn't thinking. I'm sorry that I caused a problem."

To her surprise, he laughed. "Problem? That was the most excitement I've had...well, since you threw the perfect apple pie you made at Shannon Butcher. Still, no harm, no foul. You simply did what you thought was right. No one was hurt, and you learned a good lesson from it."

"Don't try and speed up my Uncle John's chili recipe," she guessed.

"Maybe," he stated. "Although I see what you were going for and I applaud the effort. A chili needs a good long time to get the flavors developed so your instinct there was correct. However, there are a few parts of magical cooking you have to understand. First off, the reason we don't teach quick-cooking is that it's hard to control the outcome."

Paris sighed. "Hemingway told me something similar when I used the spell for gardening."

"It's important to remember, but it doesn't mean it's off-limits," he said sensitively. "The problem with it in this case is that it heightened the effects of all the spices, making those who ate the dish 'heated up' if you will."

"But no one ate the chili," she corrected.

He smiled. "That's the other piece to this perfect storm you created. Your use of aromatic vegetables like onions, garlic, and jalapenos made it so no one had to eat the dish. Once the odor hit the air, all those who smelled it suddenly had heightened emotions —making them angry."

Paris slumped. "I'm sorry that I messed up. I won't use unapproved spells without asking in the future."

Chef Ash waved her off. "Don't be silly. You gave me a sorely needed challenge. Really there was no damage done. I think you show a lot of promise, not only as a chef but as a fairy godmother."

Paris couldn't help but feel a little sorry for herself. "Yeah, but that's the thing. I'm not a fairy. Not wholly."

"You're not." He grinned. "I've never met a fairy who did what you did today with little instruction. I look forward to seeing what you create next, Paris Beaufont. You're full of surprises, and I firmly believe that's a good thing. But the person who has to believe that most is you."

CHAPTER TWENTY

"**W**hy is it that you showed up and now pies and all sorts of other food are being launched at people's faces?" Hemingway asked Paris beside her at the dinner table.

"I think food fights have long been overdue," Christine joked. Her eyes flicked up to meet Chef Ash's gaze, and an embarrassed expression crossed her face. "Not that your food should be wasted and launched at people's faces."

The good-natured chef laughed. "Food is an expression of art. I'm not offended if people throw my banana cream pies around as long as it's not because they tasted so bad that they had to get rid of it."

Christine appeared relieved. "That was the most fun class we've ever had, even though it took me forever to get that marinade out of my hair. Still, it was worth it when I threw that tomato at the back of Becky's head."

"You're not supposed to hit someone with their back turned." Hemingway mock-scolded her, although a smile hid behind his eyes.

"Yeah, because Becky doesn't take a cheap shot every chance

she gets." Christine pursed her lips. "I can't be responsible for what I did. I was under a spell. Also, Becky had thrown a pile of cabbage at Penny's face. At least I only hit her in the back with a plump tomato."

"Yeah, thanks for helping," Penny said on the other side of Christine. "Becky wasn't going to stop, it seemed."

"Maybe I'm a little offended that you all threw my fresh-farmed vegetables at each other." Hemingway pouted, but Paris could see that he didn't really mean it.

"Are you?" Christine fired back.

Hemingway laughed. "Not in the least. As you said, you all were spelled."

"Quite the spell." Christine glanced at Paris, taking a bite of her shepherd's pie. "You have to teach me how to do that."

"I'm not sure that's a good idea," Chef Ash cut in. "Besides, I'm not sure it's possible."

"Because Paris is using a hybrid of fairy and magician magic," Hemingway guessed while tearing into a flaky biscuit.

Chef Ash nodded. "Yes. I suspect she has a greater range of spells she can perform as well as not needing an instrument for directing certain magic."

"Man, you're so lucky," Christine groaned. "I want to be you and have extra powers."

"And be a total freak who everyone stares at and whispers about, with a mysterious past and strange parents," Paris teased, not offended by her friend's comments.

"Yeah, exactly," Christine answered. "No one follows my Instagram but just think if I was this cool badass halfling. Then I could get endorsement deals and free gear."

The group all laughed. Paris had learned that much unlike most of those at Happily Ever After College, Christine wasn't a cookie-cutter goody-good. Her parents had wanted her to attend and become a fairy godmother because it was a family tradition. That's why most were there, rather than because they wanted to be fairy godmothers. Paris couldn't blame them since signing on to look like an older woman when one was a young fairy wasn't that appealing to most.

Still, most of those who attended the college had gained entrance because they had the proper courteous disposition and tendency to follow the rules. Everyone knew that the rebels and bad kids went to Tooth Fairy College. However, because Christine was crafty, she'd figured out how to pass the personality part of the entrance exam, making her parents happy, but she had color and an edgy side to her that Paris appreciated.

"I don't think that it's all fun and games being a halfling, even if Paris has some extra powers," Chef Ash offered thoughtfully, giving her a caring look.

She sighed and decided not to put on the mask in front of her friends. "I'll be fine. I just want to go and find some answers."

"When?" Hemingway asked at once, urgency in his gaze.

Paris shrugged, pushing her peas around on the plate. "I'm going to go meet with my uncle tonight. That's where I have to start. He did raise me after all."

"Do you want me to go with you?" he offered, concern evident in his blue eyes.

She shook her head. "No, I should be fine. I mean, I lived on Roya Lane all my life. I think I simply need to be careful out there in the world." Paris pointed at the bank of windows, indicating the vast world unprotected by portal magic.

Hemingway didn't appear confident about this as he wiped his mouth with his napkin. "Well, if you change your mind..."

"That's so crazy that you have magician parents," Christine thankfully cut in, relieving Paris of Hemingway's pleading gaze. "Like, how two magicians made a fairy is cramping my brain."

"Science could be involved," Chef Ash offered.

"Or magic," Hemingway supplied.

"Maybe your parents used an egg donor," Penny said sheepishly, looking down at her plate at once when everyone glanced at her. "I mean, that's probably not what happened. That's a dumb idea."

"Not at all," Chef Ash corrected. "I mean, I don't know how the science could work, but it is always making progress. It would involve complex magic, but they could have used a fairy egg, and the magician's well, you know…"

"Sperm," Christine supplied with an abrupt laugh. "It's great that we're pondering Paris' mysterious conception."

Paris pushed her plate away, suddenly not at all hungry. "Yeah, it's freaking awesome."

Christine grinned at her. "I'm sure you'll get some answers. Then you have to tell me right away."

"If she wants to," Hemingway corrected, giving Paris a thoughtful expression. "You don't have to tell anyone anything. This is your business."

"Oh, she'll want to tell someone, and I'm a great listener," Christine remarked.

"Since when?" Chef Ash teased. "Can you start practicing this great listening in class?"

Christine shook her head. "You know, I think I want to freeze a bunch of my eggs. Like, a ton of them."

"Why?" Penny asked. "In case you want to have kids later?"

Christine shook her head. "No, I'd donate all of them."

"Because?" Paris drew out the word, sensing this was going somewhere unexpected.

Christine sat back with a mischievous grin on her face. "No, I love the idea of a bunch of jerks like me populating the globe."

The group laughed, gaining attention from others at the long table where most of the students were having polite conversations and not bursting out in laughter.

"I should have guessed that it wasn't for altruistic reasons." Hemingway pushed back from the table.

"You really should have." Christine pointed at something between her and Paris. "What's this?"

She glanced down at her elbow, finding a small silk pouch. Around the drawstring was a tag that said: "For Paris."

Paris frowned and looked between her friend and the pouch several times, at a loss for words momentarily. "I don't know. Where did it come from?"

Christine shook her head. "I don't know. I don't think it was there a moment ago."

Even though everyone watched her and none of them looked close to giving her privacy, Paris opened the pouch. Inside, her fingers dug around until she found a small coin. When she pulled it out, she found that most of the engravings were worn, making them difficult to decipher.

"It's very old," Chef Ash offered.

"What is it?" Penny questioned.

Paris turned it over in her fingers, not understanding why she'd receive such an object. It was silver and crudely constructed. The coin was definitely old. "I don't know."

"May I?" Hemingway held out his hand.

Paris relinquished it to him, wanting information on the object.

"I think it might be…" His gaze drifted up to Chef Ash. "Do you think that maybe…"

Without answering the cut-off sentences, Chef Ash extended his arm, opening his palm. Hemingway placed the coin in his hand.

Chef Ash studied the coin, and a smile lit up his eyes. "Yeah, this seems like her kind of work."

"What?" Paris questioned. "Whose? What is it?"

"It's hard to know for certain," Chef Ash began while handing the coin back to Paris, "but this seems like Mae Ling's handiwork."

Paris looked down the table but didn't find the fairy godmother in her usual spot. She glanced back at the coin. "The coin is her handiwork? I don't understand."

Hemingway shook his head. "No, it's been enchanted. I think that it's a protective charm." He pointed to the coin. "If I were you,

I'd have that on your person when you leave Happily Ever After on your investigations."

Paris let out a breath, grateful for the help and the information and also wishing that mystery didn't cloak everything in her life. Still, she slipped the protective charm into her pocket, feeling more secure already by having it with her.

CHAPTER TWENTY-ONE

S uddenly, standing outside the flat where Paris had grown up most of her life felt strange. Roya Lane was settling down for the night. The shops had closed, and the stragglers were finding their way to pubs or bars or other places that would take them in away from the cold London air.

Although Roya Lane was in London, it was also like Happily Ever After and not accessible to most because it required portal magic to enter. Because of mapping, many knew that Roya Lane existed in a secret place in London, but that same information wasn't available about Happily Ever After College. It did seem to be in a bubble, making it feel like it wasn't on Earth at all—although it undoubtedly had to be.

Paris started up the stairs to the second story where Uncle John's apartment was, every step feeling like it was bringing her closer to the truth. The coin from Mae Ling—or whoever—was in her pocket and that gave her confidence, although she'd never felt in danger when around Uncle John. Still, it couldn't hurt to have a protective charm on her when there was so much uncertainty in the world.

She lifted her hand, about to knock as if she was a guest. How long had passed since she'd seen Uncle John? Only a few weeks, but it felt like forever. She had moved out a while ago, but not entirely. She often went to his place, raiding his refrigerator or pestering him about one thing or another.

Still, it felt wrong to barge in when she didn't live there anymore and hadn't for a while. She quietly rapped on the door, jiggling the door handle at the same time.

"Hey Uncle John," she said, creaking the door open slightly. They had said they'd meet at eight o'clock. "It's Paris. You there?"

She opened the door all the way and found the place completely wrecked. Clothes littered the hallway, and appliances lay broken all over the floor. Paris' heart went into overdrive, beating wildly. She jerked her head from side to side, looking into the front room where she used to sleep and was now Uncle John's study, then to the small galley kitchen. More destruction.

Paris knew that she needed to proceed carefully in case the perpetrator was still there. Her uncle had taught her that much when entering a crime scene. Her heart told her something different. It said that the one person she loved most was in danger so Paris bolted forward down the long hallway to the living and dining room, unafraid if she was springing toward danger. She'd kick its ass if it were harming her uncle.

CHAPTER TWENTY-TWO

P aris halted in the center of the living room, taking in the broken furniture and strewn books and then her uncle sitting on the couch, his elbows on his knees and his head down. He brought his chin up slowly, almost as though surprised that Paris was there.

"Oh, did you call, Pare? I'm sorry. I didn't hear you."

Jerking her head around, her fist up in the air as if she might need to fight a monster, Paris drew in a breath. "What happened here? Are you okay?"

He nodded heavily. "I wasn't here when this happened."

Striding forward, Paris ducked her head into the back bedroom and bathroom, finding more the same—demolition of Uncle John's property. She returned to the living room, her heart beating rapidly. "What happened?"

"I wish I knew, Pare. I returned from the stakeout early and came home to find this, not even a few minutes ago."

Paris studied the flat, wondering why someone would go after her uncle and what they were looking for. "Wait, why did you return from the stakeout early?"

SARAH NOFFKE & MICHAEL ANDERLE

He blinked at her, his eyes red and a sobering expression on his face. "About that... I didn't want to tell you over the phone. FLEA was attacked by...well, I don't know what."

"Something attacked the Fairy Law Enforcement Agency?" Paris questioned. "Why?" As soon as she asked the question, she realized he'd already told her that he didn't know the answer.

"Pare, whatever attacked FLEA...it got Charlotte..."

Paris choked on her next breath. Charlotte had been the receptionist at FLEA for as long as she could remember. The small, round fairy always sat behind the counter, taking calls and making coffee, and offering Paris consolation smiles when she was getting in trouble for one offense or another.

"When you say got..." Paris studied her uncle, reading the tension in his every movement and expression. "You don't mean she's in the hospital do you?"

He shook his head, pain radiating in his eyes. "She's dead, and her death is a complete mystery."

"Oh, wow." Paris wasn't sure what to say or how to feel. This was all so much, so fast.

Uncle John glanced out at the chaos that was his flat. "I came back immediately, having heard about the attack. Then I arrived here and found this. I have no idea who is after the Fairy Law Enforcement Agency, but they seem really dangerous."

Paris gulped, unable to fully process the death of a woman she'd known most of her life. This was a lot. It would take time. She couldn't do it now.

She cleared her throat, straightened, and gathered strength. "Uncle John, I think I might know what's going on, although I have no idea why or how, and that's why I need your help. You have to fill in the rest."

CHAPTER TWENTY-THREE

U ncle John didn't interrupt the entire time that Paris spoke. Instead, his eyes simply shifted back and forth as if he was hearing all this for the first time. When she had shared everything she knew, Paris simply leaned against the wall with her arms crossed, checking to ensure she wasn't stepping on something and regarding Uncle John with a look that said, "Your turn."

He sucked in a breath and suddenly seemed to age ten years at once. "Pare, I-I-I...I don't know what to say."

"Why don't you start with the truth?" Her voice rose unnaturally. "Am I a halfling? Did you know about that? Is my mom Liv Beaufont and my father Stefan Ludwig? Were they both magicians who were Warriors for the House of Fourteen? Did you give me the heart-shaped locket to keep my identity a secret? Am I endangered? Is that what could have gone after Charlotte and your place? Because word has spread about me being a halfling, is something after me? Tell me what you know!"

A pained expression like when Uncle John ate too many peppers crossed his face. "Pare, I can't...I really can't."

Her eyes widened, and she wanted to yell and scream. To tell him to stop lying, but then she realized all at once that he wasn't.

Uncle John really couldn't. He couldn't tell her anything. He, like Mae Ling, had been spelled.

"Tell me who made it so you can't tell me the truth," Paris urged.

His mouth contorted oddly. "Pare, if I could, I would. I have never lied to you. I never will…"

"Then tell me, did you know this history of mine?" she asked. "At least nod. Let's play twenty questions."

A surprising smile briefly rose to his mouth. "You are your parent's child."

"Uncle John! That's what I'm talking about!" Paris roared. "You knew them! Tell me everything! What happened to them?"

"Pare, I can't. I *can* tell you that your parents were great people, and yes, I knew them, but that's the most of it," he explained. "Little things, like that you remind me of your mother every single day, can leak through, but that's all I'm allowed to say, and that's only because it's a loophole."

Paris' heart hurt—almost like the very first time, to think she was like her mother, Liv Beaufont.

"Yes, I knew your history," he stated. "But I couldn't—I can't say anything else. I'm sorry. I'm so, so, so sorry. I can't speak the words. I can't write them down. There's no way for me to tell you what I know."

"Who can?" Paris asked.

He looked at her, total heartache in his eyes. That was all Uncle John could tell her, and it was hurting him. That hurt her worse than anything she'd ever experienced.

"The Beaufonts," Paris began. "That's the key to unraveling this whole thing, isn't it?"

The man she trusted with her whole heart simply let out a breath in reply.

"Can you tell me where to find them? I have an uncle and an aunt. Clark and Sophia."

Uncle John looked surprised that she knew this information. "I can't tell you how to find Sophia. She can only be found if she wants to be."

"I'm guessing she won't want to be found by some halfling niece who has some mysterious danger taking out other people," Paris muttered and instantly felt bad for it. "I'm sorry, Uncle John. If whatever is apparently after me did this and murdered Charlotte..."

"It's not your fault," Uncle John stated at once. "But yes, that makes the most sense now. You must be very careful. You should return to the college right away. You'll be safe there."

"This is why you kept it all a secret, isn't it?" Paris asked. "Something is after me, isn't it?"

He nodded.

"But you can't tell me, can you?"

Another nod.

"All the questions in the world probably won't get me close enough," she muttered. "I simply don't know what I don't know."

Uncle John smirked. "That sounds like something your mother would have said."

Paris gave him a curious expression. "That's the second time you've said something like that in this conversation. Why?"

He gave her a serious look. "I simply couldn't talk about her before, and you didn't ask anything because of the locket. Now that you know the truth and the identity charm has been broken, I can."

Paris pulled out the locket, wondering who was behind this, both the evil person and the one who had spelled others not to talk, and also wondering if it was the same person. "This charm... you gave it to me..."

"To protect you," Uncle John stated. "Even though you've broken that spell, you must still keep the locket on you."

"Why?" Paris asked, but she knew at once that it didn't matter. He couldn't talk. As sorry as she felt for herself for being kept in the dark, she felt worse for Uncle John, who couldn't tell her what she wanted to know. She knew it was hurting him—that it had always hurt him. For whatever reason, he'd done it anyway to protect her. Now she had to figure out why without undoing everything he'd tried to do for her.

"Is there anything you can tell me?" Paris looked at him directly. "Now that the identity charm is gone…"

He nodded. "I can tell you where to find your Uncle Clark, but I'll warn you, he can't tell you anything much. He was spelled too, but he should know that the charms set up long ago are broken now. He should be alerted. We're all in danger again... Really, I'm not sure it's safe for you to be out. You should be at the college."

Paris shook her head. "I was given a protective charm." She pulled the coin from her pocket and held it up.

Uncle John sighed with relief. "Good. That will help, but please know, there's no foolproof protection. You must be very careful."

Paris didn't care if Clark wouldn't talk. She wanted to meet everyone and anyone who brought her closer to the truth.

"I can tell you that your mother was by far the best person I've ever known in my life," Uncle John continued, a fondness in his eyes. "I've missed her every day that she's been gone."

Something suddenly occurred to Paris that never had before. She was a Beaufont. Her father was a Ludwig. Uncle John was a Nicholson. None of it added up now. She knew he couldn't tell her much, but he could answer a yes or no question, hopefully.

"Uncle John, you weren't related to my mother or my father, were you? You aren't my real uncle."

A look of surprise sprang to his bloodshot eyes, and he nodded.

That one answer brought so many more questions to Paris' mind, realizing that the man she was raised by, she wasn't at all related to.

CHAPTER TWENTY-FOUR

Uncle John wouldn't allow Paris to help him clean up his place. He wanted her back at Happily Ever After College but was relieved by the fact that she had the protective charm.

Paris was more worried about him and his safety. Something had murdered Charlotte and destroyed Uncle John's apartment. She didn't think it would simply go away. Something appeared to be looking for her.

Uncle John had urged her not to worry, saying he had ways of protecting himself. Again he couldn't say much but what he did say made a chill run down her spine. "What's out there doesn't want me."

It wanted Paris. Whatever it was...

With the address of where to find Clark Beaufont in her pocket, Paris made her way down to the part of Roya Lane where she could open a portal. The streets were deserted now, and a cold wind howled down the cobbled lane.

Clark was in Los Angeles. Paris hadn't been to that city before last night when she ironically learned the truth she was currently wrestling with. Apparently, it was where her uncle lived—her real uncle. However, Paris would never think of Uncle John as anything but her uncle. Blood wasn't important to her, except in the case of learning the truth.

The area where portals were allowed was only a few dozen yards away when the howling wind picked up, nearly knocking Paris into a nearby wall. She halted, suddenly out of breath. She braced herself on the bricks with her hand, turning to look over her shoulder. It almost felt like something or someone had pushed her.

There was no one there.

The street lights were now covered in dense fog as if something had invited it out onto the lane. Paris could hardly make out where she'd come from.

Another gust surged down the street, blowing Paris' hair back and pushing her backward a few inches. She'd never experienced wind like this. It didn't feel like a regular wind at all. It felt like an attack. However, she had the protective charm and thought that should keep her safe.

On the heels of this consolation, the wind blew so hard that Paris' leather jacket flew back, nearly peeling off her shoulders. She gripped the sides, holding it tighter to her, but the winds seemed to be able to pull up the insides of her pockets. It, whatever was out there, was trying to get the protective charm off her! Uncle John was right. The protective charm wasn't foolproof. Paris knew with absolute certainty that if she stayed there, she'd lose this protection, and... She didn't know what would happen.

Paris looked back at the end of the lane. The portal area was still so far away. She didn't know if she'd make it.

She was still weighing her options when the street lamps at the portal end of the lane stole her attention as they went out—one by one.

Sucking in a breath, Paris made an impromptu decision. She

couldn't make it to the main portal area. She couldn't go back the way she came. She only had one option left.

Paris ran forward a few feet and cut down an alleyway that usually went unnoticed. She prayed that the shop she'd heard about was open. It was her only way to safety at this point.

CHAPTER TWENTY-FIVE

Paris' time on Roya Lane had told her of another portaling option. It had only ever been a rumor, but she was willing to stake her life on something so flimsy at this point.

The cutting wind raced after her as she sprinted for the shop. Thankfully the lights inside were still on. It was the only store that still appeared to be open on Roya Lane.

Maybe my luck is changing, Paris thought and pushed forward even faster. That only seemed to encourage the deathly wind that screamed through the narrow alleyway, thrust against her back, and nearly knocked her forward.

Paris had to use all her strength not to be thrown to the stone pavers where she didn't know what would happen to her.

She reached out, knowing that timing was everything. Either she made it, or she didn't, depending on how fast she was. Once inside the shop, Paris didn't know that she'd be safe. Sadly, she might bring this evil racing after her to some innocent person's doorstep. It was a risk she had to take.

The sounds of signs banging against buildings and the exteriors of the tightly congregated shops breaking echoed around Paris.

Objects torn from buildings rained down on her, but she didn't dare slow down. She didn't dare let out a breath as she neared the shop.

Ducking from a light fixture that burst, Paris covered her head with one hand as glass shards showered down on her.

Her hand was on the door handle as a chilling voice echoed at her back. Its words sounded like a guttural "No."

Not hesitating, Paris whipped the shop door open and bounded inside, slamming it behind her. She looked up at the bewildered faces of the bakery owners and the king of the fae, her chest heaving with ragged breaths.

CHAPTER TWENTY-SIX

"We're closed," a tall woman with short hair said, wiping her flour-covered hands on her apron.

Paris jerked her head to the side, peering out the window. Whatever was after her didn't come through the door for some odd reason. She wasn't complaining. In the alleyway, the winds died. The dense fog replaced it almost immediately.

"I need your help," Paris said in a desperate rush, looking back at the two women and King Rudolf Sweetwater. She would have been surprised to find him there in the Crying Cat Bakery if she had time for such things. Currently, she was trying to figure out what was going on.

"You can have help," a woman beside the other one said in a thick French accent. She had short hair too, but hers was red. "When we're open. That will be tomorrow...maybe in the morning. Hard to say. Depends on how much I drink tonight, and that depends on how much of a pain in the ass this one is." She pointed at the woman beside her.

"I love you too, dear," the taller woman muttered dryly.

"Paris." King Rudolf strode forward and looked her over. He'd dressed as regally as the first time she met him and was as handsome as she remembered. "Are you okay?"

She shook her head. "That's why I said I need help. There's something following me."

"Oh good, so you brought it here," the redhead said with pursed lips. "See yourself out, would you? And take your pursuer with you."

The other woman shook her head. "It can't get in here most likely. I have up enough wards on the Crying Cat Bakery to keep out the devil. I put them up to keep out customers, but it doesn't seem to work on the good-intentioned."

Paris tilted her head, confused but also relieved to hear the evil thing following her couldn't get her inside the shop. "You don't want customers? I don't understand."

The woman nodded. "They're bothersome. Just keep coming in and out all day long." She waved at the pastry case, which was mostly empty at this point. "They buy all our stuff and demand that we make more of this or that because they can't get enough. They never have the exact change or require us to use the credit card machine. The whole thing is a major inconvenience."

Paris glanced around the shop, wondering if she'd entered a strange alternate universe. The bakery seemed somewhat normal with large mixers in the back and bags of ingredients like flour and sugar. Overhead a few fairies flew around, cleaning or sprinkling pixie dust. "I thought the idea of a business was to be successful by having customers."

King Rudolf wagged his finger. "My friends here don't operate the same as other people."

"We aren't friends, Rudolf," the taller woman barked.

He held out his hand to Paris. "May I have the distinct privilege of introducing Paris Westbridge to my esteemed colleagues and dearest friends, Lee and her wife, Cat." The king of the fae indicated the taller woman, then the French one.

"My name is Paris Beaufont," she muttered, surprising even herself.

King Rudolf clapped his hands to his chest, shock written on his face. "You know? Who told you? It wasn't me, was it? I did black out for a few days recently but thought that I only invented a renewable resource during that time."

"You knew?" Paris had a hard time processing everything the dim-witted but also seemingly genius fae was saying. "No, it wasn't you."

He let out a breath. "Oh, that's right. I can't tell you."

"You're spelled too?" Paris questioned with surprise.

"Yeah, to be a complete idiot," Lee spat. "Will you two get out of here? I need to plan my next assassination."

"Did you just say—"

"No, we won't," Rudolf interrupted, his hands on his hips. "Didn't you hear her? This is Paris Beaufont, and more importantly, she knows she's Paris Beaufont."

Cat shrugged, toddling off for the back room. "I didn't know who I was for a quarter of a century. I kept introducing myself as Cathryn the Great because the drugs made me forget who I was, and that seemed like the most logical identity. I don't see what the big deal is. Sounds like she's simply sobered up."

"Why don't you sober up," Lee called over her shoulder as the woman disappeared into the back room.

"You knew who I was?" Paris asked the king. "In the bar, you knew? Is that why you told me about the story of Liv and Stefan, my parents?"

He glanced away. "I really can't say."

Paris sighed heavily, tired of playing this "Can't tell you" game. "What can't you say?"

"That you're in a lot of danger if you know the truth," King Rudolf stated. "That means others do too. Spells will have broken."

Paris pointed over her shoulder. "Sort of figured that out with the whole evil wind chasing me here."

Lee shook her head. "I can't stand the wind. It's always messing up my hair." She ran her hands through her tousled hair, which only made it look better. Paris wished she had that kind of luck as she combed her hands through her tangled strands.

"Did you know my parents?" Paris was suddenly bursting with so many questions for the king of the fae.

He nodded. "Your mother was the best person I've ever met. Well, besides myself. I'm the best person I've met. Most say the same."

"No one ever has ever said that…ever." Lee wiped down the countertop in front of her.

"Your father was the worst person I've ever met," Rudolf continued.

Paris gasped, not having expected that. "He was? Why?"

"Oh, he was always like 'Liv, you're the love of my life' or 'Whatever you desire, I'll give to you," Rudolf answered. "That kind of manipulation kept my best friend from spending weeks with me drunk on the beaches of Barbados. She was always like, 'I'd rather spend time with my husband than listen to your drunken drivel.' Can you believe such a thing? All orchestrated by your father's manipulation."

"Don't forget all those demons he killed," Lee added. "I mean, come on, dude. Sometimes we need a little bit of evil prowling the streets, creating nightmares and sucking out people's souls."

Paris blinked at the pair. "Are you two on drugs?"

"Tons," they both answered in unison.

Even though this interaction made Paris question her sanity, it was the first time she got real information about her parents. True, it was coming from a very questionable and probably lunatic source, but it was information, and she instantly craved more. "What else can you tell me? I want to know more about my mom and dad. How did they die?"

The light expression on the king's face fell away. "Sadly, that's about all I can say. I can tell you little things that are allowed to slip through the cracks, like that your mother loved nachos and saved my life more than a few times." He pressed his hands to his throat as if suddenly in pain. His mouth opened and closed several times, inaudible words escaping. Finally, after struggling for a moment, Rudolf sputtered out a cough. "I've said too much. Finding a loophole isn't without consequences."

Paris sighed, hoping that maybe Clark could tell her more. She'd have to start piecing together things. Her mother was good, and her father loved her dearly. She was brave, and he fought demons. That was more than she knew that morning.

"You two need to get out of here." Lee checked her watch.

Paris nodded. "Yes, that's why I'm here."

The woman gave her an annoyed expression. "You don't understand how it works, Blondie. I said you need to get out of here. Not be here. I have a hit I have to set up."

"Are you an assassin?" Paris was more curious than anything else.

The woman waved at the pastry cases. "I'm a baker."

"She's also a water treatment specialist who saves lives," Rudolf supplied proudly.

Lee rolled her eyes. "Great, now I have to counter what you've told her, or she'll get the wrong idea about me." She glanced at Paris. "Yes, I assassinate people. Lots of them. I might save villages with polluted water supplies, but I also murder. I ain't no angel."

"She only kills really evil people who deserve it," Rudolf added.

Lee shot him a murderous expression. "Would you stop it! I had a clean slate with this one to have her see me the way I wanted, and you're mucking it all up."

"By thinking that you're a good person?" Paris asked.

Lee shivered with disgust. "I hope you're not too colored by what you've learned."

"I think I know why there are so many rumors about this place," Paris stated. "I'll get out of your hair. I need to portal to Los Angeles. I heard that portal magic was allowed here, for whatever reason, even though it's usually restricted to certain areas on Roya Lane."

Lee groaned. "The secret is out. Looks like I'll have to kill everyone on Roya Lane now. I'll start with you, sweetheart. Stay still while I find my crossbow."

Rudolf shook his head. "I can take you to Los Angeles. Are you going to a Dodgers game?"

Paris narrowed her eyes at him in confusion. "No, I learned that I'm a Beaufont and a halfling with something mysterious stalking me, and no one, including you, can tell me anything. I'm going to find my relatives."

"I can tell you something," Lee offered.

"You can!" Paris' eyes widened with surprise and hope.

"Yeah, that you're going to make me late for my hit." Lee rummaged around in the back, apparently looking for a crossbow. "I hate being late. I feel like it irks the Grim Reaper."

Paris slumped with defeat. "So you can't tell me anything about my parents or past then?"

Lee straightened suddenly and thought for a moment. "Honestly, if I knew anything, I've forgotten it. Your family history isn't that interesting to me. Yes, we're all spelled."

"By who? That's what I want to know," Paris muttered to herself, knowing the two couldn't tell her.

King Rudolf strode forward, offering his arm. "I can't tell you what you'd like to know, but I can take you to see one of your relatives in Los Angeles. Clark is the second-worst after your father and about as dull as a doorknob, but he'll be interested to know your identity charm broke. Shall we go?"

Paris didn't need a chaperone, but she figured if whatever was following her went to Los Angeles, that it would be good to have extra help. She nodded and took the king's offered arm. "Yes, let's go."

CHAPTER TWENTY-SEVEN

"Where are we?" Paris asked after she and King Rudolf stepped through a portal to a very urban area.

She was worried that the evil wind had followed them, but there were no gale-force winds wherever they were—only a gentle breeze and the smell of car fumes. The sun was still shining in their mystery location, and the street in front of them was busy with shiny cars speeding by. Passing them on the streets were people dressed in many different fashions: attractive women, hip men, or those who looked like they could simultaneously pass as both.

"I think we're still on Earth, but I've messed up my portals more than once and ended up on strange planets." King Rudolf looked around. "Yeah, this is either West Hollywood, or it's that weird space station that I often confuse with the LA city."

"You... Never mind." Paris shook her head while taking in the strange smells and sights.

"Yeah, this is West Hollywood," King Rudolf finally decided. "I can tell because everyone is too cool for school." He pointed at a guy strolling past them. "You pull up your pants." Then he stuck his finger in someone else's face. "You roll down your pants." And without missing a beat, he spun and wagged his finger at a homeless man covered in newspapers. "Would you put on some pants? There are children present."

"No, there's not," the bum grumbled.

King Rudolf indicated Paris. "This one is only twenty. She's pretty much a toddler by fairy standards." He glanced at Paris appreciatively. "By magician's standards, you're simply gorgeous. Most magicians shouldn't breed, in my opinion, but it's hard to get such laws passed, even from my position. I don't understand why such ugly nerds get to pass along their homely looks when we could be expanding the fae population."

"Because then we'd have a bunch of dummies who ate dirt, and the population would surely die out in no time, making the human race join the dodo birds."

Rudolf nodded as if this made perfect sense to him. "We prefer to eat clay because of the texture, but yeah, we wouldn't last very long. But what a gorgeous population it would be for a hot minute."

"Your triplets," Paris began, following King Rudolf as he led the way down the busy sidewalk.

"Quadruplets," he corrected. "I only have three children."

Paris opened her mouth to correct him but then thought better of it and simply nodded. "Right... Your girls are halflings. Can you share a bit about their struggles, as you did before? Are there a lot of people after them because they're unique and special?"

"After them, yes," King Rudolf answered. "That's mostly because they inherited their mother's offensive ways. I can't take them anywhere without them telling someone that their blouse doesn't match their pants or they're wearing something that looks like hand-me-downs."

"That's rude," Paris agreed.

"It is, but in their defense, the elderly at the old folks' home where they volunteer don't know style. Most of them can't even dress themselves."

Again Paris' mouth hung open. She was speechless about how to respond. Paris was starting to think the joke was on her and someone was recording her to see how far she'd take these ridiculous statements from the king of the fae.

"There are quite a few men who are after my girls because they're beautiful," Rudolf continued. "Then there's the IRS, CIA, and FBI who say they've broken one or two laws. I mean really, I think those organizations need to quit hiding behind their letters and tell us what they do. How do I know what the IRS is after if they don't specifically tell me who they are?"

"That's the Internal Revenue Service," Paris muttered dryly.

"See!" King Rudolf exclaimed. "Was that so hard? But when I kept asking them who they were and what they wanted, they went on and on about tax evasion. I mean, taxes aren't something the rich even pay, am I right?"

"I think you're supposed to."

"As far as I'm concerned with the FBI and CIA, if they don't have any evidence besides those videos and firsthand accounts of treason and espionage, then I say my girls are innocent," King Rudolf stated triumphantly. "But no, besides that, no one is after my girls. However, they aren't like you."

"They *are* halflings."

"That they are," he said fondly. "You're something unique. There are three of them and only one of you. While a mortal and fae is special, that's only one magical race mixed with a bland normal one. You're comprised of two magical races."

That was surprisingly helpful and new information for Paris. "I guess that makes sense. Before, you said that your girls were bitter at you because they had trouble integrating into the world since they couldn't relate to either of their races and therefore weren't accepted. Do you think I'll have the same problem now that word is spreading? Will magicians and fairies shun me?"

"Only if they want a knuckle sandwich from Uncle Rudolf." He held up his fist and waved it in the air.

Paris couldn't help but giggle at this. She didn't even know this man, and he was calling himself her uncle. That was more than strange since she recently found out the only person she'd known as an uncle wasn't related to her, and Rudolf was definitely not her blood. Well, and not to mention they were on their way to meet her actual uncle.

"No, I don't think they'll shun you," Rudolf continued. "You'll be revered or regarded with awe for your beauty and abilities and uniqueness. I can't imagine you being outed. My girls' problems are because mortals still don't trust the magical races and there are pockets of the magical community that still think they're better than mortals. So the Captains fall into this weird in-between and can't win no matter what. Things will evolve, as they always do, and they'll make their mark. They just have to weather the storm."

"You know, sometimes you say the most intelligent things," Paris observed.

"It's because I eat organic clay for breakfast."

"Followed by the most idiotic things," Paris added.

He gave her a fond look. "You remind me of your mother so much. That sounds exactly like something she would have said to me."

"How did you meet my mom?" Paris was addicted to learning about her past, now that she wasn't spelled not to care.

Rudolf let out a strange noise and grabbed his throat, shaking his head. "Sorry, I think that falls under things I'm not allowed to say. Probably some part of it would be too much and lead to information I'm not at liberty to expand upon."

Paris grunted in frustration. It was becoming increasingly annoying that all these people connected to her and her parents weren't allowed to say anything. She simply wanted to know about the people she came from, especially when she met those who knew them, yet she kept hitting a wall. "Why would your meeting my mom lead to information I'm not supposed to know?"

"Probably because—" Rudolf coughed violently, holding his chest. It took him a moment to collect himself. Finally, he shook his head. "Yeah, that one isn't on the table either."

"What a tricky spell and a lot of them that were simply to keep me hidden from the truth," Paris remarked.

"That's nothing." Rudolf pointed down a side street. "We're this way. My wife has gone so far as to chloroform me for a solid week to keep me from learning about things she bought. We do extreme things for the ones we love."

Paris halted and narrowed her eyes.

Rudolf, sensing she wasn't beside him anymore, paused and turned back to look at her. "Did you find a roly-poly to play with? Bring him along. Maybe we can find one for me too."

Paris shook her head. "You said, 'we do extreme things for the ones we love.' Which leads me to believe someone who cared about me or my parents or both did all this, spelling everyone so they couldn't talk."

Rudolf grinned at her, a proud look in his beautiful blue eyes. "You're bright, even for being a fairy."

"Thank you." She drew out the word and tried to decide whether to be offended or not.

"I still can't give you any information," Rudolf continued. "My throat is going to be scratchy for a week based on how much I've said."

"Well, I appreciate your help and escorting me to see Clark."

King Rudolf paused. "You really should be grateful because I don't stomach the Councilor for the House of Fourteen very well. He always thinks I'm flirting with him when I tell him to take off his clothes, or he's offended when I throw his flan in the air, and it lands on the floor."

"Why would you do either of those things?"

"Because pinstriped suits belong in the trash. And I was under the impression that good flan should bounce."

"Well, thanks for stomaching my uncle to take me to meet him," she stated. "I'll admit that I'm a bit nervous. This is all so sudden and surreal. I learned yesterday that I was a halfling and a Beaufont."

He nodded and stopped in the middle of the sidewalk. "I totally get it. I was today years old when I learned that you have to look both ways before crossing the street. I mean, did you know that cars drive in two directions? It's not like in England when they go the opposite direction in one way."

"Actually… That's not really… Never mind. Yeah, it sounds like you totally get my predicament of recently learning who I am and being pursued by a mysterious evil."

Rudolf gave her an encouraging look. "I do. I really do. Cher is still stalking me because of some misunderstanding. As far as knowing who I am, well, that's a complete mystery to me. I simply crawled out of a wishing well and named myself Rudolf Sweetwater, hoping the murky details would fill in over time. That was six hundred years ago, and nothing has surfaced since. So, yes, I get it."

Paris couldn't help but laugh at the guy beside her. Yes, he had the IQ of a jar of pickles, but he was also endearing. He sounded like he was maybe one of her mother's best friends—or very committed stalkers. Anyway, it still made her proud to know her parents had royalty for friends even if he was a complete moron.

Looking up and down the busy street, Paris studied the area. "Where to next?"

Rudolf's expression turned uncertain. "That's the tricky part. Now we have to cross the street. Are you prepared to look both ways?"

Paris glanced back and forth and nodded. "I think I can handle it, although motorways aren't really my thing, having grown up on Roya Lane."

He held out his arm to her. "Well, have no fear. Uncle Rudolf is here to accompany you."

"Where are we headed?" Paris took his arm.

He pointed at a building directly in front of them. "Right there. It's where your Uncle Clark lives."

CHAPTER TWENTY-EIGHT

"There?" Paris asked in disbelief, looking at a boarded-up old storefront. Above the display window was a sign that read, "John's Electronic Repair Shop."

"Yep." Rudolf led her across the road when it was clear, whipping his head back and forth as if a car might suddenly appear.

"My uncle lives in a closed-down electronics repair shop?" she questioned.

"No, silly. That would be weird. He lives in the tiny little apartment above it."

Paris glanced up at the second story, which had a brick façade and small balcony with a fire escape ladder that led to the rooftop. "I guess that's not so bad. It's sort of charming."

King Rudolf huffed. "I guess. I mean, it's not the Cosmopolitan Hotel and Casino in Las Vegas, but it's better than living in North Hollywood."

Paris laughed. "Who would live at the Cosmopolitan?"

"Me." He proudly placed his hand on his chest. "That's where my kingdom headquarters is, but I mostly live in Canada now because everyone is much nicer there. Besides, a king doesn't have to sit on his throne to rule a race of people."

"Yeah, I guess you can rule remotely with electronics," Paris agreed.

He shook his head. "Oh no. I can't use a computer. It interferes with my genius."

"Is that the issue?" she dryly retorted as they paused in front of a set of stairs that led to the second story. Nervous butterflies fluttered in her stomach. She was about to meet a blood relative.

"I use the telepathic link." He tapped the side of his head. "Apparently, I need to have the IT department look into some bugs though, because my council constantly tells me they aren't getting my messages."

She thought about picking apart the whole telepathic link thing but instantly decided against it. "You have an IT department, but you don't use computers?" Paris questioned.

"Why is that so weird?" he questioned quite seriously. "Every king needs to have an Internal Thoughts department. Raphael, the department head, sold me on the telepathic link before I even hired him. He created his job and the department. Brilliant guy and saves us a ton on paper costs, but communications aren't what they used to be."

"I hope you don't pay him that much," Paris remarked.

"I'm not sure what I pay him," Rudolf related. "He sent it to me in a message, but I didn't receive it. He said that it got lost in the brain mainframe. I told him, 'Whatever I'm paying you, I'm going to double it so we can fix this problem.' That was twenty-something years ago, and we haven't had that problem since. He does his job so well most of the time that I never hear from him."

"You know that... I mean, he's not really... Never mind." Paris shook her head and regarded the stairs in front of her.

"Would you like to go up now or do you want to stall some more?" Rudolf questioned. "I can tell you all about the losers in North Hollywood if so. That's where the real whiners live. They're the starving artists who are all butt-hurt that West Hollywood is so much better than them so they cling to the idea that they aren't selling out to get a leading role. The real truth is they couldn't act their way out of a paper bag and would sleep with every director in town to get a job if they didn't have a whole host of ST—"

"Yeah, I think I'm ready to go up," Paris interrupted, not sure she was ready but deciding that if she listened to King Rudolf much longer, she might lose too many brain cells.

"Very well." The fae led her up to the second floor. "Get ready to be really bored. Clark Beaufont is totally lame."

CHAPTER TWENTY-NINE

The short breezeway on the second floor had several doors to different residents, making Paris think that Clark's apartment must be tiny. That took the pressure off because she worried deep down that her family were these posh types that might look down on her for living in a small studio apartment and not having much money. The thought had crossed her mind, especially when she learned that King Rudolf lived at the Cosmopolitan, but he was the king of the fae, after all.

Paris stood to the side of the door as Rudolf knocked twice. A moment later, the door opened slightly, followed by the appearance of a very attractive man with blond hair that was slicked back and brushed to the side and blue eyes. He was older than her, but as a magician, that wasn't saying very much. He could be in his forties or two hundred years old. Clark wore a pinstriped suit that reminded her of Wilfred's daily attire.

"What do you want?" He looked King Rudolf up and down with a scowl on his face. "You know we aren't supposed to talk."

"Every year since our last conversation has been a breath of fresh air, dearest Clark," Rudolf stated in a dignified manner. "I'm here because I have someone to introduce you to." He held his hand out to Paris in a presenting way. "May I have the honor of introducing—"

"G-G-Guinevere," Clark stuttered, his eyes wide and his face covered in shock. "I-I-If you're here, that means—"

"The identity charm broke," King Rudolf interrupted. "Which is why I can talk to you, although I think we should go back to not talking after this. This brief interaction with you has hurt my soul."

"G-G-Guinevere," Clark stammered again, looking between Rudolf and Paris.

"You've already said that," Rudolf stated. "I think she prefers to go by Paris." He looked at her thoughtfully. "Is that correct?"

Paris nodded. Her insides suddenly felt all smashed together. Her palms were sweating, and she was dizzy.

"You know?" Clark asked her. "What all do you know? If someone broke the charm..." He raked his fingers into his gelled-back hair and shook his head as if it suddenly hurt.

"She's aware that she's in danger," Rudolf said. "She doesn't know anything other than she's Paris Beaufont, and Liv and Stefan are her parents. I did tell her how horrible her father is, although it scorched my throat."

Clark gave him a punishing expression. "You shouldn't have been able to tell her that much. The silencing spell..."

"I didn't tell her who her parents are," Rudolf stated smugly.

"It was a professor at Happily Ever After College," Paris offered, finally finding her voice. "I found out yesterday that I'm half-fairy and half-magician and a Beaufont. I don't know how she discovered the information, but she did, and I'm here to find answers."

Clark sighed. "Then I'm afraid you've come to the wrong place."

"Uncle John said as much." Paris had expected his answer and kept her expectations low. "He also said that you'd need to be alerted about the identity charm breaking."

Clark nodded. "Yes, that changes everything. You're in a lot of danger."

"Which is why she probably shouldn't be hanging out in this hallway," Rudolf sang. "She was being pursued on Roya Lane, but I think we're safe at the moment."

"I have a protective charm." Paris patted her pocket where the coin was.

"Smart girl," Rudolf said proudly.

"Yes, but I think it only helps me so much," she said with disappointment, thinking of the cutting wind.

Clark nodded. "Yes, nothing is infallible. You should be safe in here." He pulled back the door, welcoming her into his place. "We can talk briefly, but I'll warn you, I can't say much."

"I understand." Paris took a step forward but was tugged back by Rudolf gently gripping her arm.

"My love, I leave you here," he said fondly. "I trust you'll be fine with Clark, albeit extremely underwhelmed after being in my presence."

"Bye, Rudolf," Clark said dismissively.

Ignoring him, Rudolf continued. "If you ever need anything, simply send me a message."

"Over the telepathic link," Paris stated dryly.

"Precisely!" Rudolf glanced at Clark. "I'd invite myself into your hovel of a home, but I just had my shoes shined and don't want to have to do it again."

"You weren't invited inside," Clark fired back.

"Please tell your lovely wife that I said hello and that she can do so much better than you." Rudolf backed toward the stairs and waved. "Farewell, Paris. Until we meet again."

With that, the king of the fae disappeared, leaving Paris standing in front of a stranger and the only blood relative she'd ever met...or could remember meeting.

CHAPTER THIRTY

Paris felt as though she'd stepped through to a brand-new world when she crossed the threshold to Clark's apartment. It wasn't only because she entered her mysterious uncle's home, but also because it wasn't at all tiny as she expected.

Paris halted inside the apartment and backed up, looking at the cramped hallway and the next residence's proximity. Then she stepped inside again and gave Clark a strange look.

He nodded with understanding. "Yes, it's bigger on the inside. Renovation spells."

Paris glanced around at the large and very fancy apartment. It was the poshest place she'd ever been inside.

So much for thinking my relatives won't judge me for being uncultured and poor, she thought.

A crystal chandelier hung overhead in the entryway, illuminating the bright white walls and vaulted ceiling. The marble floors matched the walls and the winding staircase that led to the second floor. Everything was white, making Paris feel like she stood out in her black leather jacket and pants.

"Please come in." Clark gestured at the long hallway that led to a large living area that was also all white with large sofas and glass tables and minimal personal effects. "The wards should keep you safe here. At least for a little while."

"From what?" Paris asked.

Clark paused beside the sofa and pressed his lips together, a look on his face that said, "I can't say."

Paris nodded. "It was worth a shot."

"Please sit." He indicated the sofa. "What do you know?"

She remained standing. "I know what King Rudolf told you and that Uncle John isn't my real uncle but you are, and Sophia is my aunt, and something is trying to get to me. I think it was using wind to try and take the protective charm off me."

Clark nodded, not sitting either. He seemed like the ultra-serious type, also very much like Wilfred, but Paris didn't mind that so much even if King Rudolf found it boring. Clark was the complete opposite of the flamboyant fae.

"Uncle John said that you should be alerted because you all would be in danger," Paris continued. "But that whatever was out there wanted me."

"That's exactly right," Clark paced, rubbing his fingers together as he did. "I should be fine here and at the House of Fourteen, but yes, we will need to set up extra protection, especially for you."

"I have the charm."

"But as you mentioned…" His sentence trailed away, and Paris got the impression that he couldn't even mention the danger that had tried to take it off her because of this silencing spell. She remembered that the little King Rudolf had disclosed had caused him pain and it wasn't even crucial information.

"I live at Happily Ever After College," she disclosed.

He let out a sigh of relief. "Good. You're completely safe there. I can't think of a better place for you. John is very smart to have sent you there."

Paris' face flushed. "Well, he didn't really have a choice."

Clark paused his pacing and regarded her with confusion. His look said, "Go on then."

She didn't know why she'd tell him about her past when she could paint herself any way she wanted, but she also reasoned that the truth would come out at some point so she might as well be honest. Honestly, she wanted to share the details of her life with him. He was her blood relative, and she wanted to know him. It was like a yearning in her soul. Paris reasoned that even if Clark couldn't tell her about her past or answer her questions, he could still share information about his life. That made her warm with happiness.

"I got in trouble," Paris stated.

"Trouble? Like how?"

"With the law on Roya Lane."

"When was this?" he asked, quite seriously.

"Oh, a few weeks ago and before that, a few weeks before. Then before that, well, I've pretty much been arrested a few dozen times."

To her surprise, Clark laughed. "You are your mother's child."

There it was again—that phrase. Everyone kept saying it lately. Paris didn't know how she could act like someone who she only had one or two fuzzy memories of. When she focused, she could see her mother's face swim in her mind, but if she focused on it, then it disappeared instantly like a dream.

"She was a rebel?" Paris wanted all the details.

Clark's face went serious again. He simply nodded. "I'm sorry, I wish I could tell you more. I'm sure you want to know everything, and you're still in shock, having just learned all this."

She sighed. "That's a bit of an understatement, but yes. I don't even know what to do at this point since no one can talk. I knew I needed to find you. Also Sophia. Can you take me to her? Uncle John said she couldn't be found unless she wanted to be?"

Clark's gaze darted to a white grandfather clock that ticked loudly. "I'd guess she'll get this news soon. If you just learned and have already been pursued, it will have spread quickly. I bet I was going to hear about it at the House of Fourteen."

Paris nodded. "Yes, apparently fairy godmothers spread information fast. It was all over the college today, and apparently, the families of the students knew. Not everyone is happy that a magician is attending the college, but the headmistress says I'm fine."

That seemed to please Clark. "Good. Yes, Willow Starr is a very competent and understanding headmistress. Still, once this information is out, it will cause more problems for you."

"Because I'm a halfling and they're rare?"

Clark chewed on his lip with that look she saw so frequently now. He couldn't say anything. "I can tell Sophia this news. She's probably on a mission."

"She's a dragonrider?" Paris remembered what Wilfred told her about her aunt being the leader of the Dragon Elite and the Rogue Riders.

He nodded. "Yes, and she'll need to know to be on guard. I'll message her."

"I know she can't tell me anything either," Paris began. "I'd still like to meet her. It would be nice to know what happened to my parents and how I became a halfling and what is after me, but since it appears you all can't tell me, I'd at least like to meet my family. My entire life feels like a lie up until this point."

Remorse crossed his face. "I'm so sorry for that, Guinevere… Paris. I really am. If there had been another way…"

"Is there something you can tell me?" Paris wondered if she could piece together unrelated bits of information. "Anything about me or my parents or my life? Maybe something about you?"

He sighed heavily as if she'd asked him to solve a complex riddle. "The silencing spell is pretty thorough. It prevents me from even telling you what my favorite color is."

Paris looked around the place. "I'm guessing it's white."

Clark smirked.

"There are apparently loopholes in the silencing spell," Paris continued. "Uncle John said the same thing about how I was like my mom, and Rudolf told me she loved nachos."

Clark nodded, a sad fondness rising in his eyes. "Yes, that's true. She did."

"You miss her," Paris observed.

Another nod. "Every single day."

"Is there somewhere I can look to find out what had happened to my parents or information on them or even a picture?" Paris pulled out her phone, realizing that it would work now that she wasn't at Happily Ever After College.

"I'm afraid not," Clark said with disappointment.

"Not even a picture?" Paris asked.

He nodded gravely. "It was for the best. To protect you. Once the identity charm broke, well, you know since you've been pursued."

"My butler at the college told me that there was information on magi-pedia.com." Hope flickered in her voice that there was something Clark had forgotten about.

"Yes, and it would simply list that Liv was a Warrior and Stefan also," Clark stated as though he was fully aware. "Everything else was erased."

Paris sat now, feeling defeated suddenly. "Why? What am I supposed to do? Hide away from something I don't know and live in confusion?"

"No," he said at once, also sitting in a white armchair across from her. "Things will come to light in time. It's simply that I can't be the one to tell you."

Paris felt tears well up in her eyes but didn't want to cry in front of this stranger. She cleared her throat. "That's what Mae Ling, a fairy godmother at the college said. She's spelled too. I don't know how to find this mystery person who can tell me the truth."

Clark thought for a moment. "Maybe I can help with that."

"You can?" Paris exclaimed, excitement beating in her chest.

He chewed on his lip again. "Maybe. First, I need to take you to Sophia."

"You will?" Paris' hopes rose. "Thank you."

"Well, it wouldn't be right not to," Clark said fondly. "She'll want to see you now that she can. I know how much it's meant to me, finally seeing you."

"It has?" Paris suddenly realized that her family hadn't abandoned her. They had stayed away from her to protect her...but why? That was the question.

He looked at her with thoughtful tenderness. "I am allowed to say that I've missed you very much and thought of you every single day, Guinevere...Paris. Sorry. That will take some getting used to. It feels so good to see who you've become finally."

"So you couldn't even check on me?" Paris remembered that Clark had told Rudolf that they weren't allowed to speak.

Clark simply nodded. "John has done a great job, it seems."

That statement brought so many questions to Paris' mind. Like, why was Uncle John the one picked to raise her? It sounded like she was somewhat safe at Clark's place or maybe with Sophia since she was a dragonrider. Then she remembered the shop downstairs and suddenly stood, a gasp falling out of her mouth.

"Is the John's Electronic Repair Store downstairs...It's Uncle Johns, isn't it?" So many threads strung together at once in her mind. Uncle John's hobby of repairing electronics. His constant interests in magitech. A past that he never talked about.

"Paris...I wish I could tell you," Clark said in reply.

He didn't have to because not being able to say anything confirmed her suspicions. It occurred to Paris that if she kept asking the right questions, she'd get answers even if those around her couldn't talk. Hopefully, Uncle Clark could help her as he'd offered with a very strong "Maybe."

A door in the back swung open, and Paris tensed, not realizing anyone was in the place but them.

"It's almost time for a House meeting," a woman said in a thick

Italian accent, striding into the room as she pulled on gloves. She was beautiful with her long brown hair and also distracted. She didn't notice Paris standing in the middle of the living room until she casually glanced up. Her expression immediately shifted to shock. "Oh, dear. You look like her."

CHAPTER THIRTY-ONE

The Italian woman's hand flew to her mouth. "The identity spell must be broken."

Clark stood and nodded. "Yes, she knows." He came to stand between the two women. "Alicia, this is Guinevere Beaufont, but she prefers to go by Paris."

"It is her name," the woman said as if this should have been obvious. She pulled off the glove she'd fitted and offered her hand, then thought better of it and hugged Paris tightly, as if they were best friends. "You are as beautiful as..."

Alicia's mouth slammed shut, but Paris was pretty sure she was going to say, "as I remembered," before the silencing spell kicked in.

The stranger put both her hands on Paris' shoulders and held her at arms' length, studying her face. "Those eyes..."

Clark smiled. "That's how I recognized her."

"How?" Paris felt like a watched monkey at the zoo.

"You have the Beaufont eyes," Alicia explained.

"This is my wife," Clark stated.

Paris remembered what Wilfred had told her. "You're a Warrior for the House of Fourteen."

"Yes," Alicia replied but didn't seem very happy about it. She gave Clark a sudden look of surprise like something suddenly occurred to her. "If she's here, that means…"

"She's in danger," Clark completed her sentence.

"Do you think he knows?" Alicia asked.

"He who?" Paris looked between the two.

They ignored her. Clark sighed. "I'd suspect so. Can you take Paris to see Sophia? I need to do something."

Alicia nodded adamantly. "Yes, and yes, you do. That's exactly what needs to happen."

Paris whipped her head back and forth, trying to figure out what they were talking about, speaking so covertly. "What needs to happen?"

Again not answering her question, Clark pulled out a phone and started messaging someone. "Hopefully, she's here and not in Scotland or on a mission."

"What's in Scotland?" Paris glanced between them.

"The Dragon Elite's headquarters," Alicia answered.

Clark's phone *dinged* a moment later. He glanced at it and sighed with relief. "Good, she's here."

"Great," Alicia stated. "I'll take her to the Rogue Riders' Mansion."

"Where is that?" Paris asked. "Is it far?"

"Beverly Hills," Clark informed her. "We'll have to skip today's House meeting. Once word spreads, the Council will know why."

"Okay, well, be careful." Alicia gave her husband a sturdy expression.

He nodded, and Paris expected that he'd lean forward and kiss her goodbye, but he simply returned the serious expression. "You too." Giving his attention to Paris, the look on his face shifted to pure affection. "I know this is confusing for you, but you're not alone in this. You have never been. We are your family, and the Beaufonts have a very important phrase."

He waved his hand at the white wall, and black cursive letters appeared. Paris mouthed the Latin as Clark spoke the words.

"Familia Est Sempiternum," he stated with pure conviction. "It means family is forever, and nothing could be more true for the Beaufonts. We uphold justice. We fight for those who need us. More than anything, we always stick together."

"Familia Est Sempiternum." Paris echoed, liking the way the words rolled off her tongue.

A small smile lit up Clark's blue eyes—the Beaufont eyes, so similar to Paris'. "I hope to see you again soon, but please be careful and return to Happily Ever After College as soon as you can."

Before Paris could reply, Clark spun and made for the door, urgency in his every move.

CHAPTER THIRTY-TWO

I n the presence of another stranger who knew Paris' secrets but couldn't tell her, she felt the continued nervousness in her stomach.

Alicia didn't say a word as she led Paris to a shiny red car parked on the streets. "Unfortunately, we can't portal to the Rogue Riders' Mansion, but it's not too far from here," she finally said, breaking the silence as she started the car.

Sensing Paris' hesitation, Alicia looked her over from the driver's seat. "Are you okay?"

Paris studied the car's interior, feeling like she was inside a spaceship with all the shiny buttons staring back at her. "I've never been in a car before."

Alicia's large brown eyes widened. "You haven't... Well, yes, I guess you haven't."

"There aren't cars on Roya Lane, and before a few weeks ago, I'd never left there," Paris explained.

Alicia nodded. "No, you wouldn't have."

"I mean, I've seen them on television and stuff, but that's about it. Uncle John has a lot of car parts around the house though, and he taught me how to change a spark plug once, so I guess I know more than I think. I've never ridden in a car."

The look on Alicia's face shifted, and she averted her eyes. "Well, I promise that I'm a good driver and your first car trip will be easy." She pointed at something beside Paris' right shoulder. "Put on your seat belt, and we'll get going."

Paris did as instructed, feeling the surrealness of the moment. She knew that she'd been sheltered living on Roya Lane but had never questioned it. Now she knew why. Spells were at work. She'd rebelled in many ways but never disobeyed Uncle John when he forbid her to use portal magic to leave Roya Lane. She only ever used it to travel from one end to the other.

When Alicia put the car into gear, it effortlessly glided along the road. Paris studied her every move as the Italian focused on the road and traffic ahead.

"Your Uncle John," Alicia began. "How is he?"

Paris sensed a strangeness in the question. "He's...well, this whole mess has given him so many new stresses, and I feel powerless. Someone or something murdered his secretary and ransacked his flat. I'm worried for him since something mysterious is out there, but he says he's protected and I'm the one who needs to be careful."

Alicia's mouth tightened. "He's right. John can take care of himself, and you're the one most in danger."

"But this thing," Paris began, wondering what this woman who would technically be her aunt could tell her, "it might come after all of you, right? Because it's looking for me?"

"I can't say," Alicia replied robotically.

Paris let out a breath, realizing that she should have expected this. "How do you know Uncle John?"

Alicia shook her head and turned onto a main road. Paris had never seen so much going on at once. The street was wide with multiple lanes and palm trees lining the sidewalk. People were everywhere, and the shops were diverse. It was so different than the cozy feel of Roya Lane.

"Can you tell me how you met Clark?" Paris attempted.

Alicia sighed with defeat. "The silencing spell is very strict."

"Yes, apparently Uncle Clark can't even tell me what his favorite color is," Paris related, realizing that was the first time she'd called him that aloud and noticing how natural it felt. "But the spell is weird because King Rudolf and Lee were able to tell me small things about my parents."

"You're talking about two incredibly powerful magical people," Alicia remarked. "Still, I'm sure they paid a price to tell you anything."

Paris nodded. "Yes, King Rudolf said it would give him a sore throat."

Alicia turned the car onto a less busy street that wound up a hill. Paris couldn't help but let out an audible gasp when they traveled up the road lined with lush bushes and trees. At the top of the hill was a massive wrought iron gate and behind it was a giant mansion that looked like something out of a movie.

CHAPTER THIRTY-THREE

Whereas Happily Ever After College reminded Paris of a grandmother's house, the Rogue Riders' Mansion reminded her of a movie star's place. The rolling green hills around the huge dwelling were so expansive and well-tended.

Alicia pulled the sports car up to the front door, which was two stories tall. The modern house had to have a few dozen rooms. A guy in strange clothing strode over as they got out of the car.

"What brings you here, Alicia?" the guy asked.

She tossed her keys at him, and he caught them in the air.

"Park this, will you?"

He gave her a look of uncertainty. "I don't know how to drive a car."

"You can ride a dragon," she argued. "It's pretty much the same thing."

He nodded. "Okay, but you can't get mad if I scratch the paint."

"I can and I will," she replied.

The guy gave Paris a strange look. "Who are you?"

"Park the car," Alicia directed and ushered Paris to the side of the house instead of the front door as she'd figured. "Sophia will be around here most likely."

Paris tried to keep up as the Italian hurried down a stone path alongside the building. She was so busy studying the various sights that she hardly looked where they were going. "What do the Rogue Riders do? I don't know much about them."

"They police the criminal world," Alicia explained.

"Isn't that the actual police's job?" Paris asked, confused.

"No, they lock them up," Alicia answered. "The Rogue Riders manage them."

"You mean they allow them to get away with crimes?"

"There isn't really ever stopping criminals," Alicia stated. "So the Rogue Riders ensure they operate inside certain parameters."

"Oh, so instead of having the criminals hide, they make everything transparent." Paris was intrigued by the idea.

"Exactly." Alicia turned the corner and Paris followed, but she immediately halted, not prepared for the sight before her.

CHAPTER THIRTY-FOUR

It had been fifteen years since Clark Beaufont had stepped foot on Roya Lane. A wave of nostalgia swept past him as he made his way down to the Fantastical Armory. The highest power had forbidden him to enter Roya Lane, but the identity charm had been broken. All rules were off—well, other than he couldn't tell Paris anything about her parents, who she really was, and what was after her. There was only one person who could.

Clark could hardly believe that Paris knew who she was. He always knew this day would come. He'd longed for it. Only once Paris knew who she was could things change, but the timing had to be right. She had to be ready. He hoped that she was.

Paris was Liv's child, so if anyone was up for the challenges coming up, it would be her. Seeing the long-lost child who wasn't a child anymore had partly healed Clark's soul. Hopefully, what happened next completely healed all the wounds.

Subner the elf looked up from his book when Clark entered. He'd pulled his long black hair back in a ponytail and wore his usual sour expression. In fifteen years, nothing had changed in the

Fantastical Armory or with its shop owner. The cases were all filled with strange weapons and random artifacts. Subner sat behind one of the glass display cases as if he hadn't moved in all that time.

"He's been expecting you," the elf grumbled.

Clark checked his pocket watch. "I guess I'm right on time for the meeting I didn't know I was going to have until a few minutes ago."

"You're late," Subner said. "You were supposed to leave right after Alicia showed up and you realized she could take Paris to Sophia."

Clark sighed. "You know, it might be helpful if you tell me this stuff in the future."

"You'd still screw it up," Subner muttered. "Everyone always screws it up."

Clark straightened when the figure entered from the back door of the Fantastical Armory. The hippie elf, who wasn't an elf but merely in that form, looked Clark over. His long brown hair hung by his face, and he wore baggy jeans rolled up to the shins and a t-shirt that read: You Are the Wind Beneath My Wings. The man before Clark might appear unassuming, but he knew better. Papa Creola was one of the strongest entities alive. He was Father Time, after all.

"Papa Creola." Clark strode forward. "You know why I'm here?"

"Yes, and why you'll pester me the next dozen times over your lifetime," he spat and folded his arms.

Clark shrugged off his cold bedside manner. "Paris—she knows who she is."

"Yes, thanks to a nosy teacher at Happily Ever After College."

"Is the timing not right?" Clark asked in a rush. "Did you see it happening this way? Could you have stopped it?"

"Despite all the rumors, I don't know everything," Papa Creola muttered. "I see some stuff. Most of it is potentials. Who knows if the timing is right, but no, I didn't see that Shannon Butcher would reveal to Paris who she was. Regardless of whether it's the right time or not, it's happened, and we have to deal with it."

Hope fluttered in Clark's chest. "Then that means we can finally bring them back."

Papa Creola rolled his eyes. For one of the oldest entities on Earth, he wasn't the most mature and definitely not very patient. "*We* can't do anything. You've always known there was no guarantee."

"You orchestrated all of this," Clark argued. "We all went along with it. Now—"

"This was always about protecting Paris," Papa Creola interrupted.

"Then you have to tell her the truth," Clark said adamantly. "She's confused, and none of the rest of us can say anything."

"Because otherwise you all would have by now and ruined everything," Papa Creola replied dryly.

"She deserves to know the truth now that she's learned her identity," Clark fired back.

"I'll tell her when the time is right."

Clark's face burned hot. "When will that be?"

"When I decide!" Papa Creola exclaimed.

Clark nearly jumped back, surprised by Papa Creola's reaction. Subner, the assistant to Father Time, simply looked up as if he was bored by this exchange.

"She's in danger," Clark said in a low voice.

"Knowing the truth isn't going to lessen that," Papa Creola stated.

"It might," Clark countered. "It might keep her from investigating and getting herself in trouble. It might give her hope. It might—"

"It might give her false hope, and that's exactly what will get her killed," Papa Creola interrupted. "When the time is right, when she's ready, if she's ready, I will tell her. Until then, you will not interfere."

"It's not like I had a choice either way," Clark said bitterly. "You've silenced us all. You're calling all the shots."

The father of time smiled slightly. "Which is the only reason that we have the slightest chance of getting Liv back."

CHAPTER THIRTY-FIVE

"That's a dragon." Paris nearly stuttered. She knew that they were at the Rogue Riders' Mansion, the base for that group of dragonriders, but she hadn't ever seen a dragon in person. Hell, she hadn't ridden in a car until a few minutes ago. It was so strange that Paris never questioned her sheltered life, but she was grateful for the way her life was opening up suddenly.

A majestic blue dragon soared through the sky, a young woman atop it. She was low on the dragon, her long blonde hair flying in the air as she held the reins, swooping one way and another as if navigating invisible obstacles.

Looking up at the dragonrider in the sky were several men. One glanced at Paris and Alicia when they paused beside them, regarding the blue dragon and rider.

"Hey, there, are you all new riders too?" One guy sauntered over. He gave Paris a flirtatious look. Unnerved by all the strangeness, she didn't have a chance to react before he draped his arm around her shoulder. "You can room with me, baby. My name is Larry, but you can call me whatever you want."

"You have two seconds to get off me, or I'm going to toss you through a window," she threatened, nodding in the direction of the mansion.

He chuckled as if she was kidding. "Oh, I like hard to get. Looks like I'll just have to try harder."

"I'd watch yourself," Alicia warned.

"You want in on this action?" The guy looked up at Alicia with his arm still draped around Paris' shoulder. "I have room for two in my bed."

"You have until the count of three," Paris warned, narrowing her eyes at the jerk.

"To kiss you?" The guy puckered his lips. "If you insist."

"One, two, three," Paris said in a rush and grabbed the hand on the other side of her shoulder, pulled it up, and ducked under it. Then she swept her boots under the guy's legs, knocking them out from under him, turning him over until he landed on his back.

The guys watching all erupted in laughter. However, the woman on the blue dragon had landed during the altercation and rushed over, her face flushed with anger. "Who are you and why are you assaulting my riders?"

Paris looked up at the woman who was both beautiful and fierce, not that the two were mutually exclusive. She knew without a doubt this was Sophia—she had the trademark Beaufont eyes.

"I warned him to get his hands off me," Paris explained, holding her chin high. "When he didn't listen, I defended myself."

Sophia scowled at Paris while studying her—confusion heavy in her eyes as though torn between defending her own or trying to decide if Paris was right. Finally, she turned her gaze to Alicia. "Who is this person you've brought that has bested one of my dragonriders straight away?"

Alicia smirked proudly and held out a presenting hand to Paris. "This little spitfire who showed this creep a lesson after properly warning him is none other than your niece, Guinevere Paris Beaufont."

CHAPTER THIRTY-SIX

S ophia's mouth fell open. Her face went slack, and her eyes widened. Paris was getting very used to causing this reaction in people lately.

Shaking her head, Sophia directed her attention to Larry, still lying in the grass. "Get up, would you? If you can't keep your hands to yourself, you're going to get the tar beat out of you." She turned to the group of guys who were gawking at them. "You lot go and practice the flying techniques." She clapped and broke their focus, making them all charge off.

Larry was slow to get up, having found something in the grass. His eyes widened at the small object, and before Paris could make out what it was, he deposited it into his pocket and took off after the others.

When they were all gone, Sophia turned to face Paris, a look of awe and confusion heavy in her eyes. "Guinevere, I can't believe this..."

"She goes by Paris," Alicia interjected.

Sophia nodded. "That makes sense. Paris Westbridge. I have so many questions."

The blue dragon glided over, dropping his enormous head down and regarding Paris with his wise eyes. He was simply breathtaking, even with the horns lining his head and the sharp teeth that Paris was certain could tear her in two with the slightest effort.

"Me too," the dragon said, surprising Paris that he could speak. "Like, why does she smell like chocolate chip cookies?" He tilted his head and gave Paris a curious look. "Do you have cookies in your pocket?"

Paris laughed, not at all expecting a majestic dragon to ask such questions. She shook her head. "No, I think it's the smell of Happily Ever After College. It kind of covers my clothes."

"It is the smell of the college," Sophia related fondly.

"You've been there?" Paris asked.

"Yes. I have a special way of visiting. My fairy godmother, Mae Ling, is there."

"Mae Ling," Paris murmured, not having expected this.

"Not to interrupt," Alicia said politely beside them. "But I don't think you all should have me intruding on this moment. My job was to drop Paris off to meet you. I'll leave her with you, Soph, if that's okay?"

Sophia nodded. "Yes, is this why Clark messaged me?"

"That's right," Alicia replied. "I'm sure you both have much to discuss." She turned her attention to Paris. "It's been a pleasure seeing you again, and I hope to get to know you better soon. Take care, dear Paris. We've missed you very much."

Paris' heart felt ready to overflow. She smiled broadly at the woman. "Thank you, and me too. Thanks for my first car ride."

Alicia simply smiled and blew a kiss, then strode toward the front of the house.

"You've never been in a car before?" Sophia asked at once, then shook her head. "Actually, that makes sense. I have so many more questions. Like, how did you find out? The identity charm...it's broken. Oh, and Clark knows. Who else? John? Wow, this is all so much, yet it's the best news I've had in a long time."

Paris drew in a breath, not sure where to begin. "There's so much to tell, yet I don't know nearly enough."

"I want to know everything," Sophia urged, breaking into a smile that made her light up. It made everything around them seem brighter too.

The blue dragon coughed abruptly.

Sophia glanced over her shoulder at him. "Oh, how very subtle."

"Well, I'm wondering when you're going to introduce me," the dragon stated smugly.

"I wasn't," Sophia teased. "I was going to send you to get us some drinks."

"You were going to send me on a coffee run, huh?" the dragon asked.

Paris couldn't help but laugh.

Sophia glanced at her and winked before returning her attention to the dragon. "Nope, I've just been reunited with my niece. Go open a bottle of champagne. That magnum I've been saving for a special occasion."

"What are the two of you going to drink then?" the dragon asked seriously. "That's just enough for me."

Sophia shook her head, holding out her hand to the dragon. "Paris, this is my dragon, my partner in policing crime, my friend, and the biggest pain in my butt—Lunis."

The huge dragon knelt one leg and bowed to Paris, making her suddenly feel very strange. "It's a pleasure to be in your presence once more, Paris Beaufont."

"Hi," Paris squeaked, finding her voice suddenly hoarse.

Sophia snapped her fingers, breaking the tension of the moment. "Now, champagne, Lun. We're going to stroll the grounds."

Lunis rose and gave Paris a commiserating expression. "You see how I get treated? I've gifted my rider with the chi of the dragon, making her stronger than any magician, and this is how I get thanked." Still, the dragon turned and sauntered toward the house, swishing his tail back and forth.

"Get the good glasses," Sophia sang in his direction. "And don't break them this time."

CHAPTER THIRTY-SEVEN

"Wow, you've had a crazy last two days," Sophia observed when Paris explained the series of events that had led her there. "I bet you feel like you're digesting an entire cow."

"As someone who has digested an entire cow, it requires a lot of sleep," Lunis chimed in. The dragon sat on the grass next to them, sipping from an oversized champagne flute.

Paris sipped her bubbly, laughed and stretched out her legs. They were seated next to a small pond with the vine-covered walls around the manor beside them. "I didn't realize that dragons were so funny."

"Oh, they aren't," Lunis replied. "Most are obnoxious sticks in the mud. I'm different."

"He's the new generation," Sophia explained. "Although many of them are a bit easier-going than the old generation, Lunis defies all of them, really pushing the boundaries."

"So those guys," Paris indicated the mansion where the others were practicing their flying skills, dragons soaring through the air in the distance. "They're the new generation?"

Sophia nodded. "Newbie dragonriders. Sorry for Larry. Demon riders take a bit more to break in."

"Demon riders?" Paris asked.

"Yeah, riders come in two different varieties," Sophia explained. "I'm an angel rider. Then there's my counterpart. They're both necessary for balance, but the demons are a little more rebellious. Good job putting Larry in his place. That guy…"

Paris smirked. "Well, I haven't conformed to the fairy godmother ways yet, although they keep trying to tame me. Not Mae Ling though. She's urged me to be myself. It makes sense that you know her because she's under the silencing spell too."

Sophia nodded. "Yeah, and the good news is that I can visit you at the college. I have access."

"That's impressive since usually, only those who work and attend can enter the grounds."

"Which is why you're safe there," Sophia confirmed. "Well, you're safe here too, but I think you at Happily Ever After College makes a lot of sense. You need your own path."

"Like, I shouldn't follow in my parents' footsteps and become a Warrior for the House of Fourteen?" Paris asked boldly.

Sophia shook her head. "You do what is in your heart. It sounds like you're already making waves at the college. I know from Mae Ling that Happily Ever After has needed change for a long time. Things are stagnant there."

Paris found it easy to talk to Sophia, who didn't seem old enough to be her aunt, although she was definitely older with the confidence and wisdom she exuded. She'd told the dragonrider all about her life at Happily Ever After College. "If Mae Ling is your fairy godmother, has she been trying to match you with a Prince Charming?"

Sophia glanced at her hand and the wedding ring on her finger. "She matched me long ago. You'll meet Wilder at some point. Mae Ling is more like my life coach. She has always helped me with cases."

Paris nodded. "Yeah, she seems to operate outside the normal guidelines of the other fairy godmothers. She's not all about Cinderellas and Prince Charmings."

"Hey." Lunis finished his champagne with a hiccup. "Why did Cinderella get kicked off the baseball team?"

Sophia shook her head and glanced at Paris. "Don't fall for his bait."

Paris laughed. "Why?"

Sophia groaned. "I warned you."

"She got kicked off the team because she always ran away from the ball." Lunis rolled over on his stomach and laughed.

"I warned you," Sophia muttered, then drained her glass. "So you're going to keep attending Happily Ever After and what else?"

"Well," Paris drew out the word. "I'm going to try to uncover my past and the web of secrets. I know you can't say anything."

"Which is why you haven't asked," Sophia offered.

"I can tell you anything you want to know," Lunis stated smugly. "I wasn't spelled."

"You also don't want to be banished to the pits of Hell," Sophia teased.

He nodded. "Which is what would happen."

Sophia must have read the confused expression on Paris' face. "It's very difficult to spell a dragon. It simply doesn't stick."

"Oh, but Lunis still can't say anything?" Hope that he could laced Paris' voice.

"He could, but honestly, we aren't supposed to talk for a reason," Sophia explained. "I know it's tough to hear, but there's a reason you don't know everything yet. When the time is right, then you will. This is the beginning, and I hope things just get better from here." She glanced at her dragon, an undeniable look of hope in her eyes.

"Things can always get better," the blue dragon agreed. "I'll help spruce up this boring convo. Why was Cinderella such a lousy football player?"

Sophia grabbed the magnum of champagne and refilled her glass and Paris'. "Lunis, you're cut off."

"She had a pumpkin for a coach," Lunis stated with a victorious laugh.

Paris nearly spat out her champagne when she laughed.

"Okay, no more Cinderella jokes," Sophia decreed.

"Fine," Lunis said smugly. "I'm taking requests. Give me any topic at all, and I'll supply you with a joke."

Sophia pointed at him with her champagne flute. "He's quite good at this. I mean, he could use his brainpower to solve the world's problems, but instead, he memorizes every single joke on the Internet."

"I invent those jokes," Lunis corrected.

Paris thought for a moment, trying to come up with something extremely random. "Okay, how about Barbie. Give me a Barbie joke."

"Easy," Lunis retorted at once. "Have you heard of the 'Divorce Barbie'?"

"Nope," Paris replied, the champagne starting to swim in her head.

"Oh, well, she comes with all of Ken's stuff." The blue dragon rolled over again, laughing.

Paris and Sophia joined him.

"That is an impressive party trick," Paris agreed.

"Although he doesn't get invited to many parties since he double-dips," Sophia joked.

"All guacamole belongs to me by right," Lunis said proudly.

Paris smiled, her cheeks hurting. "I can't believe you're my family."

"I know, you don't look anything like me," Lunis agreed with a straight face, not missing a beat.

Paris continued to laugh. "It's crazy that two days ago, I didn't know I was half-magician, and now I've met Clark and Alicia and now you all and King Rudolf. It's crazy."

"It has to be a lot," Sophia said thoughtfully, giving her a caring look.

The alcohol was making Paris tired without her consent. She couldn't stifle a yawn.

"Oh, fairy godmother college is in a different time zone." Sophia sat up suddenly. "It's nighttime there. Do you have classes tomorrow?"

Paris nodded. "Yeah, but I had to come and find you all."

"I understand." Sophia pushed to her feet and offered her hand to Paris to help her up. "There will be plenty of opportunities to catch up. No need to rush it all yet. You'll need time to process."

Paris nodded, feeling the tiredness take over her being.

"You can't portal to Happily Ever After College from here," Sophia explained. "You have to be well outside the Rogue Riders' Mansion. I'll take you down the road."

One of the dragonriders from earlier rushed over, his face red with stress. "Sorry to interrupt, but the dragonettes are at it again, about to tear each other in two, and nothing we do seems to calm them down."

Sophia grunted with frustration. "They're a particularly ornery bunch."

"Let's get out the garden hose." Lunis stood and stretched out his wings.

"I can find my way back on my own," Paris said. "You go and attend to your business."

Sophia looked uncertain for a moment but finally nodded. "Okay, well, I'll see you again soon, Paris. This has been…well, it's meant the world to me. The absolute world."

"To me too." Paris stepped forward and hugged her aunt, feeling as though the pieces of her heart were slowly mending.

CHAPTER THIRTY-EIGHT

The sun was starting to set in Beverly Hills when Paris reached the front gate at the bottom of the drive to the Rogue Riders' Mansion. Sophia had said she'd need to walk half a mile down the main road to a portal area. Lunis had offered to give her a "lift," but Paris had declined, stating that her first car ride that day was enough and she'd rather divide up the brand-new experiences.

Once on the sidewalk, Paris stood frozen, the surreal aspect of the moment hitting her. She was in Beverly Hills, California. She had a family and was part-magician. She'd ridden in a car and met a dragon that day—and her world was only starting to open up. Paris couldn't imagine how much things would change, but she couldn't wait to tell Uncle John all about it.

Feeling around in her pockets for her phone, Paris realized something immediately. Her heart suddenly sank. She hoped she was misremembering and checked her other pockets, but all she found was her phone. That meant the protective charm must have fallen out when she body-slammed Larry.

She remembered then that he'd found something of interest in

SARAH NOFFKE & MICHAEL ANDERLE

the grass. That had to be the coin that served as a protective charm.

Gulping, Paris glanced both ways down the dimming busy street. Soon it would be dark, and she had half a mile to cross in either direction to get to safety. Turning back, Paris considered stepping across the threshold into the protective area of the Rogue Riders' Mansion. She would be safe there and could possibly retrieve the coin.

She also considered that she'd look like a fool if she accused Larry and he didn't have the protective charm. It would be her word against his. On top of that, if she couldn't find it, she'd be depending on her aunt to get her back to the college safely. All in the first hour after meeting her. Paris didn't want anyone to see her as weak and incapable. Also, Sophia and Lunis were busy taking care of the fighting dragonettes.

Paris shook her head as though making a nonverbal movement would strengthen her resolve. She had to do this on her own. It was simply a half-mile walk in a fancy area with probably lots of police forces. She hadn't felt the violent wind or any other signs of the danger on Roya Lane since coming to Los Angeles, so there was little reason to conclude that she was in trouble right then.

She took a step forward and paused as if checking the universe to see if it struck back after she decided to proceed without help. Nothing happened.

Letting out a steadying breath, Paris took another step and another, picking up her pace as she continued down the manicured sidewalk.

Pausing at an intersection, Paris nearly laughed, thinking how silly she'd been to worry she was in danger. All the new meetings and information was making her paranoid. This evil villain who had killed Charlotte apparently knew to look for Paris on Roya Lane, but that didn't necessarily mean it would know to follow her to Los Angeles. The world was a very large place.

When it was her turn to cross, Paris stepped out into the inter-

162

section, hearing a strange sound. Since she'd never been in a large city or any city at all, Paris figured the noise was normal, like an ambulance. It sounded like a train going by overhead. The noise was everywhere and drummed in her chest like a bass drum. It vibrated the pavement under her feet.

That's not what unnerved Paris the most. It was the reaction of those on the streets around her. People looked around with fearful expressions on their faces.

"What is that?" Paris heard someone ask in an urgent rush.

"That doesn't sound good," another stated.

Many turned their faces to the sky as if expecting aliens to crash down and invade Beverly Hills. Some started to run as if they'd spotted the source of the noise, which was growing louder.

Paris decided that this wasn't a normal thing in the city and took off, running as fast as possible. Maybe it wasn't the danger from Roya Lane, she reasoned. She hoped it was a different threat that she could outrun or wasn't coming after her at all.

Using a spell to enhance her speed, Paris easily passed the others on the street, although she didn't like the idea of leaving them behind to face whatever was the source of the noise. Still, she had to get to the half-mile mark. She figured it wasn't that far ahead.

To her relief, the noise died down as though she was getting far enough away. Also about the same time, all the people who had been strolling down the sidewalk disappeared. The sun seemed to go down instantly, casting everything in darkness.

Paris didn't speed up, but she noticed how the yards with mansions that she passed all suddenly appeared like haunted houses. Then the chilly, cutting wind hit her in the back and nearly threw her to the ground. Paris couldn't deny it any longer. The evil from Roya Lane was after her, and she didn't know how to fight it. Without the protective charm, she feared it could take her down. All she had as an option now was to hope she got to the half-mile mark before the monster got to her.

CHAPTER THIRTY-NINE

Throwing up her hand, Paris projected a portal, hoping that it opened in the distance, meaning that she was close to the half-mile mark. The good news was that it did. The bad news was that it was still twenty yards away.

The worse news was that the train noise overhead had returned, and it was deafening now. The roar was so loud it made Paris' teeth chatter, and her eyes water like it was taking over her body from the inside out.

Her feet moved fast on the pavement, but she didn't think it was quick enough. She felt like the wind had already caught her in a net and was about to grab her.

Everything was moving by her so fast on the sidewalk that it all looked like a blur. Which was weird when Paris could have sworn that she saw a black and white cat simply sitting on the curb, looking at her nonchalantly as she passed in a mad rush to save her life.

She would have dismissed the strange animal precariously positioned in a weird place, but it seemed to give her a look of reassurance. That's when she realized that she was losing her mind.

The portal was only ten yards away. So close—and still so far away as the roar of the train-like monster bore down on her. The wind overhead started to spiral like a helicopter's rotor wash, sending her hair every which way. She felt something resembling arms wrap around her.

Then the voice seemed to speak from inside her.

"Finally," it whispered darkly, a ravenous yearning in its essence.

Paris pushed forward harder but instantly felt something tug her backward. The sensation was like hands grabbing her by the shoulders, holding her in place. Her feet moved, but she remained in the same position as if she was on a treadmill—like she was in a bad dream. The harder she pushed, the more she ran, the more she stayed in the same place.

Paris screamed in frustration and fear, wishing she'd made a different decision. Wishing she knew what had hold of her. That's when she decided to face the nightmare holding her in place and turned to look at the monster. It was definitely a monster, but unlike anything she'd ever seen.

What held her didn't have hands or a body or anything else human as far as she could tell. It was simply a cloud of black. Despite it looking undefinable, what it made her feel wasn't—dread. Never before had Paris felt more despondent than she did at that moment. Wars waged in her. Sadness ran rampant. Her spirits were buried in the true gloom of a hell that she never knew and realized was the reality of the world around her. Paris suddenly felt she'd never be the same. That the world as she knew it was over. That every day would be torture if the sun ever rose again.

The black monster opened its mouth of smoke and torture—or that was what it seemed. Its tendrils wrapped around her arms and pulled her back, not just holding her in place. Paris knew what would happen next—the beast would suck her in. She'd be swallowed whole and gone forever.

Unsure what to do next, Paris sent out a simple plea to whoever could hear it. "Please help me," she whispered to the wind as the darkness neared, covering everything she could see.

Paris was certain she'd feel death next. Or the absence of feeling. Nothingness. That she'd die and who knew what would happen then.

Instead, she dropped to the pavement as if she'd fallen from a great distance. She landed on her feet and promptly fell to her tailbone and rocked back before popping up on her feet again.

Paris couldn't believe it. The blackness disappeared as suddenly as it had appeared. The roaring noise ceased so abruptly that she felt deaf. The lights in the houses and the street grew brighter until the road felt normal and not like it was seconds away from being pulled into a nightmare.

Standing squarely in the middle of the sidewalk was the black and white cat, with a strangely knowing expression on its face. The black monster was gone, but Paris had a feeling that she shouldn't push her luck. It wouldn't be gone for long.

Giving the bizarre cat one last look, unsure whether to thank it or run from it, Paris turned and dared to put her back to the animal. She hurried down the sidewalk, making for the portal in a few seconds—grateful when it swallowed her whole, taking her to Happily Ever After College where she was safe once more.

CHAPTER FORTY

P aris was breathless, sweat dripping from her brow and her
heart racing when she stumbled through the portal to the
charming and secure grounds of Happily Ever After College. It
almost seemed too silly to think something was awful out in the
world when she looked at the pristine, idyllic manor before her
and the Enchanted Grounds.

She glanced over her shoulder at the portal that had closed
straight away and knew that the evil she'd experienced in Beverly
Hills wasn't a dream. Somewhere out in the world—and thankfully, far enough away that it couldn't get her at fairy godmother
college—was a danger so dark and evil that it wanted to swallow
her whole.

Why? she wondered. Also, equally perplexing, what had rescued
her when death seemed so imminent? Was it the strange black and
white cat? Or something else? One thing was certain. She wasn't
leaving Happily Ever After College unless she had protection, and
when she did, she'd be much more careful with it—not allowing
some dragonrider thug to get it from her.

Paris regarded the estate before her, grateful to be back after all her adventures. She's met her Uncle Clark and his wife, Aunt Alicia. She'd ridden in a car and seen a dragon. However, one of her favorite parts was Sophia. How could Sophia, the small and unassuming but confident leader of the Rogue Riders, not be her favorite part of the strangest and most awesome afternoon of her entire life?

Paris remembered that before she'd realized she'd lost the protective charm that she meant to call Uncle John. It would be late on Roya Lane. It was late at Happily Ever After College, and the sun would soon rise for another day of perfect weather. Paris decided she'd save the call for the morning, after she'd gotten some sleep and time to process all of the amazing things she'd seen and learned.

CHAPTER FORTY-ONE

Paris awoke to a strange tapping on her forehead. If she weren't so exhausted and hadn't registered that the source of the pestering had a fluffy tail stretched over her head, she would have assaulted it.

Peeling open one eye, she regarded Faraday sitting on her chest with a beyond-annoyed expression. "Why is it that you woke up this morning and decided you wanted me to kill you?" she muttered, still unable to open both eyes all the way.

A *tinging* noise vaguely registered as the squirrel flicked his tail and hopped off her onto the bedside table. She followed him with her gaze, noticing that beside him was the fairy alarm clock, which made the chiming noise and threw pixie dust into the air.

"I have no desire to perish today," Faraday chirped. "It's just that your alarm has been going off for a half-hour, and I thought you were the one who had perished since you hadn't awoken."

Paris bolted upright. "It has? Am I late for class?"

He shook his head matter-of-factly. "By my calculations, with your bare minimum morning routine, you'll still make it down to breakfast on time even after waking up late. I've even factored in a few minutes in case today is the day you decide to brush your hair."

Paris rolled her eyes. "Why start today or mess with perfection?" She ran her hands through her wavy blonde hair, which probably could use a washing more than brushing.

"Seems that you had an adventure," Faraday observed, watching as Paris attempted to get out of bed, feeling less rested than she would have liked.

"Why? Because you were following me?" Paris stretched and willed her blood to start flowing.

"I wasn't following you." He sounded offended.

"Oh, then what did you do last night?" she asked.

"Research," he answered simply. "And you?"

"The same. That dragon was something else, wasn't it?"

He shook his head, looking disappointed with her. "I wasn't following you. But I would have liked to have seen one. What kind was it?"

"A blue one," she dryly retorted while trying to find some clean clothes in her drawers, which was difficult with Faraday's constant rearranging. "Would you stop messing with my clothes?"

"They happen to be in my bed," he countered.

"Which is in my drawers," she fired back. "I thought you were going to take the sock drawer."

"I'm trying out a few to discover which one is the most conducive for the best sleep."

"Why don't you find one before I discover which instrument is the most conducive for murdering you efficiently?"

"Someone woke up on the wrong side of the bed," he teased and scurried over to the windowsill.

"Someone woke up with a squirrel on their chest," she muttered, finally finding some clothes that would work. They were her usual uniform basics that the college had thankfully furnished although she refused to wear the blue gown. They could have forced her into it by withholding clean jeans and black t-shirts, but they didn't.

"So, are you going to tell me what happened when you were gone?" Faraday asked.

"I met my family, and they told me nothing of any use about who I am or my parents."

"That's unfortunate," he said sensitively.

She nodded while looking out the window where the sun was rising over the Enchanted Grounds. "It is. They seem to be wonderful people who love me...loved me. I want to know more about them even if I don't know more about the secrets."

"I gather you'd like to know both," Faraday offered.

"I really would. But I get that it will take time so I'm not going to be some whiny girl who cries because my life was a lie, and it's slow going to uncover the truth. I'll keep following the clues."

"I respect that attitude," Faraday said proudly. "It seems you don't have to rush to discover the truth."

"Oh, I forgot to mention that some shadowy black thing nearly killed me by trying to suck out my soul." Paris made for the door, desperately wanting a shower.

"I feel like you should have led with that part," Faraday stated tersely.

She turned her head to smirk over her shoulder. "Here I thought you were following me and already knew about the monster and the strange black and white cat."

"Black and white cat, you say?" Faraday asked. "You saw a cat?"

She turned to face him directly and tipped her head. "Yeah. Why does that interest you?"

"No reason," Faraday said at once. "Just seems strange. That's like saying you saw Godzilla attacking a city and a mouse scurrying through the streets. Like, one is of supreme interest, and the other doesn't seem worth mentioning or noteworthy."

"Yeah, I guess I see what you mean." For some reason, she thought that wasn't altogether true, and Faraday was unnerved by the mention of the cat. "I had the impression that the black and white cat saved me, but I was sleep-deprived and running for my life, so I was probably hallucinating."

"Probably," Faraday muttered, looking out the window.

"What are you doing today?" she asked. "More research?"

"It's Tuesday!" he chirped excitedly as if that should mean something to her.

"I do love Taco Tuesday," she joked.

He shook his head. "I prefer sandwiches."

"I don't think Sandwich Saturday has the same ring to it."

"It should be a thing," he declared. "Tuesday is when the Serenity Garden is off-limits."

"So, like a mischievous squirrel, you're going to go and investigate it then?" she inquired.

"Naturally, and not to be mischievous but simply to resolve the mystery," he stated.

"Just like you came here to Happily Ever After College," Paris observed. "You simply have to go where you're not supposed to, don't you?"

"Says the girl who was outside the college all night after being told it was dangerous," he countered.

"Touché," she mumbled, thinking that she'd need another protective charm before she could venture out again, which definitely needed to happen.

"Well, will you do me a favor and when you leave the college again on your family history investigations, please let me know?" Faraday asked.

"Why?"

"Because that way a black and white cat doesn't have to watch your back." He flicked his tail. "Or whatever saved you from the monster."

She laughed, not expecting him to say this. "You think you could have saved me from the black soul-eating beast?"

The squirrel shrugged. "Probably not, but at least I could be there to help. Two heads are better than one, and I'm good at thinking my way out of things."

Paris considered the squirrel for a moment. He was asking to go on missions with her, knowing that something deathly was pursuing her. For some reason, that spoke more about his loyalty to her than making her skeptical about his motives. "Yeah, sure, Faraday. I'm off to get ready. Have fun investigating and try to stay out of trouble."

"As always, same to you, Paris."

CHAPTER FORTY-TWO

P aris only had one thing for breakfast, and she had a lot of it. Coffee.

She was grateful that she'd managed to put herself together and make it to her Art of Love class on time after only a couple of hours of sleep. Since there were no open seats at the back of the room, it forced her to take one in the front row.

Headmistress Starr looked up at her from her front desk with a polite smile on her face. She was writing a note with a quill pen as if she'd jumped out of the 1800s. "You okay, Paris?"

Stifling a yawn, Paris nodded. "I was up late."

Maybe respecting her privacy or perhaps assuming that she'd been busy investigating her past, Willow simply nodded, rose to her feet, and looked around at everyone. "Good morning, class. Yesterday we discussed the famous romantic comedy *Sabrina*. Studying romantic movies, books, and poetry teaches us about the art of love and how two people can fall for one another. However, it's important to note that sometimes—actually, most of the time—two people don't simply meet and it's love at first sight. Most of the time, there's something that serves as an obstacle to keep them apart. In the case of the movie *Sabrina*, it was Linus being a worka-holic and Sabrina's desire to flee back to Paris, which she deemed safe since that's where she was once happy."

The headmistress picked up the quill on her desk and twirled it. "Today's lesson is a little less cheerful but just as important. Although love ballads tell us about how people feel when in love, it's equally important to understand how they feel when love doesn't work out whether unrequited, lost, or missed."

On the surface of everyone's desks appeared little bluebirds and two tiny rosebuds with no stem.

"These, as many of you know, are music players." Willow glanced at Paris. This information was obviously for her benefit since she was the newbie to the college. "You place the rosebuds in your ears, and the bird will sing you a song in your head."

Wow, Paris thought, wondering if this technology was ahead of its time or behind it. There was no question that it was whimsical.

"Your task today is to listen to the song I've chosen for each of you," Willow continued. "They are songs about yearning, lost love, or heartbreak. Your job is to try and grasp these obstacles that our charges will inevitably face and help them understand how to overcome them. It simply is unrealistic to think all our matches will go off without a hitch. Usually, couples break each other's hearts a few times before they truly fall in love. That's because the heart is so fragile and falling is a very vulnerable affair. Many of the songs I've chosen are about these experiences. It will be your job to help our Cinderellas and Prince Charmings to work through the heartbreak and find their way to each other, which is rarely a flat, straight path."

The headmistress looked around at the class as though expecting questions. Paris didn't have any. This lesson made the most sense of any of them so far. Learning how to garden or dance or cook to create love for two people was a little abstract. However, she could understand that creating love would involve a lot of obstacles. The path of love would have to be the most treacherous of all.

Suddenly, the inscription on her locket rose to her mind: "You have to keep breaking your heart until it opens."

Paris figured that it was much like this for two people finding love. It seemed unrealistic that two people would rush into each other's open arms and live blissfully for the rest of their days.

Instead, their interactions would be full of protective glances and terse words with hidden meanings. When she or he didn't respond the way the other expected, there would be disappointment. Maybe one would rush off, deciding that they were better off without the other person, trying to convince themselves of that when in reality they only wanted that love.

That all made much more sense to Paris than the fairytale love where a woman put on a dress and strode into a ball and found her prince. Even the idea that he sought her out and simply put a glass slipper on her foot and they rode off into the sunset was unrealistic. Life was full of mundane Tuesdays and bills and getting the kids to soccer practice and planning for retirement.

Happily ever after was everyone's goal, but in between, there were daily stresses and little disappointments. They never told that in Cinderella's story.

Maybe if they did, so many women wouldn't be searching for someone to rescue them, Paris thought and picked up the rose "buds."

She would have preferred if Cinderella told her stepmom to shove it, went out on her own, and put herself through school, learning a skill other than cleaning someone else's house that paid the bills and gave her confidence. That would have been a much better story than a prince fixing all her problems.

In this fantasy, Cinderella would meet Prince Charming while attending night school and they'd banter over drinks, teasing each other with playful looks. Maybe he wouldn't call her right away. Or perhaps she'd pretend not to be interested. There'd be some rough patches until they realized they only ever wanted each other.

Between the beginning of their story and their happily ever after is when they'd write or play the heartbreak songs, which seemed like the best, most realistic story to Paris. She'd read that story. She'd listen to their music.

Paris thought that even if they had to deal with the mundane Tuesdays and carpools and insurance premiums and whatnot, her Cinderella and Prince Charming would have true happiness. They'd almost always curl up together in each other's arms at night, grateful that they fell in love the way they did because it made them have to work for it. That to Paris was true love. That was the kind the stories and the songs should be about.

"Paris, did you hear me?" Willow stood in front of her desk.

She wasn't playing the music from her songbird, but Paris' mind had trailed off in the fantasy, and she hadn't been listening to the headmistress.

Pulling out the rose "buds," she offered an apologetic smile. "I'm sorry. What did you say?"

Thankfully Headmistress Starr didn't appear offended by Paris being distracted. "I assigned everyone to review their song and give a full report on its significance for creating love. I understand it's not an easy assignment since you're new to this class and asked if you had any questions."

"Oh." Paris glanced down at her songbird. A small "Play" button was on the top of its head. "No, I think I'm good for now. I'll let you know."

Willow nodded acceptingly. "Very good." She glanced out at the class and pressed her hands together. "Well then, go ahead and put in your buds and get to listening. There are tissues in the back for those who need them."

CHAPTER FORTY-THREE

P aris hit the button on the top of her songbird, and a deep soulful voice filled her head.

The female singer told a story of standing at a train station and watching a lover leave. The guy said, "I want to see the world," and she replied, "Go."

Paris felt a prickle in her throat as the singer continued to tell of her heartbreak. The song lyrics detailed how the woman felt lost without the person that she'd let go. It brought so many ideas to the surface for Paris about how a person could be so strong, then losing one seemingly "small thing" could make them so weak.

Before, she wasn't sure what this analysis report that Willow asked for would include. Paris quickly retrieved paper and a pen from her desk, afraid that her ideas would dissipate if she didn't get them out fast enough.

It occurred to her that the woman telling the heartbreak story had told her lover to leave, not realizing how important he was to her. Still, if she hadn't, she'd never have known. That was part of their tale to happily ever after. They had to lose each other to realize how much they loved one another.

"That's the way real love happens," Paris wrote with a firm period as she quickly finished her report.

She glanced up, surprised to find Willow and Mae Ling huddled at the headmistress' desk. Paris pulled the rose "buds" from her ears and realized that without the music playing in her head, she could hear them easily.

"Amelia Rose's company, Rose Industries, is growing fast," Willow explained to the professor, "but with it, so is the competition. She and Grayson McGregor have met a few times to negotiate competitive terms, but it always turns into a heated argument."

"Because the two have chemistry, but they're fighting it at this point," Mae Ling declared.

Willow nodded. "I think so too. They feel the spark, but right now it's creating an explosion instead of a warm, nurturing fire."

"Amelia is bitter about how Grayson treated her at their first meeting." Mae Ling glanced at a report on the desk. "Grayson, it appears, doesn't like that she was able to create a company from the ground up seeming overnight that could threaten his."

"Yes, although I think in a different light, he'd be very impressed by her," Willow stated. "Amelia only ever interviewed with Grayson's company, McGregor Technologies, because she respected it so much."

"What they appreciate about each other is now tearing them apart." Mae Ling sighed. "She has ammunition to take him down, and he keeps fighting back. If they simply called a truce, they'd realize they were perfect together. They're both strong and incredible. Imagine what they could do together if they weren't sabotaging each other's efforts."

"That's the thing." Willow flipped through a report. "In an attempt to destroy each other's companies, they're polluting the area around them, creating rivalries between employees, and instigating bad relationships. The whole thing is spreading, diminishing love, and you know how that goes…"

Mae Ling nodded heavily. "It's like a disease."

Paris found she was standing before she knew it. Her feet took her forward quicker than she realized, and she stood in front of the headmistress and Mae Ling. "I think I know how to fix Amelia and Grayson," she said to her surprise and theirs too.

CHAPTER FORTY-FOUR

"Paris, although I appreciate that, you're supposed to be working on your assignment," Willow said.

"I've finished." She turned to retrieve her report and noticed that all the students were either still listening intently to their songs or writing out their reports. Feeling a little too quick and short-sighted, Paris flushed and handed the paper to Willow. "I guess I could have added a little more or something."

The headmistress ran her eyes down the report and laid it down, giving Paris a proud smile. "Not necessarily. More isn't always better. This is a very insightful analysis."

"Do you think it's correct?" Paris asked.

"The thing about love is there is usually no right or wrong," Willow explained. "Like any art form, it's subjective. I would agree that in some cases, two lovers have to lose each other or be separated somehow to appreciate one another fully. However, the phrase 'distance makes the heart grow fonder' isn't really accurate. Distance is tough for two lovers, but the key is to find out if that space makes the heart realize what made it beat faster in the first place."

"So my report is okay?" Paris' heart beat faster from merely the idea that she rushed the assignment.

"It's more than okay," Willow said. "Now, I think we owe you our attention because if you have any input on our Amelia and Grayson situation, I'm all ears. How about you, Mae Ling?"

The other professor nodded. "Yes, I think a fresh perspective is exactly what we need."

Paris wanted to ask Mae Ling about being Sophia's fairy godmother but knew the timing wasn't right. She tabled the conversation for later when they were alone.

"Well, I'm sorry if it wasn't okay, but I overheard you both," Paris began.

"We weren't talking in private," Willow offered.

Paris nodded, letting out a breath. "Anyway, I was listening to the situation with Amelia and Grayson, and it seems that since they're two people who are at odds, we can't have their past erased. Like the song, we have to use the bad experiences to make them appreciate each other and realize what they're missing. They need to have their obstacles between them turned to their advantage."

Willow absentmindedly twirled her long bluish-gray hair around her finger. "Yes, that makes sense. We have to hope the rivalry brings them together and makes their love stronger." She glanced down at the papers in front of her that detailed the situation with Amelia and Grayson. "I'm just not sure how. They're after the same niche in a small industry, cutting each other around every corner to get ahead. Each day the war gets hotter between them. Neither seems close to backing down."

"I think we need more information," Paris suggested.

"Well, the report from Saint Valentine's office has offered us information about what's happening in the media and public memos," Willow stated and sighed. "Honestly, I think we might have to turn this over to a higher-level fairy godmother at the agency or Matters of the Heart. It's just that the case originated here with one of our professors so it fell under our jurisdiction. I never imagined that it would create so many negative effects that keep getting worse."

"What we need is information that's not public," Paris stated with a sly smile.

"What do you mean?" Willow asked curiously.

"I mean that we need to go incognito." Paris wasn't sure if she should proceed with this idea, which was undoubtedly against standard fairy godmother protocol. However, she reasoned she was already in headfirst. "I propose that we investigate their two separate corporations from the inside and figure out how we can bring them together while they're trying to tear each other apart."

When she was silent, so were the other two fairy godmothers. They simply blinked back at Paris, making her feel very self-conscious.

After a long bout of silence, Paris finally cleared her throat. "I mean, it's probably a bad idea, and you should do whatever it is that you normally do in these circumstances. Ignore—"

"What we normally do," Willow cut in politely, "isn't working. We keep trying to put them together and try to negotiate, but it only incites them more. I think we're missing something crucial in this situation. Mae Ling, what do you think?"

The other fairy godmother nodded. "I agree. We're trying to get them to get along, but maybe there's another part of this that needs our attention first. Maybe they aren't meant to get along, not at first to fall in love. Paris makes a good point. The only way we're going to know what gets them together is to gather more information."

"Very well," the headmistress stated with finality. "I'll assign two students to go in covertly and discreetly gather information on the companies, but absolutely nothing else."

She glared up at Paris with a strange stern expression that was rare to see on the headmistress' face.

Paris couldn't help herself. "Why are you looking at me like that?"

"Well, isn't it obvious? I expect you to be one of these students. To be honest, I think we'll need someone with your kind of expertise to accomplish this."

"Expertise?" Paris questioned.

Willow gave her an embarrassed look. "I mean someone who knows how to break the rules, which is what we'll have to do to get into the corporations to research them from the inside."

Paris laughed. "That would be me. I'm most in my element when I'm doing that."

Thankfully the headmistress smiled too. "You'll be partnered with an experienced student. Your job is to collect information for us to use to help these two lovers. That's it."

Paris nodded, pride spreading across her chest. "Yes, and I'm up for the challenge."

Willow softened, smiling at Paris. "I figured you'd be. I think you'll do an excellent job."

CHAPTER FORTY-FIVE

Because the Amelia Rose and Grayson McGregor situation was so dire, the headmistress ordered that Paris get ready to leave straight away for the investigations. Not used to having fairy godmothers sneak into corporations in disguise, Willow was at first at a loss for how to get them into the businesses.

Paris, who had been sneaking into bars well before she was allowed or just plain sneaking around Roya Lane all her life, had a few ideas. She took the rest of the morning to develop some strategies while Headmistress Starr recruited the other student.

Hardly taking time to chew a protein bar, Paris called Uncle John to update him and get some tips. He answered on the first ring, sounding concerned.

"Are you all right?" he said instead of "Hello."

"I'm fine." Paris briefly filled him in on what she'd done the night before. He seemed relieved that everything had gone as well as it had. It probably helped his anxiety level that Paris left out the part about losing her protective charm and encountering the dangerous entity. Remembering that she'd first met the monster on Roya Lane, Paris suddenly tensed.

"Have you seen anything strange on Roya Lane?" she asked her uncle. "Like, whatever could have attacked Charlotte?"

He blew out a breath over the receiver. "To be honest, I haven't left the flat since it got ransacked, too busy putting everything back together."

"I could have helped you," Paris protested. Her magic was stronger than her uncle's from an early age. She'd always wondered why—and why he preferred not to use magic, but when he did, he employed a screwdriver to funnel it. A conduit for their magic was apparently common for most fairies but not for Paris. She'd never needed a wand or object to perform magic. Now she knew why. She was half-magician.

"I'm fine," he stated adamantly. "I know you're going to worry, but I'm fine here. Others are searching Roya Lane, and the portals are heavily monitored now. If there's something here, we'll find it. It's doubtful that anything that isn't supposed to be here will be able to get back in again."

Paris sighed with relief. She knew whatever had been after her on Roya Lane was most likely what attacked her in Beverly Hills. Hopefully, that meant it, whatever it was, couldn't get back into Roya Lane, and Uncle John was safe.

"Hey, you told me about Clark and Sophia. Oh, and I forgot to mention that I met Clark's wife, Alicia." Paris filled in more of the details. "She asked about you."

"Did she?" Curiosity edged his voice.

"I guess you can't tell me anything about how you know her since you can't tell me how you knew my mom and dad." There was a hint of hope to her voice.

"I wish I could," he muttered.

"Well, does a black and white cat have any significance to you?" Paris asked. "I saw one in Beverly Hills and got a strange impression from it as if the animal wasn't normal."

"How so?" John asked quickly.

"Just odd timing of seeing the creature." Paris left out the point that it appeared when she was being chased and again when the monster disappeared.

"Pare, you know I wish I could tell you something about him."

"Him?" Paris questioned. "That must have slipped through one of the loopholes on the silencing spell. So you do know a black and white cat then? Should I stay away from him? Or is he good, like my friend Faraday?"

"Faraday?" John questioned.

With all the excitement, Paris had forgotten to tell her uncle that she had a talking squirrel as a roommate. "Oh, yeah, this chatty squirrel followed me through a portal. His name is Faraday, and he says the strangest things. He's been sleeping in my sock drawer."

"Hmmm...that's odd..."

"Why?" Paris instantly responded.

"It just is," he said simply over the phone, but Paris got the distinct impression he knew more than he was letting on. *What did it matter though?* she reasoned. *He most likely couldn't say anything.*

"So the black and white cat." Paris looped back around to the previous topic. "Is he good or bad? Can you at least tell me that?"

There was a long pause. Finally, John said, "What does your instinct from the interaction say?"

So he couldn't answer even that question, Paris realized. She thought about seeing the cat and his calm demeanor as havoc was ensuing around her in Beverly Hills and later when he appeared right as the monster disappeared. There wasn't really anything concrete from the experience to help her. "I don't know."

"Well, be careful." He exhaled a tired sigh. "But you already know to do that. I'm glad you're back at the college now."

"I'm about to leave," she admitted sheepishly.

Another sigh. "To investigate?"

"No, strangely enough, Headmistress Starr is sending me on a mission."

"Already?" Uncle John sounded shocked and worried. Maybe also proud.

"Well, yeah, the idea for the mission was sort of my idea," Paris stated. "It's not their traditional fairy godmother mission. It involves using disguises to sneak into a corporation for research."

Uncle John sighed. "Who better for such a job? You've been trying to perfect that disguising spell since you were tiny, all so you could play pranks on me."

She laughed. "I remember that one time you came home to find a gnome sitting on the couch."

He chuckled. "I nearly tossed you over the balcony before you shifted back. Soph is good at that t-t-t..." Uncle John's words cut off, and Paris assumed the silencing spell had closed that loophole before he could finish his story.

"Aunt Sophia?" Paris asked. "She's good with disguising spells?"

There was no answer, but Paris thought she knew it anyway.

"You're a master at sneaking in places," Uncle John began. "I remember when I got the call that someone had infiltrated the Official Brownie Headquarters, and they thought it was my niece."

Heat rose in Paris' cheeks. "What can I say? I was curious how that place operated. There's no door. You see the little Brownies disappear into a solid brick wall, so I took their form and snuck in."

"Which got you into their headquarters but promptly kicked out."

"Don't worry," Paris reassured him. "I won't get caught this time. These are mortals we're dealing with and standard security measures. I only have to have a good story and some credentials, which is where I hoped you could help."

"Go on then." He still sounded uncertain of the idea.

"Well, Willow is going to get us added to the calendar as consultants who are visiting the corporations today," Paris explained.

"That sounds like a 'you' idea."

She nodded although he couldn't see it over the phone. "It was. That gives us a reason to be there, but they do have top-level security due to the nature of the rivalry, which is what we're trying to squash to create love."

"Is it okay if I stop you and say how proud of you I am?" Uncle John asked. "You're using your powers for good now. This is great work and so much better than getting into trouble on Roya Lane."

"I would argue that my work on Roya Lane was good too. I stopped bullies," Paris argued, but Uncle John didn't respond to that. It was a sticking point with them and always had been since he firmly believed it wasn't her business to police the streets of Roya Lane. Finally, Paris said, "Yes, thank you. I'm glad you're proud of me."

"I've always been, but now even more so."

"Anyway," Paris continued, "we'll need to show some ID. I remembered that you once had a cool badge that would change to show the credentials for whoever you were trying to be."

"Yes, it's magitech," John stated. "The person you're showing it to sees what they need to allow you to pass. That way, you don't have to make up the title, in case you're wrong and it's not a high enough security level for what you need."

"That's brilliant," Paris nearly exclaimed while striding back and forth in her room, getting more excited for this mission. "I told Headmistress Willow about it, and she said you could send it to us through a bread box. Does that make sense?"

He chuckled. "I haven't used that in forever, but yes. Since they don't get mail at Happily Ever After College, there's a single place on Roya Lane where people can send things there securely. It's a bread box in one of the retail shops here. One must know about it to use it, and it's always there because the store owner refuses to sell it, knowing its purpose."

"That's so cool. So, I hoped you could loan me the magitech ID for this mission and pass it through the bread box."

"Pare, I'm more than happy to send it to you. It won't be a loan.

SARAH NOFFKE & MICHAEL ANDERLE

I think you're more in need of keeping it than me with the work you'll be doing."

"You're giving me the magitech ID?" Paris asked.

He paused. "Well, you have to promise to use it only for good. No sneaking into the President of the United States' Oval Office or anywhere else because you're curious."

"Or want to get a selfie behind their desk." Paris laughed.

"Yes, another thing you'd do." He chuckled. "I'll send it over in a few moments."

"Thanks, Uncle John. I better get ready. We're leaving soon."

"Okay, well, take care and keep me updated. And Pare?"

"Yes?"

"I know things are changing a lot and are confusing, but you'll always be my family, no matter what."

"Always," she repeated. "Familia Est Sempiternum."

A sound of surprise echoed over the phone. "Yes, the Beaufonts have always had it right. Familia Est Sempiternum."

CHAPTER FORTY-SIX

As instructed, Paris waited in the entryway of FGE. She didn't have to wait long because soon Mae Ling appeared from her office, holding two objects in her hands. One Paris recognized and one that she didn't.

The magitech ID looked ordinary to the unsuspecting eye. It appeared to be a real badge inside a folded leather case. Paris took it when Mae Ling handed it to her wordlessly, disbelieving that it was hers! That was like the coolest prize ever, but she wouldn't abuse its powers, although her mind was already busy pretending the places she could go.

Paris opened the magitech ID and found that as she expected, the inside was blank. That was because she wasn't trying to trick herself into believing she was any particular person. To a security guard or whoever, it would show them what they wanted to see to grant her clearance.

"Thank you," Paris said to Mae Ling.

"We've put your name on the list of visitors for Rose Industries as Emma Blackstone," Mae Ling stated. "For McGregor Technologies, they 're expecting a Gemma Whiterock."

Paris laughed. "You don't think those names are too similar?"

"I think they'll be easy to remember," Mae Ling countered.

"Or I'll get them mixed up," Paris teased.

"Try not to," Mae Ling warned, handing over a second object. It was a figure of an angel. "We both know that you can't leave here without a protective charm. It's unfortunate that you lost the other one."

"You know about that?" Paris nodded. "Of course, you know about that."

"This one," Mae Ling indicated the pin, "can be fastened to your clothes so hopefully you don't lose it again or have it taken from you, although it's impossible to guarantee this."

"So I can't have protective charmed boots or socks or something that someone couldn't take off me?" Paris kidded.

"Everything can be taken off you," Mae Ling corrected, not at all amused. "The protective charm spell only works on objects that can be somewhat easily removed. That's part of the caveat of the spell because with magic, there's always a counter. An object can protect you from something, but it has to be one that someone can take from you rather easily."

"So no protective charmed tattoos, then?" Paris asked.

"That's right," Mae Ling affirmed.

"I have a question," Paris began.

The fairy godmother nodded. "Yes, Sophia is one of my charges."

Paris blinked at Mae Ling, wondering how she knew the question before being asked, but that was on the long list of mysteries about the enigmatic woman.

"Does your being her fairy godmother have any relation to your secret advice and help with me?"

"My job is to promote love," Mae Ling answered. "Helping Sophia Beaufont supports that goal. Helping you supports that mission. The fact that you two are related isn't really a factor. The Beaufonts happen to have ties to justice and peace."

"Wilfred said that the Beaufonts were tasked with protecting magic," Paris offered, remembering what the butler had told her.

"That's true," Mae Ling said simply, not expanding as Paris had hoped.

"I have so many questions that can't be answered," Paris related, wishing the fairy godmother could help.

"Easily," Mae Ling corrected. "In time they will be." She pointed toward the front door. "Now, the second-year student we've assigned to go with you is on the front porch, so please don't keep her waiting any longer. The faster you both recover covert information from the companies and return, the sooner we can determine a plan to fix things with Amelia Rose and Grayson McGregor."

Paris nodded and headed for the door. She glanced back once more before opening it, surprised at who she found waiting for her.

CHAPTER FORTY-SEVEN

"You're my partner on this mission?" Paris blinked as Christine grinned back at her.

"Of course you're the newbie who gets to go on this crazy awesome mission!" Christine exclaimed, throwing up her arms in excitement. "Seriously, in my next life, I get to be a crazy awesome magician-slash-fairy hybrid so I get to be all badass and do cool stuff."

"Well, you're going on this mission with me," Paris countered. "I'm not going on this mission because I'm a halfling. It's because the idea of sneaking into the dueling corporations was my idea. Apparently, I have the spy and rule-breaking skills that others at the college or the other fairy godmothers wouldn't have to complete the job."

"I was told that I needed to accompany a first-year and was totally stumped on who it could be since first-years don't get missions ever," Christine explained. "Really, it's rare for second-years, but Headmistress Starr said she thought I might be a good fit for this one."

Paris winked. "Because you have a rebellious tendency."

"The headmistress said you'd explain the mission details," Christine continued. "All I know is that it involves investigating, which sounds fantastic."

"You're going to love it." Paris was excited as she pinned the angel charm on her shirt securely. "We have to use disguises to sneak into two different corporations."

Christine glanced up at the heavens. "I don't know who sent Paris Beaufont here, but thank you. Simply thank you."

Paris giggled. "We're trying to dig up as much internal information as possible about these corporations and their CEOs who are fighting instead of falling in love. We have to find out how to get them to stop warring and put up their white flags."

"So she can put on the white dress, and they can make love, not war?" Christine supplied.

"Yep, I couldn't have said it better," Paris answered.

Christine greedily rubbed her hands together. "I can't wait for this. So we sneak. Do we need to bust some kneecaps so we can gain entry?"

Paris shook her head. "No, we're going to do this peacefully since we're fairy godmothers and all."

"Sounds less fun, but fine," Christine muttered.

"We get to be fake people, with fake magical badges," Paris sang.

"I'm already happier," Christine stated.

"More importantly, you'll need to change." Paris pointed at the blue gown. "Sorry, but no one is going to believe that you're a professional consultant dressed as a fairy godmother."

Christine lowered her chin and regarded Paris with hooded eyes. "You look like you just got finished besting a giant at a pool game in a dive bar."

Paris pointed a finger at herself and blinked. "Watch this then and be amazed." Her leather jacket, pants, and t-shirt became a professional black business pantsuit with a starched gray blouse and practical heels. On the lapel of her blazer was the protective angel charm that Mae Ling had given her. "What do you think?"

"Other than you're going to a funeral?" Christine asked.

"Yes, besides that…"

"Well, you look brilliant," Christine announced. "I would never guess that you're a rebellious halfling there to steal all my corporation's secrets."

"Now we need to deal with you." Paris raised an eyebrow, waiting for Christine to remove the gown.

She grabbed the hem of her gown, her excitement palpable. "I'm more than happy to get rid of this thing." Pulling off the silk gown in one swift movement, the fairy before Paris transformed all at once. Whereas before she sported the grayish-blue hair like all the other students and professors, save for Paris and Mae Ling, Christine's natural hair color came to life.

As Paris had suspected all along, her friend with the long, straight locks was a redhead. It was weird to see her with freckles and orangish-red hair that made her appear her age—or younger. Under the robe, she'd been wearing a pair of jeans and a t-shirt too.

"Hey, Red." Paris winked.

"Heeeeey," Christine sang, seeming more herself without the gown covering her.

"Now we have to do something about your clothes since professional consultants don't dress so casually."

Christine shrugged. "I'm not so good with disguising magic. I'm not sure if you've heard, but it's advanced magic, changing appearances and all."

Paris shrugged. "I started early because pranking my uncle was top of my priorities."

Christine pressed her hands to her chest. "I truly think you're my soul mate in a lot of ways."

Paris laughed, thinking of how to dress Christine to fit her style but also be professional and believable. "How about this?" She flicked her hand at her friend and her appearance instantly changed, putting her in a navy blue pencil skirt, matching blazer, and a ruffled white top—all of them complementing her red hair, which was now in a French twist. To complete the look, Christine wore silver hoop earrings and black heels.

Her mouth fell open as she peered down. Christine turned to face the windows on the front porch, taking in her appearance. "I. Freaking. Love. It!"

Paris beamed. "Good. Now I think we're ready to go be spies."

Christine held her hands up excitedly. "I freaking love this. Please don't ever leave the college while I'm here."

Paris cast her a sideways glance as they started forward, off the porch. "I have zero plans of going anywhere."

CHAPTER FORTY-EIGHT

Faraday scurried down the drainage pipe onto the Enchanted Grounds and in the direction of the Serenity Garden. He didn't like that he hadn't been with Paris the night before when she was investigating. It shouldn't have fallen on Plato to help her. That was his responsibility, although he admittedly had fewer options than the lynx. Still, Faraday had his brains and a few tricks up his sleeves—well, if he had sleeves instead of squirrel arms.

He'd known from spying on Paris that she had a new protective charm, a sidekick, and a mission for Happily Ever After College and therefore shouldn't need him. Not yet, at least. He'd be there for her when she went on her next Beaufont fact-finding mission.

For now, Faraday's curiosity led him to the Serenity Garden. He simply had to know why it was off-limits on Tuesdays. That was such a random day to close it, and all his calculations had crossed off the idea that it shut down for fertilizing, statue-washing, or any other plausible excuse.

He'd watched the Serenity Garden for the last two weeks before, on, and after Tuesday. He hadn't noticed any supplies or equipment brought in or taken away from it around then, making it unlikely that it was closed for maintenance.

All that meant Faraday needed to investigate and get answers.

Checking to ensure that the Enchanted Grounds were deserted between the mansion and the garden, Faraday hung back in a rose bush, scanning the area. Most of the students would be in class at that time. Usually, Hemingway was tending to the horses around then. The Wilfreds, well, they were all over now, but that wasn't an issue. Chef Ashton was almost always in the kitchen before lunch. That meant Faraday could pass more easily between the mansion and gardens, going unnoticed, although he was always careful as he'd promised Paris. The last thing he wanted to do was cause her problems. He was there to make her life easier after all.

Faraday slipped out from the prickly bush and made it to the Serenity Garden entrance marked by an arbor covered in climbing roses. Like most things at Happily Ever After College, there wasn't a lock on the gardens to discourage trespassers from entering, although it was closed on Tuesdays. Most who attended the college weren't like Paris Beaufont and didn't break the rules. Of course, there were bullies like Becky Montgomery. Or others who didn't have the best behavior for whatever reason, but most of the students did as instructed. The rebel rule-breakers went to Tooth Fairy College down the way.

A quick check over his shoulder ensured that no one was watching. The usual giddiness that marked an occasion where he'd make a discovery returned. Faraday turned and scampered into the Serenity Garden, which was full of roses, topiaries, and beautiful statues, interested in what else he'd find.

He had scurried into the center of the first main area when he realized what was so different about the garden from other days. It had taken a moment for things to register. Then events had moved too quickly for him to deal with properly, and more importantly, escape from.

The statues in the Serenity Garden were moving. They were alive. Now they had him cornered...

CHAPTER FORTY-NINE

The new clothes made Paris feel like an imposter already, and she had to remind herself that she had to own the appearance. No one would automatically guess that she wasn't Emma Blackstone. People usually wanted to believe that a person was who they said they were. Plus, she had a badge.

The front lobby of Rose Industries was pretty impressive, especially considering that Amelia Rose had only started her company recently. Paris realized that she kept checking over her shoulder as they strode into the lobby of the skyscraper in London.

"What's the deal?" Christine asked at her side.

"Evil thing that could be following me because I'm a halfling," Paris answered in a whisper.

"Oh, is that all," Christine said sarcastically. "Here I thought you had real problems."

"Nope, just trying to fix the meter of love so the world doesn't crash and burn while also trying not to have my soul sucked out by an unknown evil."

Christine rolled her eyes. "If it makes you feel better, I burned my tongue on some hot tea earlier, and if that wasn't enough, I stubbed my toe on a garden gnome. I'm certain that the little sucker cursed me as he hobbled off toward the Bewilder Forest. He's probably going to do something awful to me, like overly prune my plants or unfertilize them. They're vindicative little devils who hold a grudge even if you apologize for punting them across the Enchanted Grounds."

Paris shook her head. "I can't believe I've even pretended to have problems when in your presence. Thanks for humbling me."

"You're welcome," Christine sang as they sauntered up to the metal detector and security checkpoint.

Security at Rose Industries was tight not only because their CEO was paranoid that Grayson McGregor would ruin her, but also because the technologies they created were incredibly expensive and patent-pending stuff that could shatter the world if released before they were ready.

The company created things that took small tech and made it nano-sized. Their technology took an app and made it more of a thought. It bordered on magitech, but for mortals. That's one reason that McGregor Technologies and Rose Industries were fighting so much. They were genius parts of the tech world, and their CEOs were as smart as they came. The truth was they were both full of passion, and if harnessed for one another, they could do even greater things as a true power couple. Currently, while at odds, they were dangerous dictators with nukes aimed at each other.

"Who you here to see?" the security guard at the first station asked.

"Amelia Rose." Paris pulled out her magitech badge. "My name is Emma Blackstone, and we have an appointment with her." She opened the badge and flashed it at the man.

His eyes widened, and he grinned, showing a row of crooked yellow teeth. "Wow, the Chief Engineer for NASA. We haven't had anyone of your caliber at Rose Industries."

"Well," Paris drew out the word, realizing she shouldn't expand much to keep her cover.

"And your friend?" The guard pointed at Christine.

"That's Wistine Celsh, my assistant," Paris said at once, reversing the initials of Christine's first and last names.

"Very good." The guard indicated they could move on to the next phase of security clearance.

"Wistine Celsh?" Christine asked. "Cute. Now my alias will always be that because no one will mistake Christine Welsh for that."

"I know," Paris whispered over her shoulder.

They paused at the metal detectors in front of a tall security guard. "Hold up your hands when you enter and halt until it finishes scanning you," the guy informed them.

Paris waited until he waved her forward, then strode into the metal detector and held up her hands, her blazer and shirt rising to show her midriff. The machine scanned and flashed green.

"You're clear, sweetheart." The guy waved her out of the machine.

She strode out, waiting for Christine to clear the scanner.

"Nice abs, sweetheart." The security official glanced at her sideways.

Paris gave him the side-eye. "They're rock solid. Nice head. I look forward to smashing it against something as hard as my abs if you don't take your eyes off me," she stated as Christine struck a pose.

"Hey, it was a compliment, sweetheart," the guy complained as the detector flashed green, clearing Christine. "You don't have to get all bent out of shape."

"How about you not comment on my body, and I won't bend you out of shape?" Paris threatened.

Christine strode out of the machine, grabbed her by the arm, and hauled Paris toward the elevator. She didn't release her until they were in the closed compartment alone.

"What?" Paris dusted off her sleeve, although it was fine.

"You just have to start a fight, don't you?"

"He was insulting," she complained.

"Although that might be true, you realize that you don't have to attend every argument you're invited to, right?"

Paris blinked at her friend and deflated, never having heard it put so eloquently. "Yeah, no, I guess I don't."

CHAPTER FIFTY

The secret of the Serenity Garden was fascinating, although Faraday was still uncertain what he was seeing. Many times, he'd explored the English garden full of stone statues of regal-looking men in formal attire and women in maids outfits and simply thought their appearance was to reiterate the formality of Happily Ever After College.

Whereas the stone statues had been gray before, now they had color and movement. They appeared very much alive although there was something wrong with their actions. They were robotic and didn't seem to flow naturally.

Faraday had often gotten the impression that he was at a formal dinner party when in the Serenity Garden, and all the statues were the servants. Some of that observation was because many of the figures resembled Wilfred with his three-piece suit and tails. Several of the sculptures looked very similar to the magitech AI butler in features. Some were younger or older or had their hair parted on the other side, but they all gave off that impression of formal servitude.

The female statues were similar in their attire, and their

features didn't vary much. There were roughly two dozen living sculptures in the garden, and they were all in a circle around Faraday presently. There would be little hope of escaping from them, and maybe that was okay.

At first impression, Faraday didn't think he was necessarily in danger. The statues that had come alive might have cornered him immediately. They might be doing some strange things like swinging their heads strangely or opening their mouths and abruptly closing them. Some might be singing senseless songs. However, they weren't attacking him.

"W-Wh-What are you all?" Faraday stuttered, his eyes scanning as he turned in a circle, noticing all the strange characters around him.

A man dressed in a black suit and tie with short brown hair and a mustache stepped forward and bowed. "At your-your-your service Ma-Ma-Master. I am Alfred and ready to assist you."

"I am Alfred, and I am ready to assist you," all the male statues chorused around the squirrel, their heads bobbing sideways strangely.

They all had the same British accent as Wilfred, but their voices were mechanical.

A woman in a long black dress and apron curtsied before Faraday. "It is a pleasure to serve you, Master. Please just say my name, and I'll appear to assist you."

"You can call me Mary," all the women statues said in unison.

Faraday pieced it all together. "You all are magitech AI servants." He was still missing a giant piece of the puzzle. Why would the fairy godmothers have a bunch of strangely operating AI servants in the Serenity Garden that only came alive on Tuesdays—the one day it was forbidden to enter the area?

"May I get sir anything?" the first Alfred to introduce himself asked. "Master must be tired after the long journey. You've been gone for ages."

"I have?" Faraday scratched his head.

"For a very long time," the first Mary said. "We have not seen anyone in many decades."

"You haven't?" Faraday watched as one of the butlers turned, doing something near the large cascading fountains.

That Alfred spun proudly, brandishing a tray with a teacup and saucer. Faraday had often seen this prop on a few of the stone statues and wondered about it, but now it looked as real as the ones inside FGE.

"Sir, would you like some rainwater?" Alfred asked. "I have a lovely variety from the east part of the garden."

Faraday shook his head. Something was obviously wrong with the magitech AI servants. Definitely a few screws loose, although Faraday didn't know that any of them contained a single real screw. He was uncertain of the physical hardware that made up the magitech AIs, although investigating Wilfred had been on his to-do list.

"Would sir like some bark and worms with his tea?" one of the maids said at Faraday's back.

He spun to find one of the Marys holding a tray, and on it were pieces of tree bark arranged neatly and wiggling worms beside it.

"I'm fine, thank you." Faraday heard something behind him. He turned again to find one of the Marys washing the fountain's side, which was a typical job for a servant to do. Except that it was an outdoor fountain—and she was doing it with mud.

"Oh, I can never get that spot out," the maid fussed. "I will simply be at this all day." She had covered one entire side of the once-pristine fountain in thick mud.

Faraday suddenly felt like he was in a strange dreamland. Almost as if he was a regular person in the ordinary world who had fallen down a hole of sorts into a bizarre wonderland where people had weird birthday and tea parties. The notion struck Faraday as an interesting one, and he made note that someone should write that story at some point. Maybe he would and call it *Faraday in Curiosity-Ville.*

For the time being, he needed to figure out what was going on in his reality.

"Does sir take rust or salt in his tea?" an Alfred asked while stepping forward, carrying his tray of teacups filled with grass shavings.

That was when Faraday realized what was wrong with all these magitech—they were all insane. That wasn't a very technical term nor an acceptable scientific assessment, but he knew he was correct. Whatever minds these magitech AIs had, they'd lost it. Or maybe that was the issue all along, he pondered. These servants were the mistake prototypes created before Wilfred, who was an impressive piece of magitech.

The question now for Faraday was, why were these living statues all here in the Serenity Garden? More importantly, why did they come alive on Tuesdays?

To answer that question, Faraday needed to test his hypothesis on the AIs being flawed models.

"Can you tell me where the conservatory is at FGE?" Faraday asked the nearest Alfred.

The butler held his chin up high. "Certainly, sir. It's on the main space station, twelve paces past the entrance to the underground unicorn."

"Thank you," Faraday chirped.

Yep, the AIs were insane. Faraday's next hypothesis was that their physical hardware must not have paired correctly with their magitech programming. To test that one, he'd have to get a closer look.

"Can I get one of you to open your control panel so I can examine it?" Faraday asked.

"I will satisfy that request from the master." One of the Marys stepped forward, and a panel on her front popped open.

Faraday climbed up onto a nearby pedestal and waved the maid forward. "Please come here so I can take a closer look."

Like a door opening to reveal a whole new world, the panel on the front of the AI showed her insides, and it was simply incredible. It also explained exactly why the magitech acted so strangely. From Faraday's initial observation, he could tell that their hardware wasn't the type that would be compatible with magitech. They had their robotic bodies and computer minds, but to pair that with magic required that the hardware was flawless, and a quick assessment told Faraday that technical bugs riddled these servants.

"Very interesting." Faraday poked around at various wires inside the AI. He had hypothesized that although Wilfred had a physical body, it was housed somewhere like a computer's mainframe. Faraday hadn't found that location in FGE yet, but it was on his list of things to do.

Once he'd found it, he could confirm his other hypothesis, which was that the magitech AI butler simply projected a holographic image of himself when paged at various places inside the mansion. However, it was the magic that made it so he took a physical form, allowing him to do chores and serve.

However, his assessment of this maid told him that initially, the fairy godmothers had tried to create physical bodies for the AI servants and pair them with magitech. The result was…well, it was what Faraday was looking at all around the Serenity Garden. The servants were crazy, and that might be due to a whole host of factors.

Faraday assumed that the fairy godmothers figured out their mistake after several dozen trials and realized that the AI had to be "housed" somewhere locally first. Otherwise, it appeared that the magic overwhelmed the technology, making the servant act in untraditional and illogical ways. It made sense to Faraday because the magic to make a robot come alive, as Wilfred did, would have to be vast.

Furthermore, these servants would be confined to their physical bodies, making them limited in how well they could take care of FGE. Maybe that was why there were so many of them, Faraday observed, regarding the servants. Initially, the fairy godmothers must have thought they'd have a large staff to care for the estate.

When these AIs didn't perform correctly, they must have come up with the Wilfred solution, which required only one physical location and potentially a thousand projections of the butler to do the work around the college. It was simply incredible, and Faraday reveled in his findings. This was precisely why he wanted to come to Happily Ever After College. Well, a bonus reason to the one that brought him there.

The question remained, why were the flawed AIs there in the Serenity Garden and why did they come alive on Tuesday? Sometimes the best way to discover the answer was simply to ask the source. It was the most straightforward and efficient approach, although he wasn't sure if any of them could answer since they all were insane.

Faraday stepped back from the maid with the open panel and peered around at the others. "Why is it that you all are here in the Serenity Garden?"

"The fairy godmothers put us here," one of the Alfreds answered.

Faraday flicked his tail. "Right. My question is, why?"

"Because they didn't want to get rid of us," a Mary stated.

That made logical sense. Of course, the compassionate and loving fairy godmothers wouldn't want to destroy their creations, even if they were flawed.

"Why is that you come alive on Tuesdays?" Faraday questioned.

"That is our day to enjoy the life we were given," one of the nearby butlers answered. "We were created to serve, and that's what we desire most. Will Master require me to turn down his bed? If so, I'll grab the can opener and pliers."

There it was, Faraday thought victoriously. The magitech AI servants were very much alive, like Wilfred. The fairy godmothers not only didn't want to "kill" them but thought they should offer them a life. The problem was that this wasn't the life they wanted because it wasn't how they were programmed. Without being able to serve, they were unhappy. Moreover, a lack of experiences made it impossible for them to evolve and become sentient, as Faraday thought was Wilfred's case. So the AIs were restless on Tuesdays, quite literally losing their minds.

Faraday shook his head. "No, thank you."

The talking squirrel wasn't sure how to fix this situation, but he wanted the opportunity. First, he'd have to do some research in FGE. He climbed down the pedestal and made for the Serenity Garden's exit, but most of the maids and butlers moved to create a tight line, blocking him from leaving.

"Where is Master going?" one of the Alfreds asked.

"I was going back to FGE to look into something," Faraday answered.

"Master can't leave," a maid said flatly. "We have waited a long time to be of service."

"I'll come back," Faraday stated. "I need to—"

"Master is free to roam through the Serenity Garden," a butler informed him. "But under no circumstances will he leave now that he has finally joined us."

Faraday turned in a circle, noting that the other AI servants had moved into various spots, blocking any possible place for Faraday to escape.

CHAPTER FIFTY-ONE

When the elevators opened on the top floor of Rose Industries, a tall red-haired man with the most freckles Paris had ever seen greeted them. Christine had a fair amount of freckles as a ginger, but she wore them well, almost like jewelry or an accessory of sorts.

This guy looked like he was a handful of freckles away from having a complete tan. His red hair was bright and almost made him appear alien-like, as did his slanted dark green eyes.

"Hello and welcome to Rose Industries," the man greeted them as they exited the compartment. He extended a long-fingered hand to Paris. "I'm the CFO, Bryce Tyler."

Paris wrung his hand and introduced herself and Christine with their aliases.

"Amelia asked that I give you a tour before you meet with her," Bryce offered. "We are both very interested in what you can provide us from a consulting aspect that would allow us to level up our business."

"We're looking forward to working with you." Paris tried to sound professional but felt like an imposter. She never had to act professionally a day in her life and felt like there was a large sign on her head that said "spy."

However, Bryce didn't seem to notice as he led them through a long hallway with glassed-in walls. Various things appeared to be on exhibit in the rooms. On the other side was another glass wall, but this one showed the view from the skyscraper's top floor, which gave an impressive view of the Thames River and London. Amelia Rose had built this company fast, and it appeared she'd dipped into Bryce's pockets to fund it in style, which was information the fairy godmothers knew from the report.

"I think seeing some of our cutting-edge concepts for future products will give you an idea of where the company is going," Bryce explained. "Since you signed the NDA before you arrived, we have full confidence that what you learn here won't be leaked outside these walls." He narrowed his eyes. "We have a cutthroat competitor that will sink to sick levels to gain an advantage, even if that means stealing what rightfully belongs to us."

The headmistress and Mae Ling must have taken care of the nondisclosure agreement when they set up the appointment with Rose Industries.

"This competition?" Christine prompted while striding beside them.

Bryce paused at the end of the long, bright hallway that made it feel like they were on the roof of the building, out in the open since it was mostly glass. He pointed out the window to another tall skyscraper across the Thames. "It's our neighbors there, McGregor Technologies. Their CEO will stop at nothing to try and ruin our good reputation, steal our employees to learn insider secrets, and race to secure patents before we can. Grayson McGregor doesn't even go through the full testing procedures before he puts something on the market. We have it on good authority that their technology is probably responsible for several small office fires due to faulty wiring. That hasn't been proved yet, but it's only a matter of time."

"What would happen to them?" Paris questioned.

"Well, it would be enough to shut them down completely," Bryce answered. "That would surely sully their reputation, and there would be no coming back from it. Then McGregor Technologies would have to close down, but knowing Grayson, he'd come back under a different name with another shady business model. It's hard to kill a rat."

That sparked a hint of an idea in Paris. Not a full one, but something she thought she could flush out with more information.

"If you'll follow me, I'll show you our newest technologies." Bryce led them back the way they'd come.

For ten minutes, he droned on about advanced technologies that should have been of interest to someone. However, the CFO was about as animated and engaging as a box of Q-tips.

"Now, if you follow me in here, I'll take you to meet with our CEO, Amelia Rose." Bryce approached one of the only solid doors on that floor since everything was mostly glass.

He opened it to reveal a sleek office with modern furniture, a floor-to-ceiling glass wall at the back that had the same view as before, staring straight across the Thames River at McGregor Technologies. Sitting behind the desk was a beautiful woman who had her brown braid over one shoulder and wore a smart business suit.

Amelia Rose looked up when they entered and stood to greet them. "You must be the consultants we're looking to hire. Please come in."

The woman strode around the desk and offered them her hand. That's when Paris noticed it and had to work to keep the look of worry off her face. On Amelia's left hand and so big that someone could probably see it from outer space was a shiny and gaudy engagement ring.

CHAPTER FIFTY-TWO

A melia Rose couldn't be engaged to Bryce Tyler. That would put a wrench in the whole plan to hook her up with Grayson McGregor, her one true love.

"Pleasure to meet you." Christine stepped forward and shook the CEO's hand, covering for Paris, who was still working to keep the dismay off her face.

"I trust that Bryce gave you a good tour." Amelia indicated the chairs in front of her desk as she resumed her seat. "Did you show them the over levels?"

"I didn't, dear." He awkwardly stood to the side.

Amelia glanced at him, and Paris wasn't sure if the reaction was because he'd used an affectionate term for her in a professional setting or because he'd disappointed her with his bad tour-giving skills.

"The tour was probably sufficient for us to start creating plans for Rose Industries." Paris crossed her legs the way she saw ladies do on television.

"I probably should have done it myself." Amelia studied her

computer screen momentarily. "It's just that I'm busy with sending out a press release."

"I don't think you should send that out, dear," Bryce said with a tight smile.

"I'm well aware of what you think, Mr. Tyler." Amelia sounded overly formal, her tone clipped.

"Press memo?" Paris asked.

Amelia rolled her eyes and spun in her chair, putting her back to them as she stared across the river. "It's a preemptive measure. McGregor Technologies has made private threats that they'll expose bad working conditions in our factories, which would bring us a huge human resources headache, if not worse. You see what we're up against and why we need to find a way to level up the company?" The CEO wore a furious expression when she turned back.

Paris nodded. "I do. This press memo?"

"Grayson is full of empty threats," Bryce cut in. "Our factories are fine, and he's only trying to goad you into this. If you release a preemptive press release stating that our working conditions are fine despite an anonymous claim, that's only going to shine a spotlight on us. He's trying to get us to hang ourselves with our own rope."

"If I wait to see whether it's an empty threat and he does take something to the press," Amelia began, her words terse, "I lose the advantage of cutting him off."

The couple stared each other down, frustrations bouncing back and forth between them silently. The tension was palpable.

Paris glanced at Christine, who seemed to read her expression with a minute nod.

"It sounds like a risky situation," Christine supplied sensitively. "Have you tried talking with Grayson McGregor to come to a resolution?"

Bryce laughed, but the sound lacked any joy.

Amelia shook her head. "There's no talking to that man. Every time I'm in the same room with him, he makes me so angry, I lose my words. He gets under my skin so badly."

Paris smiled inside. Getting under one's skin was also code for chemistry in her opinion. If one didn't care what another person thought or did, they wouldn't have the power to irritate them. However, she suspected that Grayson had the reins on Amelia's emotions and vice versa.

The hint of an idea from earlier was starting to unfurl for Paris. She thought she knew where to start with getting these two love birds together, but it wasn't going to be easy or straightforward, and it would require a hell of a lot more research and coordination. Since she had everything she thought they needed from Rose Industries, she wanted to visit McGregor Technologies to dig up information from their side. Time was a factor, and they couldn't afford to stick around and watch Amelia give Bryce dirty looks any longer.

CHAPTER FIFTY-THREE

This was definitely not good, Faraday thought as he backed up from the entrance guarded by the deranged magitech AIs. He consoled himself that the servants only came alive for one day a week, but what if they could overpower those wards now that they had a master to serve and therefore the motivation to do so?

Furthermore, by the way that one of the Mary's was sweeping with an imaginary broom and looking at him, he was starting to fear for his safety. "I think you're overdue for a bath, Master. Why don't I go boil you a bath?"

"I'm good," Faraday squeaked, scurrying several yards away to a grassy area. He was looking over his shoulder, his heart rapidly beating when he slammed into something solid that hadn't been there a moment prior.

The squirrel looked up at an Alfred whose leg he'd collided with. The butler had appeared out of nowhere, holding a pair of gardening shears that Hemingway must have left lying around. He motioned with them, making a chopping sound.

"Would sir like his hair cut now?" the butler asked. "It's overdue, and your tail is quite long. Actually, tails are out of fashion for lords of your stature. Why don't we get rid of it entirely?"

Faraday's large eyes bulged even more, and he scampered around the butler, dashing between various servants stationed in multiple places. He would have tried to scale the stone walls around the Serenity Garden, but they were clean of vines that he could climb. The walls were slick and smooth as if polished regularly. They probably were.

Feeling like he was running out of options, Faraday ran straight for a well in the middle of the garden. He planned to jump onto its high walls to get a view around the Serenity Garden to find options. However, one of the maids dove in front of him, her arms wide.

"Sir, I really must ask that you tuck in for the night," she said in a wicked voice, her eyes sinister. "You know how Master gets if he doesn't get enough rest. Come here, and I'll tuck you in properly." She held her hands out in a choking motion.

Not thinking of anything but self-preservation, Faraday threw himself into the air, flicking his tail to propel him in the direction of the well where he intended to overshoot the walls and risk falling into the center. He could swim if needed, but hopefully, he'd be able to climb back out once the servants took their breaks —if they took breaks.

The squirrel flew through the air and expected to land in the dark and damp well in water. Faraday was surprised and a little bruised when he landed on top of a bunch of parts—not just any, though. They were pieces of the magitech AI servants, all dismantled and lying at the bottom of the well. They were exactly what the talking squirrel needed to get out of the Serenity Garden.

CHAPTER FIFTY-FOUR

"Oh, yes, more disguises," Christine said with delight as she and Paris hid in a back alleyway on the other side of the Thames, opposite Rose Industries.

It was time that they snuck into McGregor Technologies, but that would require a different appearance in case anyone was observing or sneaking around—like them.

"How do you want to look?" Paris asked, tapping her chin. "Ever wanted a bob or black hair or to be pixie short?"

"No, no, and no," Christine stated. "I'd like to be blonde with shoulder-length hair and half-magician and half-fairy."

Paris tilted her head. "That identity is already taken and a little overrated if you ask me."

"I'm not." Christine held her arms wide. "Make me look like Paris Beaufont. I want everyone to gawk at me, the girls to hate me, the boys to wonder, and—"

"The evil mystery soul-eating entities to come after you," Paris interrupted.

Christine looked up suddenly. "Not that last part. On second thought, make me a guy named James who has a plain appearance and a forgettable face. I always thought that was the best appearance for robbing a bank."

"Christina," Paris purposely said her friend's name wrong to irritate her. "You can't rob a bank after this...or before this...or really at all."

"Because..." Christine drew out the word and regarded her fingernails as though she was bored.

"Because you're a fairy godmother and our job is to create love around the world. Or at least not to destroy it with bank robberies and whatnot."

Christine shrugged. "You don't know. Bank robberies might be what makes this world go 'round. *That* might be the key to love."

"I doubt it," Paris grumbled. "But if plain James is what you want, that's what you get." She flicked her wrist at her friend, and her appearance immediately shifted from pretty Christine with strawberry hair to a nondescript guy with drab brown hair who was instantly forgettable.

"I like it," Christine said, looking down at her appearance. She angled toward Paris. "And you?"

"I'm going to be James' middle-aged mom named Beverly, who is tired of putting up with his lazy ways." Paris flicked her finger at herself. She shifted until she looked like a pudgy woman with curly brown hair and a frown-filled face with twinkling brown eyes.

"What's our cover for getting into McGregor Technologies?" Christine looked impressed.

"Well, we already have appointments as consultants." Paris held up the magitech badge. "Our credentials are whatever they think they are."

"Right on!" Christine cheered in a deep voice, throwing a fist in the air.

CHAPTER FIFTY-FIVE

Whereas Rose Industries had a modern feel with its glass walls and high-security team at the elevators, McGregor Technologies felt more like they were walking into a cigar lounge.

The wood-paneled walls in the lobby were rich and warm, making the space feel dark. There was a pretty woman with a perky blonde ponytail sitting behind an elegant desk. She smiled at the mother-and-son team when they approached.

"You must be the consultants here to see Mr. McGregor," the woman said, flipping through an appointment book. "He should be able to see you right away, but first, can I see some ID from you both?"

Both, Paris thought. At Rose Industries, the security guard only needed to see hers. She only had one magitech ID badge.

She pointed at the guy next to her and shook her head. "This is my son, James. I can vouch for him. He doesn't have any identification because he can't get his lazy butt off the sofa long enough to get one. Hopefully, my credentials are enough." Paris flashed the badge, and the woman's eyes widened.

"Well, it makes sense that Mr. McGregor would hire only the

best design consultants for this project," the secretary said, an impressed look flitting across her face. "Michelle Bordeaux, I've heard you're the best interactive designer in the world. Your adventures are world-renowned."

Not having expected this, Paris simply nodded.

"My mom is the best," Christine said, her voice deep.

The secretary nodded. "I can't wait to see what you do with the space. I'll take you to meet Mr. Grayson. He's excited about the project."

Paris nodded again, not sure what to say and thinking that she might blow her cover if she said anything at all. She and Christine followed the woman through a door at the back of the room. Paris turned and mouthed to Christine, in the form of frumpy James, "Interactive designer?"

Christine smirked, apparently finding this all entertaining.

Paris didn't even know what an interactive designer was. What did it mean that this woman, Michelle Bordeaux, created world-renowned adventures? She knew she'd find out, but she hoped that she didn't have to say much in the process.

At Rose Industries, Paris had collected a good bit of information that she thought could work for the plan starting to unfurl in her mind. However, the project would need more. Plus, she needed to know what was happening at McGregor Technologies.

Dark wainscoting covered the bottom of the hallway's walls, and a blue and green plaid wallpaper covered the rest.

The carpet running down the length of the corridor was a warm green. Paris suddenly felt like she was in a hunting lodge—not that she'd ever been in one.

The secretary led them to an office at the back of the hallway. All the other doors were closed, not giving Paris any clues about what went on at McGregor Technologies.

The woman knocked on the door and waited briefly before opening it and poking her head inside. "The design consultants are here to see you, Mr. McGregor."

THE MYSTERIOUS LOST CHILD

"Please send them in," a man directed from inside the office.

The secretary opened the door for Paris and Christine, welcoming them into the office. It was similar to the lobby with dark wooden furniture. Thick curtains hung in the large windows and old books lined one wall.

Behind the desk was a very handsome man with short brown hair and kind blue eyes. He wore a navy blue suit and showed a dimple when he flashed a toothy grin. "You're the consultants from Escapism Designs?" There was an edge of doubt in his voice.

The secretary nodded. "Yes, they sent Michelle Bordeaux."

The look of skepticism fell off Grayson McGregor's face. "Oh, wow. That's very impressive. What an honor."

"And my son, James Bordeaux," Paris said, indicating Christine next to her.

Grayson stood and strode around the desk, similar to Amelia Rose's approach during their introduction. He offered a hand to her. "I apologize for sounding uncertain earlier. It's just that although I've never met or seen any game designers, I've heard they're usually young and hipster types. You're—"

Game designer? Paris wondered. *What the hell did that mean?*

"Old and pudgy," Paris supplied seriously. Once Grayson started to look a little offended, Paris laughed, dismissing his nervousness. "Oh, I get it. Most don't think I look like a game designer, but I assure you, I'm the very best, so appearances can be deceiving."

Grayson chuckled. "You have quite the reputation, and now I'm really excited to see what you can do for me."

That was the question that worried Paris. What exactly did Grayson want them to do for him? How could she use that to find helpful information for how to pair him with Amelia?

The door at their back opened and a tall woman wearing way too much makeup, an outfit that looked like one of those bizarre contraptions that runway models wore, and a spray-on tan materialized. "Gray, we have reservations tonight at..." The woman with dark brown hair studied the mother and son. "I didn't realize you had company."

"Oh, Tee, these are the consultants who are designing my escape room in the basement," Grayson said in an excited voice. "Meet Michelle and James." He glanced at Paris. "This is my fiancée, Tee."

An escape room, Paris thought, wondering what exactly that would entail. And fiancée? She was already tired of both Amelia and Grayson making things so difficult for the fairy godmothers. Couldn't they just stop their feuding and fall in love already? It appeared that first, the fairy godmothers would have to break up some unhappy couples. Then they'd have to orchestrate a lot more.

"Nice to meet you." Paris discreetly glanced at the woman's hand where she indeed had a large diamond engagement ring.

The woman didn't reply. Instead, she stared at Grayson. "I thought we were making the basement into a Pilates studio."

He shook his head. "You know how much I want an escape room for the employees. It's my hobby, and it will promote team-building and problem-solving skills."

"Pilates will give them better posture and rounded behinds," Tee countered.

"I'll partner with a local gym and offer the employees discounts on memberships," Grayson stated.

"I think it would better if you took them to Escape Rooms in London instead and made a Pilates studio in the basement." Tee pouted with overly collagen-injected lips.

"We've already discussed this, and I've made up my mind," Grayson urged through clenched teeth. "The employees are getting an escape room."

Paris let out a breath of relief. She knew what an escape room was. They were complex puzzle-type rooms that several people went into and had to find a string of clues to break out of. Usually, it involved all sorts of brain-buster skills, and team players had to rely on each other to succeed. She thought it was a brilliant idea for a corporation to invest in for their employees. The fact that Tee was so unsupportive and selfishly driven would make getting the couple to break up easier.

"Fine, but I'm in charge of the design for the penthouse," Tee said smugly.

Grayson rolled his eyes and shook his head. "Whatever you want, I guess."

"That's what I want," she stated tersely. "We have reservations tonight at the Ritz-Carlton."

He sighed. "I'm kind of tired and would prefer a night at home."

"I'd prefer a fancy dinner," she said flatly and spun to march off, her stiletto heels unfortunately not breaking and making her fall. Paris had practiced restraint, not using magic to mess up Tee's high heels.

Grayson offered a polite smile to the mother and son. "Sorry for that. Things are a little tense around here with some industry turmoil, and it has us both on edge. Shall I show you the basement and the space you'll be designing for the escape room?"

Paris and Christine simply nodded, both of them teeming with excitement about all the important details they were learning on their covert mission.

CHAPTER FIFTY-SIX

Thankfully, because the parts littering the bottom of the well in the Serenity Garden were magitech, they would work for what Faraday needed. Otherwise, he could piece them together a hundred different ways, and they would never work.

The squirrel had to dig pretty deep to find all the different parts he needed, including a screen, a circuit board, a transmitting device, and a few other things. The deranged AI servants were all huddled around the well, peering down into it and chanting senseless babble.

"Master needs to be turned down, and the bed has to go to sleep," a Mary stated.

"The hounds are ready for your afternoon fox hunt. Good news, today you get to be the hunter and the fox," an Alfred informed him.

Faraday shook his head while screwing pieces into place. "You all are a bunch of nutters. Go and clean up the garden or something."

"If that's what Master wishes, that's what Master gets," a maid chimed. "As long as Master doesn't try to escape again."

"I'll go and sweep the dirt path," a butler sang, striding away.

"I'll go and organize the vines covering the gazebo," a maid stated. "They're all tangled."

"Just one more little connection and…" Faraday clicked a button on the device he'd cobbled together with the loose magitech parts. It wouldn't work very well, but it should do well enough. There was no keyboard, so his communication options with it would be limited. He hoped that he remembered Paris' mobile device number correctly.

He'd paired his device so that it would link to her phone and only hers, but that could go one of two ways—it worked, or it didn't. Then he didn't know what his options would be. Maybe a lifetime of being waited on by the worst servants in the world. This was what his curious nature got him, yet again. It always got him into trouble, and yet, the talking squirrel doubted that it would be his last investigative mission if he survived this.

Nothing happened on the device when Faraday pressed the main button. He gritted his teeth and jiggled some wires. Sometimes things needed overly technical methods to fix problems. Sometimes it simply required jiggling some connections.

The screen lit up, and Faraday nearly yelped with excitement over his first stage of success. Now he had to hope that he had a connection. He was in the bottom of a well, inside a bubble that was unmapped and out of cell range for most. Paris had reception enough to make phone calls, which was what gave him this idea. However, he didn't have a microphone, so the clever squirrel had to go the extra mile. If this worked, maybe he could make changes to Paris' phone so it could text.

There was also the possibility that because of the intensity of the magitech parts and the untested nature of the device that it could blow up, sending the squirrel flying. The only consolation there was that it might project him over the walls of the Serenity Garden and to freedom—if it didn't kill him.

Faraday held his breath and watched the screen, hoping that he could get the device to connect. Everything was riding on this.

His tiny squirrel heart leapt when the device showed a connection. Now all he had to do was use the rudimentary system to send a message to Paris that hopefully, she could understand.

CHAPTER FIFTY-SEVEN

As with Amelia Rose, Paris quite liked Grayson McGregor. He was obviously intelligent with business sense and had a thoughtful concern for his employees' wellbeing. Paris would have felt sorry that he was engaged to a first-class spoiled brat succubus if her instinct didn't tell her that was part of the equation.

Paris reasoned that sometimes a person had to be with the wrong person to recognize who the right person was when they came along.

"You mentioned industry turmoil." Paris found it harder to keep up in her pudgy form as she and Christine followed Grayson down to the building's basement.

He nodded. "One of the reasons that I want an amazing escape room experience for my employees. Rose Industries across the river has been trying to steal my workers. I think that if I enhance their work-life experiences, they'll be less likely to jump ship."

"Have you thought about providing them free lunch?" Christine said in James's form, the loafer that played video games in his mother's basement. "People love free food."

Grayson shook his head. "I wish that's all it would take. Rose

Industries is cutthroat. They've been enticing my employees over to them by offering them premium benefits packages, ridiculous amounts of vacations, and company cars."

"They sound awful," Christine said dryly.

He cast an annoyed expression over his shoulder as he paused in front of a door on the lower level. "Believe me, I can't blame my employees for taking better offers, but it's hurting my business."

"Maybe you should try and get a job over at Rose Industries," Christine joked.

To Paris' surprise, Grayson chuckled at this. "I would, but I can't stand their CFO, and it's all about who you work with."

Interesting, Paris thought. Grayson hadn't said the CEO, Amelia, was who he couldn't stand. Instead, it was Bryce Tyler. She understood after spending an hour with the guy. He was definitely on the list of most boring people ever and reminded her of a lizard that walked upright. However, not mentioning the CEO made one thing abundantly clear—Grayson had feelings for Amelia. There was undeniable chemistry between them.

He pulled back the door to the basement and held out a welcoming hand to them. Paris stepped through, and the overhead lights all flickered on throughout the huge space. Like an underground warehouse, the room went on for at least fifty yards. It was very industrial in contrast to the warm floors with wood paneling above them.

The floors were all concrete and the walls and ceiling unfinished. Other than that, there wasn't much to the space, merely a lot of potential. Paris' mind started calculating all the possibilities. She never imagined that she'd be creating and building an escape room, but the more she thought about it, the more she realized that was exactly what she needed to do.

"As you can see," Grayson held his arms wide and regarded the area proudly, "it's a blank slate."

"Yes, I have lots of ideas of various ways we can build out the square footage for a fantastic escape room experience," Paris stated.

"You do?" Christine sounded surprised.

Paris narrowed her eyes at her friend.

"I mean, of course you do, Mom."

"Why don't you go and take measurements, son?" Paris waved Christine away.

"I would, but I forgot my measuring tape, especially the one that's a bazillion miles long," Christine joked.

"Don't worry," Grayson interjected. "I can send the measurements to your office. Escapism Designs."

"Actually, you should send them to me directly." Paris pulled out her phone. "Let me get your direct line, and I'll message you my phone number."

"Oh, great idea," Grayson said. "My number is—"

The CEO's words were interrupted by the horrified look that jumped to Paris' face. She had several messages from a number she didn't recognize.

They read:

"**Par**"

"**Far here**"

"**Help!**"

"**Trapped**"

CHAPTER FIFTY-EIGHT

P aris left Christine with Grayson to get his contact details, stating that she had to rush off for a design emergency.

Rushing through the portal to Happily Ever After, Paris didn't stop running until she came to the Serenity Garden's entrance. That had to be where Faraday was and had gotten himself into trouble. It was a Tuesday, and she knew he was curious about why he wasn't supposed to go in there on that day. It seemed that he'd found the reason and it was dangerous.

A ton of large stones blocked the arbor covered in climbing roses that led to the Serenity Garden. *That was weird,* she thought. What could pick up all the boulders from the retaining walls and place them in front of the only entrance to the Serenity Garden?

Paris pointed her finger at the stones, considering that maybe she could blast them apart. Then she realized that she could also hit much more, and since she didn't know what was on the other side, that was probably too much of a risk.

Standing back, Paris looked at the stone walls that enclosed the Serenity Garden. They were slick with little way to be climbed, almost as if someone hoped to prevent this. Paris was in over her head now, she realized.

She sighed and admitted that she would have to enlist help.

Not only was Paris going to have to reveal something she hoped to keep covered up, but she was going to look foolish right after she had a small victory with the Amelia and Grayson case. She slumped, then trudged off for the FGE.

To Paris' relief, Mae Ling was in Willow's office when she knocked. That made her feel better since the fairy godmother always seemed to be on her side. Not that Willow was out to get her or anything, but she was more objective with Paris.

"Paris, are you and Christine already back from your investigations?" The headmistress looked surprised to see Paris.

"I'm back," she answered. "Christine remained, but overall the mission to find information was successful. I think we've dug up some things that will help get Amelia and Grayson together, but it will be complicated, not straightforward."

"Well, please come in and tell us what you learned." Willow waved at the large armchair next to Mae Ling.

Paris shook her head. "I would and I will, but right now, I need your help with something."

Willow tilted her head, confused. "Help? From us? Well, of course. What is it?"

"Well," Paris drew out the word after inhaling, preparing for what she had to confess. "There's this talking squirrel named Faraday who I met right before the first time I came through the portal to Happily Ever After College. He's very scientific-minded and wanted to come here with me to research how the college works. He's been living in my sock drawer, and now it appears he's gotten himself in trouble. That's why I need your help."

Paris held her breath after completing the sentences in quick succession.

Willow blinked and didn't say a word for a moment as if she expected Paris to laugh and say, "Just kidding."

"A squirrel...who talks," the headmistress said slowly, as though trying to digest the concept. "You understand that even in the magical world, animals who can talk are very rare and almost always suspect. Magic that would do something like that is simply too mysterious."

"I understand." Paris twisted her fingers in her other hand. "I don't know much about Faraday, but he's...well, he's my friend."

"I would hope so if he's been sleeping in your sock drawer." Willow glanced at Mae Ling. "Did you know about this?"

"No," Paris said at the same time that Mae Ling nodded.

Headmistress Starr sat back in her chair and sighed. "Of course you did. I swear you know everything that goes on, it seems, and yet you don't tell me most of it, I believe."

"I tell you what's relevant," Mae Ling stated simply. "More information isn't always better. Believe me. It's overwhelming. I don't know everything. Just some stuff. Casanova mentioned that he sensed a new creature on the grounds of the college recently."

Casanova was the large fluffy orange cat that usually slept in the sitting room at the front of the mansion.

"I thought you said that talking animals were rare and suspect," Paris argued.

Willow nodded. "Casanova can't talk freely. He's a tattle cat."

"A what?" Paris asked.

"A tattle cat," Mae Ling repeated. "It's a cat who can only talk to tell on something wrong that someone is doing."

"That's right," Willow affirmed. "Usually, he tells us that Becky is planning a mean prank on someone or a student is stealing beauty potion ingredients from the greenhouse. Small things."

Paris nodded. She'd been suspicious of the fat cat since Mae Ling had thrown him out of the sitting room before their first meeting.

"Your squirrel," Willow began. "What kind of trouble is he in?"

Paris gulped. "He went into the Serenity Garden."

Willow's eyes widened and darted to the flowery wall calendar with cherubs on it. Her mouth popped open. "It's Tuesday."

"Which is why he snuck in there," Paris explained. "He wanted to know why it was off-limits on Tuesdays."

Mae Ling nodded. "Now he must be held hostage."

"Well, can you blame them?" Willow said to the head professor. "They must be lonely. We knew that was a growing potential."

"Who is lonely?" Paris looked between the two.

Ignoring her, Willow began worrying her hands, rubbing them together. "I feared this would happen."

"Which is why we never wanted to risk anyone encountering them on their day off," Mae Ling stated.

"Feared what would happen?" Paris questioned. "Whose day off?"

"They don't have their intended purpose," Mae Ling continued with her attention on the headmistress. "We knew they'd grow restless."

"Now I bet they're holding this talking squirrel hostage," Willow added.

"They who?" Paris' face flushed red with frustration.

Both fairy godmothers looked at her.

"Paris, we have to tell you a history of Happily Ever After College that few know about," Willow began, her voice suddenly grave.

CHAPTER FIFTY-NINE

"So you kept a bunch of deranged magitech AI servants?" Paris was in awe after hearing the hidden history, not sure if she should be touched or repulsed.

Willow sighed, obvious stress lining her features. "We knew that they weren't right and sometimes dangerous. Some of us suspected that they would grow increasingly crazy, but they were also alive. It didn't feel right to get rid of them."

"But they're machines," Paris argued. "It sounds like they're far more machine than Wilfred, who I contend has sentient moments."

"That's true," Mae Ling affirmed. "Still, due to their magical aspects, the robots felt real to us, so we decided not to destroy the remaining staff."

"It was our mistake that created them," Willow admitted, guilt heavy in her eyes. "So we decided to spell them into statues in the Serenity Garden but would release them on Tuesdays. Not only could we not destroy the butlers and maids, but we wanted them to have a semblance of a life—even if for only one day a week, we thought they should have freedom."

"Now my overly curious squirrel has gone in their territory, and what? They're holding him hostage?" Paris tried to piece it all together.

Willow nodded. "Most likely. On the rare occasions that any of the staff has peeked into the gardens on Tuesday, it was obvious that the AIs were even more deranged than when we created them and growing restless since they were programmed to serve and can't do that. We hoped they'd simply enjoy their time off on Tuesdays, but increasingly so, I've feared that was not the case."

"They sound downright dangerous." Paris started to get angry that the fairy godmothers had allowed such a potential threat to exist at the college.

"They can't leave the gardens though," Willow argued.

"They also have the power not to allow whoever mistakenly goes in there on Tuesday to leave," Paris countered. "Faraday said he was trapped, and I saw that they'd walled up the entrance with large stones."

"This problem could resolve itself," Willow mused, looking at Mae Ling.

The professor shook her head. "I wouldn't rely on that option. Yes, the spell is supposed to freeze them to statues at midnight on Tuesdays, but we've known that they can break that spell if properly motivated. Although they can't leave the garden no matter what."

Willow nodded. "Which is why we never allowed anyone around them. They're motivated mostly by the idea of having someone to serve."

"Great, so the mad AIs have my squirrel held hostage as their master," Paris muttered, thinking of their options. "Can Wilfred reason with them, as one of them sort of?"

Willow shook her head. "Good thought, but Wilfred's programming makes it difficult for him to leave the mansion. This is his domain, and we learned from many mistakes when we created the first set of staff."

"What options do we have for rescuing Faraday?" Paris asked. "I know that I snuck him in here and he shouldn't be at the college, but at the time I was nervous, and he offered to be my friend. He really is all right. I'll get rid of him if you help me rescue him."

Willow smiled politely. "I'm not sure that you having a friend when your life was turning upside down was such a bad idea. I bet he's been a comfort to you during this strange time. Now, your life is even more chaotic than before." She glanced at Mae Ling. "If we assess that this Faraday isn't a harm to the school, do you think he should stay?"

"I think so."

"Thanks," Paris said with relief. "I don't think he's a danger. He's just a curious weirdo who talks like he swallowed a dictionary."

"That is quite interesting." Willow stood, a new determination suddenly in her eyes. "Well, it appears we're going to have to go rescue this strange creature, who I must know more about."

"How are we going to do that?" Paris asked.

Willow picked up the quill on her desk, turning it in her fingers. "Unfortunately, I think we're going to have to do something that we've put off too long."

Paris lifted an eyebrow curiously.

"Sometimes we avoid putting something or someone out of its misery," Willow began speculatively. "I think that many times we're deluding ourselves into believing that we're doing it for them when in reality, it's our emotions we're protecting. The fairy godmothers kept the malfunctioning AIs because we told ourselves it was wrong to terminate them, but their life hasn't been good. It's time that I make the hard decision and end the experiments that went wrong once and for all—freeing them at last."

"[illegible] do we have [illegible]?" [illegible] I stuck [illegible] but at [illegible] the time I was nervous and [illegible] to be my [illegible] is all right. [illegible]

Willow smiled [illegible]. "[illegible] having [illegible] when your [illegible] up [illegible] your [illegible] more [illegible], then before [illegible] Mac [illegible] that the Faerie [illegible] should say?"

"[illegible]."

"[illegible]," [illegible]. "[illegible] thing, he's a dinger [illegible] just [illegible] who talks like he swallowed a [illegible]."

"That's [illegible]." Willow [illegible] a new determination [illegible] going [illegible] to go [illegible] strange creature [illegible] more [illegible]."

[illegible]

[illegible]

[illegible]

[illegible] a [illegible] should [illegible] that [illegible] we were [illegible] it [illegible] The fairy [illegible]

CHAPTER SIXTY

"How do you suggest we get into the Serenity Garden?" Paris led the two fairy godmothers out to the Enchanted Grounds.

"Well, that's a first." Willow took in the walled-up entrance. "The AIs must be riled, having their first visitor in a very long time."

"Which supports our assumption that they probably won't let Faraday go easily." Mae Ling studied the rock wall.

"We can try a disassembling spell." Willow waved her quill at the wall. Nothing happened. "That's odd."

"Not if there are multiple layers of reinforced rocks behind it," Mae Ling offered. "A disassembling spell only works on that which you can see."

Willow chewed on her lip, thinking. "We could try a dissolving spell."

Mae Ling considered this and shook her head. "I'm afraid that would cost too much power."

The headmistress sighed and turned to Paris. "You'll have to be patient with us while we work this out. Combat magic isn't something we're accustomed to using. Really, we rarely use any spells of this sort. For fairy godmothers, it's almost always about creating something rather than destroying it."

Paris offered a wicked smile. "Good thing that I'm half-magician and we're notoriously known for destroying things and starting wars."

"I'm afraid that is partly true," Willow said.

"Although they've also been responsible for stopping many feuds and creating peace," Mae Ling added.

"Well, today, let's put those magician powers to good use." Paris cupped her hand around her mouth. "Faraday, get away from the entrance. We're coming in!" she yelled, realizing she alerted the AIs to their presence but assuming it was worth it to let Faraday know to get to safety.

Paris waited for a few moments for the squirrel to take cover before she pointed her finger at the rock barrier and muttered an exploding spell. Almost immediately, the stones blasted back from the wall, exploding into the Serenity Garden and sending a gust of dust and dirt at the three women. They all shielded their faces, Willow squealing suddenly.

When the explosion settled, Paris dared to remove her arm from her face and check the others over. "Are you okay?"

The fairy godmothers were fine, although in rare form. Dirt covered the usually pristine headmistress, and Mae Ling's usually black hair looked gray from the gravel dust.

She shook it out and wiped her face. "I'm fine." She looked at Willow, who nodded while brushing off her dirty blue gown to no effect.

Paris craned her head to peer into the garden, but all she could make out was the rubble from the explosion of rock she'd caused.

Willow placed a hand on her shoulder and stepped around her. "I think I'd feel most comfortable if I went in first."

Paris nodded, not wanting to argue although she was pretty

sure the headmistress had never clocked a giant or had a gnome in a headlock.

Holding her silk gown up so she could step over the strewn rocks without tripping, Willow proceeded into the Serenity Garden, followed by Mae Ling. Paris was on guard as she entered behind them.

She'd always thought of the space as peaceful and perfectly manicured with its many stone statues and topiaries and rose bushes. However, it was unrecognizable with many of the plants covered in debris and an army of magitech AI servants all standing at attention in front of them.

Whereas before the men and women statues had been gray and still, now they were full of color and animated.

They stood in several orderly rows. There had to be at least two dozen of them, all facing off against the fairy godmothers with menace on their faces. There was no sign of Faraday.

"Well, maybe this won't be so difficult," Willow muttered from the corner of her mouth. "Maybe we can have a reasonable conversation with them."

The headmistress cleared her throat and lifted her chin, peering out at the army of AI servants. "Hello! We come in peace to retrieve the squirrel you have and deactivate you from further opportunities to create harm to others."

A soft groan escaped from Paris' mouth.

Willow glanced at her. "What? I think honesty is the best policy."

"Unless that honesty is regarding deactivating those who you've labeled deranged," Paris whispered.

"Well, they might respond well to my straightforward approach." Willow glanced at the AIs.

Their heads turned one way and the other as if they were taking in their surroundings. Then one of the men dressed in a suit similar to Wilfred's stepped forward, and his eyes flashed red.

"Master is ours for eternity. We live only to serve him and live we shall do, from now until forever."

The butler took another step forward, and the rest of the staff followed him as they marched straight for the three women, menace unmistakably filling their every movement.

CHAPTER SIXTY-ONE

The headmistress held up her hands. "We come in peace. There's no reason for violence."

"I think we're past that." Paris sprang into fight mode. She grabbed a pole being used to help a sapling grow upright and tugged, hoping to pull it from the ground and use it as a weapon. It broke at the base, creating a makeshift quarterstaff Paris could use to defend herself.

Willow backed up a few steps, nearly falling on her gown. To Paris' surprise, Mae Ling disappeared.

Oh, good, when the going gets tough, the mysterious fairy godmother disappears, Paris thought, watching as several women dressed in maids uniforms marched in her direction. "Miss looks tired. We will put her to sleep." They held out their hands in a choking gesture.

"I'm good." Paris backed up. "I had lots of coffee, and you trying to murder me is putting some pep in my step."

"Stay back." Willow pointed her quill at a gang of approaching butlers who moved robotically. "I don't want trouble."

"Miss made trouble for herself when she banished us to the

garden," the front man said. He halted, and so did the others behind him. Then he bent, pulled up a bush, and held it out to her. "We made you dinner and insist you eat it all."

"Wow, these guys are real fruitcakes," Paris remarked, her attention darting between the maids cornering her and the butlers surrounding Willow.

The butler, as if practicing his pitching skills, pulled his arm back with the large thorny bush in his grasp and hurled it at the headmistress. She screamed, and Paris was about to jump in and defend her when the fairy godmother did the unexpected. Headmistress Starr slashed her quill through the air and deflected the attack, sending it back at the man, covering him in loose bits of dirt, leaves, and twigs.

Nonchalantly, he brushed himself off. "That was very unwise of you, Headmistress. Do you know what happens to naughty ones? They are banished to the Serenity Garden and made into statues. Get ready to be frozen."

Paris could have sworn she saw Mae Ling materialize on the other side of the AI butlers, but when she blinked, the figure was gone or never there to begin with.

The halfling brandished her pole and whipped it back and forth, keeping the maids back from her.

The butlers moved forward, going after Willow again. The fairy godmother surprised Paris once more, pointing her quill at a sprinkler spigot in the ground between her and the butlers and muttering an incantation.

Water exploded up from the sprinkler, covering the AIs. It didn't stop them as Paris had hoped, but it seemed to disorient them as water seeped into their electronic bodies and caused malfunctions—well, more malfunctions. Paris guessed that the servants in statue form were protected from water damage but otherwise were less resilient to its effects.

Moving slower, like squeaky tin men, the butlers clumsily advanced with steam rising from their chests. Willow darted around them, able to outmaneuver them since the water delayed their actions. The headmistress was drenched now but appeared relieved when she made it out of the clutches of the grabby butlers. However, her problems were hardly over when she made it out of the sprinkler area and to a plaza where more AI servants crowded around her quickly.

Paris didn't know what happened next because her efforts to keep the maids back by whipping a makeshift staff around weren't working anymore. The servants were adapting their approach.

One had picked up a small birdbath and was marching in her direction. "It's time for a bath, Miss."

Paris shook her head. "Thanks, but I already bathed today, and I prefer not to clean myself in things where birds have washed."

Using the same spell as before, Paris flicked her head in the direction of the stone birdbath. It exploded, hurling large chunks at the maid and knocking her onto her back. The sound of metal on the cobbled path was a nice indication of Paris' success—if ending crazy AIs was part of the goal, which it was.

Another maid retrieved a sundial on a small base from somewhere and, copying Paris, held the bottom like a sword.

"Oh, cool, you had to get a bigger weapon." Paris rolled her eyes. Suddenly her wimpy little pole didn't seem fit to go up against the stone pedestal with a sundial at its end.

"If Miss would like the bigger sword, she can have it," the maid remarked in a sickly sweet voice before launching the large object at Paris.

She ducked as the rotating structure nearly took her out—it grazed her hair as it passed overhead. The sundial and base broke into bits on the wall behind her.

Paris shook her head. "You all don't play nice, and you don't play smart either. The rule is, when you have the advantage, meaning the bigger weapon, you keep it." She spun and whipped the pole so fast that it blurred in the air. A piercing sound like that of glass breaking shot from the object. It grew hot in her hands, and instinct took over as she felt energy pulse down from her fingertips and shoot straight out of the makeshift staff.

She shot forward and continued her spin. The pole collided with the maids trying to attack her, cutting them in two, although she hadn't thought that it was sharp enough for that—only a blunt assault. Still, three of the maids split in half, and the rest backed away after seeing what happened to the others.

Paris didn't think that would be the end of their efforts, so she lunged with her weapon held ready and a threatening look in her eyes. She suspected that the other servants would reconfigure and develop another strategy to attack, but she'd be ready.

Meanwhile, Willow had backed herself into a corner. Literally. The AI servants had her cornered against the stone wall at the back of the garden. Her hands were in the air, and she was shouting pleas. "I'm sorry that I didn't deactivate you sooner and had you live here. I was trying to give you a life."

"Our life is in service," one of the butlers said. "Now we serve to end you."

Paris was about to abandon her position when something between her and the headmistress appeared from the well in the middle of the Serenity Garden. It was a little brown squirrel, his tiny arms on his hips, reminding Paris of the strangest, most unassuming superhero ever.

"As your master, I order you to stand down and not harm Headmistress Starr," Faraday said.

Pride for her fierce little friend materializing suddenly filled Paris. She wished that she knew where Mae Ling was though.

All the servants stopped their fighting and bullying and turned to face the squirrel. They bowed or curtsied and nodded.

"Yes, if that's what Master wants," the butler in front of Willow stated. "We won't harm a hair on her head. Do we have to allow her to keep her head though?"

Faraday nodded. "She keeps her head and everything else."

"Very well, Master," one of the maids said. "She and her friend will stay with you, and we will serve you all—forever."

Faraday sighed and glanced back at Paris. "That's the crux. I can order them around, but I can't get them to let us go. Hope you packed some cheese sandwiches."

Paris shook her head, glancing at the entrance with disappointment. The maids she'd been fighting, the ones she hadn't finished with the unexpected magic, had moved in front of the opening and blocked it once more. These servants were the most unhelpful that she could imagine.

"Yeah, it appears the battle isn't over," Paris muttered. "Looks like we're going to have to destroy them all or they'll never let us go."

Willow, who was still literally cornered, didn't appear to like this idea. Faraday didn't look ready to fight either, despite his imminent blockade by servants who had discovered his whereabouts. Paris glanced around, surveying the area until something unexpectedly disarmed her. She whipped her head around to find a maid had snuck up on her with a shovel and knocked the pole from her hand.

Paris sighed. "Damn it, again a better weapon than I had."

The maid looked ready to bring the shovel across Paris' face when something swooshed through the air and landed on the high garden wall, stealing everyone's attention.

To Paris' surprise, it was Mae Ling standing majestically on the stone wall with her hands in a prayer position and a challenging glint in her brown eyes. Before Paris could wonder what would happen next, the fairy godmother threw her arms out wide. Something rippled through the air like a wave, broadcasting across the Serenity Garden. It hit every single one of the magitech AI servants and froze them at once—putting them back into the forms of gray stone statues.

CHAPTER SIXTY-TWO

B efore Paris could rejoice at their victory, or Willow could enjoy the freedom of not being cornered, or Faraday could thank Paris for coming to his rescue, Mae Ling tumbled forward and landed on her back on the grass in the Serenity Garden.

All three sprang into action, running in the fairy godmother's direction. Paris was the first one there, her fingers on Mae Ling's pulse. She was alive, but barely. Her eyes were closed but moving under the surface of her lids.

"What happened to her?" Paris asked when Willow arrived, running her eyes over the passed-out woman.

"The amount of energy she had to expend to do that..." She didn't finish her sentence, simply nodded behind her where the magitech AI statues were frozen once more.

Willow felt various places on Mae Ling's wrists before standing. "She'll be okay, but we need to get her inside. I can grab her hands if you get her—"

Running footsteps cut her off. Hemingway materialized at the Serenity Garden's entrance, his eyes darting all around in horror before landing on the three.

Faraday glanced up at Paris. "I think you'll have some explaining to do."

"I think you're the one who has things to explain, talking squirrel," Paris said dryly and waved Hemingway over. "Can you please come and help? Mae Ling needs assistance. Can you carry her into the house?"

Hemingway didn't ask any questions about the destruction around them, the talking squirrel, or why Willow looked like she'd been through hell and back. He simply rushed over and scooped the passed-out fairy godmother into his arms. "Where do you want her?"

"Third floor," Willow stated and hurried after him, the groundskeeper not wasting any time taking Mae Ling to get help.

Paris, knowing she wasn't allowed on the third floor, stayed behind with Faraday. Willow and Hemingway would ensure that Mae Ling got the help she needed. There wasn't much left for her to do except maybe clean up the Serenity Garden a little, although she wasn't sure where to start. The place looked like a battlefield.

She looked down at the squirrel and pursed her lips. "Did you get your curiosity satisfied?"

He nodded. "You're not supposed to come into the Serenity Garden on Tuesdays because that's when the statues come alive."

"Nooooo," she said sarcastically.

He nodded and gulped. "They're magitech AI servants that didn't turn out right."

"What gave it away?" She kept up the mocking.

"When they offered me tea with rust and salt and tried to boil me," he stated seriously.

"I guess you figured out why the fairy godmothers kept them around then?"

He nodded. "I suspect they didn't have the heart to terminate their projects so they tried to give them some sense of freedom, not realizing that they were programmed to serve and would never feel complete otherwise."

Paris sighed. "I hope they've learned their lesson now. Sometimes you have to end something out of kindness. Keeping it alive isn't always for its own good."

Faraday shivered before looking up at Paris. "Thanks for coming to help me. I wasn't sure if my communications would work."

"Whatever you did to send me text messages from here, well, it's pretty impressive for a squirrel to pull off," she stated proudly. "Or even a person."

"Thanks," he chirped. "Maybe I can make your phone receive text messages while you're in Happily Ever After College."

"That would be nice." Paris headed for the exit, thinking she could use a shower and maybe a good night's rest after the long night before and the day she'd had. "Are you going to tell me how you, a squirrel, were able to send me those text messages with whatever you had?"

"Leftover magitech parts from the AIs," he supplied. "And maybe, but not today. I'm hungry."

"Fine," she acquiesced. "Then maybe later. Perhaps tomorrow night when I'm more back to normal."

"Maybe," he chirped. "I was thinking of exploring the Bewilder Forest tomorrow night. You know it's off-limits after sunset."

Paris sighed but smiled. She knew that even if the looney squirrel got himself into trouble in the Bewilder Forest, which he undoubtedly would, she'd still come to his rescue.

That's what friends did for each other.

CHAPTER SIXTY-THREE

Paris hadn't been able to rest or shower, knowing that Mae Ling had passed out. Instead, she paced back and forth in front of Headmistress Starr's office. The woman had to return at some point, and Paris could get an update.

Footsteps in the quiet corridor made Paris spin to see Hemingway striding in her direction with a curious expression on his face.

Paris rushed for him but stopped short. "How is Mae Ling? Will she be okay?"

He nodded, immediately putting her at ease. "She'll recover completely. She's a tough one. Tougher than most fairy godmothers, I'd say."

Paris pulled in a breath, thinking of that spell she used to put the magitech AI servants back into statue form. She'd checked several times, and they were all like that, none of them moving again even though it was still Tuesday.

"You want to tell me what happened in the Serenity Garden?" A crooked smile appeared on his handsome face.

Paris hesitated. "I'm not sure what I can tell you…"

"You mean about the Wilfreds that went wrong and were only allowed to be free on Tuesdays or the part where the talking squirrel came into the mix, and you were obviously involved?"

"Yeah, pretty much all of that." She leaned against the wall, feeling hungry and tired and especially torn in several directions.

"Well, I care for the Serenity Garden, so Headmistress Starr had to tell me why I couldn't go in there on Tuesday," he explained. "So I'm one of the few privy to the facts about the magitech servants, who I hear are nutters."

Paris laughed. "Yeah, they were certifiably crazy."

Hemingway studied her for a long few seconds and finally pointed toward the dining room. "Want to grab something to eat? Dinner is going on."

She shook her head. "I'm not much in the mood for a bunch of chatting people."

He understood and offered a caring smile. "Then let's go scrape the pans in the kitchen. Chef Ash always makes more than an army can eat, and there are always leftovers. He won't be in to clean up for an hour or so."

Before Paris could protest, Hemingway grabbed her by the arm and hauled her toward the kitchen. He didn't release her until they were in the chef's domain, where he made a beeline over to the stove and peered into the various pots and pans. "We have mashed potatoes, macaroni and cheese, and creamed spinach. What would you have, madam?"

Paris grinned. "I'll take the mashed potatoes."

He nodded, pulling a spoon from the tasting cup and handing that with the pot to her. Hemingway took the macaroni and cheese and another tasting spoon and joined her at the kitchen's central workstation, where they leaned over their warm pans and ate directly from them.

"So, Mae Ling?" Paris asked. "She really is okay?"

"She'll be fine," Hemingway stated. "She exhausted herself. The question is how."

"She turned all the crazy magitech AI servants back to statues," Paris answered.

"That would do it." He shook his head, impressed. "Now the question is why were you all in there when the Serenity Garden is off-limits."

Paris took a bite of the creamy mashed potatoes, wanting to dive into them and away from her problems. However, she knew the answers weren't in the velvety spuds, even if that felt like the way to save the world.

"My talking squirrel snuck in there." Paris covered her mouth to obscure her words.

Hemingway leaned on his elbows, angled in her direction. "Sorry, I missed that. Did you say that your 'smocking quarrel tucked hair?'"

Paris laughed. "My talking squirrel snuck in there," she said more plainly.

"Oh, this wouldn't happen to be the little guy leaving footprints in and around the Enchanted Grounds?"

She shrugged. "How am I supposed to know? I can't keep up with all the woodland creatures in this place."

He nodded. "I'll assume it's the one that belongs to you. So, a talking squirrel, eh? Who sneaks into places? Did he know the Serenity Garden is off-limits on Tuesdays?"

"Why do you think he was there?" she countered and took another bite.

"Not a dumb talking squirrel then."

"I'm sorry about the Serenity Garden," Paris apologized, realizing what a big job it would be to clean up. "I'll help you put it back together."

He waved her off. "First off, students don't do chores. Second, despite what you think, my job isn't onerous. I like working with my hands and getting things done. There's a sense of completion to that kind of work. Third, Headmistress Starr didn't say much before she sent me down to talk to you, but she did tell me that the

Serenity Garden wouldn't be closed on Tuesdays anymore, so I have an extra day every week to get things done."

"She sent you down to talk to me?"

Hemingway nodded. "She knew you'd be worried. Said I could probably find you pacing in front of her office, and she was correct."

"Well, Mae Ling…" Paris left the rest of that thought unspoken. "How could I not be worried? It was quite the eventful afternoon. Is the headmistress okay?"

A laugh burst from Hemingway's mouth. "Yes, but I've never seen her look so disheveled. There was rock in her hair. What did you all do?"

"We fought a small army of magitech servants," Paris answered. "The headmistress was pretty good at it. She has some combat potential."

Hemingway whistled and shook his head. "I swear, you're shaking things up, making our headmistress fight AIs and bringing a talking squirrel onto our campus. Tell me about this curious little guy."

Paris smirked. "Maybe I'll bring him by to meet you at some point. For now, he's been grounded to my room, although I should fetch him a cheese sandwich."

"And therein lies the reason you collect a midnight snack each night." Hemingway winked.

"Faraday is a long story, is all," Paris stated.

"With a name like Faraday, he'd have to be."

"You're one to talk, Hemingway."

He smirked at her. "Same to you, Paris Beaufont. Have you thought about my offer to accompany you on your adventures to discover who you are?"

"I have," she said simply. "But I have a protective charm." Paris pointed at the angel pin on her jacket. "Honestly, it's a lot more dangerous than I thought. I wouldn't want to drag you into anything."

He lowered his chin and regarded her with hooded eyes. "That's exactly why I offered to help. Because of the danger aspect."

She shook her head. "I can handle myself, although I appreciate it."

"I don't doubt that," he countered. "Sometimes it's nice to have help when you're doing something as complex as digging up secrets from a hidden past or dealing with a mysterious danger."

"Thanks." Paris finished the last bite of mashed potatoes and felt perfectly full. She could eat that for dinner every night. "I'm good for now, but I'll let you know." '

He gave her a skeptical look. "Excuse me if I think you'd rather wrangle an army of giants on your own before you asked for help."

"I asked the headmistress and Mae Ling for help with the Serenity Garden," she argued.

He threaded his fingers together and stretched them in front of his face. "That's good. It shows that you know when you're in over your head. I suspect, from the little time I've known you, that the water is going to keep rising in your land. If it gets to be too much and you want a life raft, you can always call on me. I'm no fairy godmother, but I think I'd be helpful in a pinch."

CHAPTER SIXTY-FOUR

Paris awoke early, hoping to get a chance to check on Mae Ling somehow before classes started. However, an envelope with her name on the front in flowery handwriting lay on her bedside table, next to the fairy alarm clock that hadn't gone off.

When she sat up in bed, Paris noticed Faraday staring straight at her. "It appeared a few moments ago," he said, sensing her question.

"Any clues as to how?"

"Magic," he guessed.

She shook her head, the tiredness in her brain making it hard to think. Still, she opened the letter and read the beautiful penmanship.

Dear Paris,

I knew that you'd be concerned about Mae Ling and wanted to assure you that she continues to make progress. She drained her magical reserves, but all she needs is rest to recover. Worry no more. You'll see her soon. She asked about you when she awoke briefly, and I told her that you were also fine.

In that regard, I want to thank you for...well, being an influence on me without maybe realizing it. I've never been in any battle or used any magical spells to protect myself, and it felt...good. I must reflect on the feelings more, but for now, that's all I have to say on the matter. I don't know that combat magic is right for fairy godmothers, but before, I firmly believed it wasn't. Now, I'm not sure...

Last, I think you've been through a big ordeal. It's impossible to keep the chatter about the Serenity Garden from the college since it's off-limits now on a Wednesday while Hemingway does repairs. Therefore I think it would be better for you to take another much-needed break to avoid the questions and speculative gossip. Please take this time to do what you need to for your health and wellbeing, whatever that might be.

Christine has returned from the investigative mission in London and reported but said that she thought you had more ideas on how we could use the information. I'll wait for your full briefing on the matter tomorrow. Until then, please rest, recover, and do whatever will help you to feel more focused.

You may not realize this, but the college needs you. Fixing the Serenity Garden, which has long been a source of brewing problems, is an example of that, even if you brought a talking squirrel into the college to do it. I still look forward to meeting Faraday properly, but until then, I hope you two take care of each other.

Sincerely,

Headmistress Starr

Paris lowered the letter, unsure what to make of it.

"Did she mention me?" Faraday asked at once.

"Did who?" She played dumb.

"Well, I assume based on deduction that the note is from Head-mistress Starr. The note from your Uncle John had different penmanship. I suspect that Mae Ling is still recovering. I don't take Hemingway as having bubbly writing. Who else would send you a letter?"

Paris rolled her eyes. "She wrote of nothing else but you."

"Oh." He hopped off the dresser and arrived at her feet on the bed. "Do you think she wants me to interview for a professor position?"

"Not just yet," she teased. "I think a formal meeting happens first. Then we pick out your blue gown, and before too long, you're teaching the science of attraction."

He tapped his chin, thinking. "There is a lot of science to the chemical reactions that go with love. First, you have lust, which is supposed—"

"Please don't make me toss you out the window so early in the morning." Paris threw herself back on the pillow. "My aim is prob-ably off, and I'll launch you into the wall. Then there will be a squirrel stain on the stone."

He grimaced. "You're not a morning person, are you?"

"I'm not a 'manage a talking squirrel's ego first thing in the morning when I have my own problems' person," she countered and put down the note. "I'll remind you that you created a lot of problems for me already."

Faraday quickly scanned the note. "It sounds like I did you some unknowing favors. The college, too. The Serenity Garden has long been a problem that the fairy godmothers didn't have the guts to deal with. You gave the headmistress courage."

Paris grabbed the note but soon smiled. "He talks. He reads. Do you do math too?"

"What kinds?" he questioned. "I'm not a fan of geometry, but in a pinch, I can get by. Trig, algebra, calculus, statistics—those are where I really shine."

Paris shook her head on the pillow. "Seriously, how did I get so lucky to have the illusion of a talking squirrel who does the most ridiculous things as a roommate?"

"Oh, no," he disagreed. "You know I'm not a figment of your imagination. Others have seen me now. The headmistress isn't going to kick me out. She wants a meeting. Wilfred and I are associates."

"Friends," Paris corrected. "In the real world, where weirdos like you don't live, we call the people we talk to friends, usually."

"Says the person who didn't have friends until recently," Faraday retorted, but there was a fondness in his voice. "It sounds like you have a day off. What are you going to do?"

"Work on my base tan," she instantly responded. "Take up surfing at the beach. Maybe take one of those cool online master-classes. Oh, perhaps do a puzzle if I start to hate my life and want to feel bad about myself."

"I'm excellent at puzzles," he offered. "Do you think that's the best use of your time with everything going on?"

"Well, there's always teaching you how to pick up on the subtle hints of sarcasm," Paris stated blandly.

"Oh, so you weren't planning on going to the beach, then?"

"I can't stand sand in my clothes," she muttered.

"I thought you'd never been to the beach because you'd never been away from Roya Lane," he argued.

"Well, there was a beach shop on Roya Lane that had virtual, magical experiences that they guaranteed felt one hundred percent real, and man, one day at a virtual beach or otherwise is enough for me."

"I'm not much of a beach-goer either," Faraday admitted.

"Because you can't swim?"

"Because I burn like a lobster."

She shook her head. "I guess I need to take my day off to do some more Beaufont family investigations. I just don't know where to look next. I've met Clark, Alicia, Sophia, and her dragon. There aren't any more living Beaufonts. I don't know where to look next for clues about what happened to my parents or this evil following me."

"Oh yes, the whole where to look conundrum," Faraday agreed. "It's always hard to know where to find answers before you even know what you're looking for. I mean, you know you need answers, but you're not even entirely sure what all the questions are. You don't know what you don't know."

Paris sat up, struck by his words. "I said something similar to my Uncle John. I mean, there's not knowing what I don't know. Then there's not knowing what I don't even know."

He nodded thoughtfully. "Which means you don't know the questions to ask or where to look. Maybe that's where I can help. What is it you want to know?"

She huffed. "Come on now. You already know that I need answers."

Faraday shook his head next to her on the bed. "It's an exercise, Paris. Go with it."

"Fine." She sighed. "I want to know what happened to my parents, which no one can tell me."

"Why?"

"Why can't they tell me or why do I want to know what happened to my parents?"

"Whichever you most want answered."

"Well, I'd like to know what happened to my parents because I think that will tell me why no one can talk and why there's something after me."

"And they were..." He let the question hang in the air.

"Magicians."

"Who were?" he prompted.

"Warriors for the House of Fourteen." For the second time,

Paris bolted upright. "Do you think I need to go to the House of Fourteen to investigate?"

"Do you?" he asked.

"Well, it makes sense. That's where they worked, so I might find something about them there," Paris reasoned. "I mean, everything else about them has been pretty much erased. The House of Fourteen, from everything I've heard, is pretty much cloaked in mystery and secrets so maybe there's something hidden there. If only I can get in there somehow. Do you think you can sneak me in there like you snuck into the Serenity Garden?"

"I don't think I'd have to," Faraday answered. "I'm not certain about this, but my various studies have supplied me with information on many topics on magical organizations. The House of Fourteen is one of them. Only Royals or those who sit on the Council like the Mortal Seven can enter the House of Fourteen."

"So you think I can enter?" Her heartbeats suddenly increased with excitement.

"It goes to reason," he stated matter-of-factly.

"Oh, but you won't be able to come with me." She deflated slightly. "You asked to come on the next adventure."

Faraday shrugged. "That's fine. I'll stick around and keep a lookout."

"You'd do that for me?" she asked fondly.

"You returned from your first mission early, when first-years never get one, to save me so yes, I think I'd do that for you. And a lot more too."

Paris smiled. "It wasn't really a mission. Only investigations. Honestly, I think it's because the fairy godmothers wouldn't know how to sneak up on a comatose sloth. It's not a part of their usual practices."

"You're changing all that," Faraday pointed out.

"I'm only doing what Mae Ling told me to and being myself." Paris felt a pang of emotion for the fairy godmother who had displayed great skill and power, sending all the AIs back to statue form. Paris still didn't know how she did it and reasoned that no one ever might.

"Well, the headmistress seems to recognize that you have something to offer and is open to it," Faraday stated.

"I think she doesn't have anything to lose at this point, but I'll take it." Paris crossed her legs and sat up taller. "The only problem with this whole House of Fourteen idea is that I have no idea where it is. The rumor on Roya Lane has always been that its location is top-secret."

"That's true and not merely a rumor," Faraday confirmed. "However, for those who like to research secret places with unique magic, its location might not be so secretive even if a certain squirrel hasn't been inside the actual building."

Paris leaned forward and looked directly at the talking squirrel. "Faraday, do you know where the House of Fourteen is?"

He nodded gleefully. "I'll take you, but you have to take pictures once you're inside."

CHAPTER SIXTY-FIVE

"**I**s this a joke?" Paris stepped through the portal to Santa Monica, California, and saw the Pacific Ocean crashing on the beach in front of her.

"If it is, then I'm confused on the punch line." Faraday hopped through the portal after her.

"I just got finished telling you that I don't like the beach. Then you lead me here, which is quite clearly a beach." She held her arm up in the direction of the long stretch of beach and the pier in the distance.

"Right," he chirped. "But it's not like you have to dive into the water to get to the House of Fourteen."

"I don't?" she asked skeptically.

"Well, I'm not certain how you get in there, but it's not on the beach," he stated matter-of-factly.

"It's not?" She glanced around the busy boardwalk where they stood. Tourists and surfers and girls in short skirts strolled by, all of them too cool for school. Paris was fairly certain she would create a school one day that was too cool for all these hipster types. Then what would they do?

"By my calculations, the House of Fourteen is straight down this boardwalk, approximately two-point-three kilometers away," he stated.

"Can you be more specific?"

"Well, it's… Oh, that was sarcasm again, wasn't it?"

"Yes, and we're continuing your education on the subject. Currently, you're failing the course."

He huffed and hopped after her as she started down the boardwalk paralleling the Pacific Ocean. "I've never failed a class in my entire life."

Paris paused, looked down at the squirrel, and squinted at him. "Why would you fail a class that you couldn't attend?"

"I meant the classes I pretended to attend when spying on them in squirrel form," he said in a rush.

Paris nodded. "Yeah, fine. I'm not in the mood to dissect whether you're telling the truth or a squirrel or an illusion so just tell me where this House of Fourteen is."

"Down here, next to a taqueria," he stated.

She nodded. "All-powerful magical governing agencies are located next to taquerias and on boardwalks clogged with overfed tourists."

"I'm not sure," he replied. "I've not been to many—oh, wait—sarcasm again."

"You're failing my class." She took a moment to soak in all the strange sights, smells, and sounds around her. Paris had seen a ton of new things in the last couple of days. She'd ridden in her first car, seen her first dragon, walked the streets of West Hollywood, and watched magitech AIs come alive. Still, walking down the boardwalk in Santa Monica might have taken the cake. There were just so many…freaks.

Everything seemed to be vying for her sensing. There was the cart of fried funnel cakes asking for her taste buds' attention. Then the musician playing drums in the sand, not to mention the acrobats playing on the rings. Paris felt as if she could be lost in this area for the rest of her life and not see it all. Yet, she wasn't there to take in all the uniqueness of this strange new world. She was there to learn about the world she came from—the House of Fourteen.

"I think this is it." Faraday suddenly interrupted her reverie.

Paris halted and looked around. "What? Where? Here?"

Not much had changed about their surroundings. There was something called a taqueria and a souvenir shop and another store that looked like a closed-up palm reading shop. However, Paris expected to find a huge skyscraper for the House of Fourteen like the headquarters for Rose Industries and McGregor Technologies. This only seemed like more of the same.

"Yeah, according to my research, the House of Fourteen is in the palm reading shop," Faraday answered.

Paris pointed at the run-down store that was two stories and had a palm printed on the front of the door and a faded sign in the window. "That? That's the House of Fourteen?"

"According to my research," he repeated.

Paris shook her head. "I'm not sure if I should be more concerned that everyone is watching me talk to a squirrel or that I'm taking advice from said squirrel."

"If you look around, I think you'll notice that talking to a squirrel is about the most normal behavior down here," he stated.

Paris glanced around. A guy with a large albino python on his shoulders was letting women pet it. Another character very poorly pretended to be a statue but chased tourists when they turned their backs. She didn't appreciate the statue aspect after her last adventure.

"Yeah, I guess you're right." Paris centered her attention on the palm reading shop. "So do I just go in and ask to see the person in charge of the House of Fourteen?"

"That seems a little too straightforward," he muttered. "I thought you were the sneak in type."

"I usually am. Maybe I'll go in and pretend to get my palm read and get the lay of the land."

"Good idea," he agreed. "Only Royals can enter, so you should be good."

"Okay." She exhaled. "Here I go."

Paris strode forward with determination, grabbed the door handle, and pushed, but it was locked.

She glanced back at Faraday with defeat. "They're closed."

"Try knocking," he suggested.

She nodded. "Okay, I'll knock."

Paris lifted her fist and rapped hard a few times, making her presence known.

Nothing happened.

She looked back at the squirrel. "Any suggestions?"

He opened his mouth to answer, but the crowd on the boardwalk suddenly parted as a howling wind shot down Santa Monica Boulevard. Paris didn't have to wonder where it was headed or who it was after.

CHAPTER SIXTY-SIX

S he jerked around and looked straight at Faraday, hoping that he had advice for her as tourists screamed in the distance and food carts flipped over.

He did, and it was explicit. Faraday jerked his head to the side, taking in the barreling wind, and shot Paris a look. The squirrel's tail straightened and his eyes widened with alarm. "Run! Run and don't look back, no matter what!"

She didn't hesitate, sprinting in the opposite direction of the howling wind that sounded like it was causing havoc in her wake. She hoped that Faraday got away, but something told her that the crafty squirrel was resourceful enough to escape it.

If Paris was honest with herself, she knew what this unique wind was after. It had a feeling to it as if branded. She never thought that wind or any other element could feel unique, but this did. It wasn't any usual wind. It felt like a person or a spirit—and evil. Paris could almost hear a voice on the wind's current. She felt something yearning to reach out and grab her.

She pushed her arms back and forth, her feet hitting the pavement hard as she maneuvered around the distracted tourists on the boardwalk. They spooked when she ran past them, then the wind racing after her assaulted them. It was gaining on Paris.

Although Paris didn't know where she was headed, she knew she had to keep moving. That had been Faraday's advice, and she trusted it. The wind had found her, maybe knowing that she'd go to the House of Fourteen or prowling around that area for whatever reason. However, it had found her, and she had to flee from it. She had the protective charm attached to her shirt, but she knew that wasn't enough.

Maybe if she got far enough ahead, she could open a portal back to Happily Ever After College and jump through and escape. There was also the very real possibility that she'd bring through whatever was racing after her now. Then she'd endanger the school and be trapped there with it. No, her best option was to get far enough away to escape. Maybe open several portals if that's what it took.

Paris ran like she never had before. Sadly, the wind was pushing at her back and sending her hair all around her head. It had caught up with her. She felt like she'd already lost this race that she'd never signed up for.

The wind started to slow her down, and Paris felt out of options. She wasn't sure what to do. Then her shirt tore slightly around the angel pin. Paris slapped her hand over it, securing it in place. She couldn't lose that. The last time, she'd felt that blackness. The evil. The doom everywhere. That's when whatever was following her could do what it came for...

In front of her, the boardwalk was still busy. As Paris raced toward Venice Beach, she didn't take in her surroundings, simply swerved when she encountered tourists or darted into the sand when someone was unwilling to move although she was yelling.

The sand always slowed her down. On her last detour, it sought to destroy her. Paris tripped on something in the sand and fell face-first, rolling over from the momentum and landing on all fours. She really, *really* hated sand now as she spat some out of her mouth. However, what she loathed more was the wind, which was all around her now.

On all fours, unprotected and having lost any head start, the wind ripped at her, taking what it wanted most at that moment before it took the real prize—the protective pin that Mae Ling had given her ripped off and flew into the beach area, burying itself deep in the sand.

Paris instantly decided against trying to find the charm. She was out of options. Instead, she hauled herself to her feet and sprinted faster than before, remembering how the darkness tried to suck out her soul last time. She couldn't allow that to happen— not again. And she couldn't rely on a black and white cat to save her.

No, Paris was on her own. That meant that she might be about to die on her own.

Tears of fear ached in her throat, but she pushed forward around crowds. The blackness started to take over the boardwalk and blot out the lights—blotting out everything and sending the tourists screaming to unseen corners. Everything was a blur.

That's why Paris was surprised when the portal materialized right in front of her. She had an impromptu decision to make. Run around the mysterious portal that she didn't know where it led or who created it. Or use it to run from something she was pretty sure she couldn't otherwise escape.

In the end, there was only one decision. Paris dove forward and launched herself through the mystery portal, unsure what she'd find on the other side.

CHAPTER SIXTY-SEVEN

"I s she dead?" a raspy voice asked from the distant corners of Paris' consciousness.

Someone else sighed with annoyance. "Of course she's not."

"Well, do you want me to throw you a sword to finish her off?" the first voice asked, making Paris fight to regain full consciousness. Coming through the portal had done a number on her.

"Would you stop it?" the second voice urged. "She's stirring."

Indeed she was. Paris could feel her body move, although her limbs weren't doing exactly what she was asking. Still, it was close enough if flailing her arms was what she intended.

She expected to open her eyes and find herself in a death chamber about to be eaten by a dead ten-headed beast. What she didn't expect was to find a weird elfin hippie staring back at her. She blinked several times, wondering if she saw Satan in the wrong form—or maybe the right one—maybe hippies were really forms of Satan.

"Oh, there you are." The man shook his head and stood from his crouched position.

Paris put her hands down, finally having control over them,

and felt the floor under her. It was a grimy thin carpet. She blinked up at the dusty lights overhead and smelled the tobacco in the air. Turning over, she coughed, waiting to be attacked. When she wasn't, she pulled in a breath and turned her head to the side, taking in the stranger next to her.

He had stringy brown hair and an unreadable expression. Even stranger than finding this hippie standing next to her was that he was wearing jean cut-offs, cut way too short, and a t-shirt that read, "My other ride is a hookah."

"Who are you?" she sputtered. "Where am I?"

"Oh, good she can talk," the first voice said. It was unseen.

Paris pushed back onto her bottom, glancing around. She was in a shop of sorts. Sitting behind a nearby countertop was a sullen-looking man with a black ponytail who was reading a book and appeared completely disinterested in this whole situation, although she was sure he was the one full of insults.

"You're on Roya Lane," the hippie elf in the ridiculous t-shirt said.

Paris nearly jumped to her feet, wondering how she'd gotten back there. Then she remembered the portal. That led her to wonder where this shop was that she'd never seen. She stared around at all the strange weapons and artifacts in glass cases.

"Where am I on Roya Lane?" Paris asked.

The man sighed. "Specifically, you're in the Fantastical Armory."

She closed her eyes, thinking. "That one shop at the end of the eastern side of the lane? It's been closed down for…well, ever."

The guy nodded. "Yeah, well, I had other business to attend to."

"With no concern for my business," the man behind the counter chimed.

"Your business is my business," the man said sharply.

Paris shook her head, trying to push up to her feet, but discovered her muscles were shaky. "What did you do to me?"

"Saved your butt," the guy with the black ponytail answered

bitterly. "You're welcome. Or maybe we should drop you back in Santa Monica so you can die?"

The guy with brown hair shook his head. "She's staying here. At least until we talk. Then she'll go back to Happily Ever After College."

"You know about all that?" Paris again tried to make it to her feet and finally did but had to steady herself on the counter.

"Yeah, I know about Happily Ever After College," he replied.

"Is Faraday okay?" Paris asked, all the recent events rising to the forefront of her memory.

"Oh, cute," the man behind the counter grumbled. "She cares about the squirrel. Just like what's-her-face."

"You know her name," the guy in the t-shirt griped as his face flushed red. He turned back to Paris, his demeanor shifting. "Faraday is fine. The more important fact is that you are fine."

Paris pulled in a much-needed breath. "Okay, then my first question is, who are you?"

"We maybe shouldn't rush into that just yet," the man answered.

"Why not?" Paris fired back, finding her strength.

"People don't always respond well when they find out," he replied.

She threw up her hands. "I knew it. You're the devil. I'm in Hell."

"Yes, Hell is an armory at the end of Roya Lane," the man in all-black replied. "Award a Pulitzer Prize to this lampshade."

Paris pointed at the man. "What's his problem?"

The hippie elf shrugged. "Where do we start? He had a bad childhood. Years of neglect. Working as my assistant is a thankless job. Currently, I think he's going through a quarter eternal life crisis. The last one was much worse."

Paris blinked, wondering if she was still sleeping. When her current reality didn't clear, she let out a breath. "Again, will you tell me who you are?"

"How about a drink? Something to eat?" the guy asked.

"Her glucose levels are fine," the man behind the counter stated matter-of-factly. "So is her hydration. Her hair could use a brush, but I suspect it always could."

"Seriously, is this a prank?" Paris squinted to try and see out the dirty front glass window. There was a street, but it was hard to make out much more or if it was Roya Lane.

"Paris, this isn't a prank," the guy with stringy hair replied. "This is the biggest thing I've orchestrated in quite some time. It's of supreme importance and it all hinges on you, which is why I've been reluctant to bring you on board. Despite my efforts, the time-line has been rushed."

"Which is more than ironic," the man in black cut in.

"Thanks," the hippie elf said, not sounding like he meant it.

Paris shook her head. "Can someone please tell me what's going on?"

The man before her took a step closer and offered a kind look. "I know this might sound crazy—"

"You'd be surprised what I can digest," she cut in.

He nodded. "Well, get ready for the craziest because you're about to get it. I'm about to tell you exactly what you want to hear. I'm about to tell you the truth about your parents and your past and everything else because I'm the only one who can."

Paris' mouth fell open and hung that way for a long time. Finally, she recuperated and swallowed, her throat dry. "You are? Why and how and most importantly, my first question. Who are you?"

The man before her who seemed so small and unassuming sighed in defeat. "I'm the one, the only, Father Time."

CHAPTER SIXTY-EIGHT

"Fa-Fat-Father Time," Paris stuttered, trying to understand how this man—man, she repeated in her mind—was the person who constructed all of time and was all-powerful. She'd heard rumors of him. Heard he was in hiding for one reason or another. Still, they were all rumors. Here he was in front of her. Or some looney-tune was and doing an excellent job of faking her out. How did she get Father Time to prove who he was without turning this whole thing into a side show?

Paris leaned up against one of the cases and rubbed her eyes. "How...why...I..."

"You're Guinevere Paris Beaufont," the man began in a bored tone. "You were born twenty years ago to Liv Beaufont and Stefan Ludwig. The details of that won't convince you, but I'll tell you that your first distinct memory is when your Uncle John pushed you on the swings at the park on the west end of Roya Lane. That's when I allowed you to start having your memories, not erased or implanted, at age five. Other vivid memories for you would be waking up and demanding he make his famous French toast, which you both know came from a box. You used to sleep outside his door because you wanted to be close to someone but didn't want to tell him you were too afraid to sleep on your own. You always hung outside that sketchy bar on the lower third of Roya Lane because you knew that's where thugs who take advantage of the little guys hung out and you liked to make them pay." The guy let out a breath and looked suddenly heavy and older. "Do you want me to go on with facts that will convince you that I'm Father Time?"

"Not really," the guy in black stated. "Talk about a bore-fest."

Paris pointed. "If you're Father Time, who is that jerk and where do I deliver his knuckle sandwich?"

The hippie nodded. "That's Subner. He's my assistant. Don't worry. You'll warm to him."

"I doubt it," Subner contradicted.

"Well, he and your mother had a rivalry, and they haven't settled it yet," the guy said.

"W-W-Wait," Paris argued, holding up her hands. "Did you say they haven't settled it, as in present tense? Like, they could?"

The man stating he was Father Time nodded. "Yes, but for that to even be a potential, we need to have a very important conversation."

"Which means you need to stop asking dumb questions," Subner added.

"It would be easier if you weren't making me want to punch your face," Paris said to him while looking around Father Time.

"Just like her mother," Subner grumbled.

Father Time nodded. "Let's hope."

Paris shook her head. "I really don't understand. Can someone who isn't a jerk tell me what's going on?"

"I'm Father Time," the hippie began in a calm tone. "Those who know me well call me Papa Creola."

"Papa Creola." Paris tried out the name.

"Wow, good job," Subner muttered. "Next, let's have her master finger-painting."

"Is he really your assistant?" Paris pointed at the guy. "Like, I can help you find someone loads better. Or anyone else at all. He's, like, the worst and that's saying a lot."

Papa Creola nodded. "I'm pretty grumpy once you get to know me. Subner is a ray of sunshine in comparison. The job of time is a thankless one."

"You don't seem so bad to me," Paris observed.

"I'll admit, this reunion means a lot to me, and I'm something that I rarely am…"

Paris remained quiet, waiting for the man before her to continue.

"Paris, meeting you in person, face-to-face, marks a remarkable opportunity for us all. If you're here, that means we might be able to start a new chapter and end the dark one we've lived. You being here, well, it simply makes me hopeful."

CHAPTER SIXTY-NINE

P aris only had one question. "Why?" She wasn't sure she was
buying all this, but what else could she believe at this point?
This guy, well, he did know things he shouldn't, and there was
something timeless about him. He apparently could answer the
questions that no one could. The test would be to see if he did.

"'Why' is probably the last part that I can explain," Papa Creola
stated. "I think it's better if we back up. You have a lot that you
need filled in first."

"Should I put on the hot chocolate?" Subner asked. "I have
some arsenic for yours, Paris."

"Thanks, but I take mine plain," she chimed.

He nodded. "Maybe you'll try some of my special brownies."

"Can't wait. Can you put them in a to-go container, then shove
them up your—"

"It's remarkable how much like your mother you are," Papa
Creola said with a fondness in his eyes.

"Yeah, why don't we talk more about that and what happened
to her and my father and that deadly wind that took yet another of
my protective charms?"

Papa Creola nodded. "Your mother worked for me on special cases. She was my right-hand field agent, ambassador, delegate, and—"

"General pain in the ass," Subner cut in.

"Anyway, that doesn't pertain to your situation," Papa Creola stated.

"No, it seems irrelevant," Paris said dryly. "My mother worked for Father Time, which is totally normal."

"She does that one thing I can't stand," Subner grumbled.

"Breathe?" she asked.

"Joke," he retorted.

"I'll keep it up then," she fired back.

"My point is," Father Time began matter-of-factly, "Liv's history doesn't pertain to this. Your history started when your mother became pregnant with you. I'll run through the facts fast, so pay attention."

"You're asking a lot," Subner jibed.

Father Time drew in a breath and started talking at rapid speed. "Your father was a demon hunter who had been bitten by a demon. However, your mother, Liv, had helped to track down the demon and found the cure, ensuring your father didn't turn into one too. Unfortunately, the blood of the demon was still strong in him, and they both knew it. When she found out she was pregnant with you, she knew she had to find a way to fix things. Otherwise, there was a chance you'd be part demon since your father's cure might not work to fix their unborn child."

"This is not at all where I thought the story was going," Paris said dryly.

"Just wait," Subner added. "It gets worse."

"Anyway, Liv sought out a genie's lamp," Papa Creola stated.

Paris cut him off with a laugh. "We're still telling a real story and not a farce, right?"

"Try and keep up, Blondie," Subner scolded.

"Liv believed that if she asked a genie to fix her baby, she could avoid you becoming a demon," Papa Creola explained. "It did work, in theory. However, your mother, suspecting that the tricky genie had played a trick, as genies tend to do by granting wishes but causing other complications, investigated. That's when she found out right before your birth that you weren't a demon, thankfully. To everyone's surprise, you were part magician and part fairy."

"That's how I became a fairy." Paris nearly gasped. It made perfect sense.

"Yes, but that was only the beginning for your parents and you," Papa Creola resumed. "You see, as you've learned, halflings are rare. They're powerful. Maybe what you don't know is they have a huge life source that certain entities crave. Once you were born, one of the most powerful prophecies to ever be told was recorded. It spoke of a child who was the first fairy and magician ever to be born. I can't tell you all of that since it includes you, as I'm certain you realize. What I can say is that it told of an evil entity who we call the Deathly Shadow. The prophecy stated that from the moment of your birth, it would come after you and that if it ever got you, our planet, time and space, humanity, peace, and love would all hang in the balance."

"The Deathly Shadow is bad," Subner muttered. "It's like Wednesdays."

"Thanks," Paris replied. "I think we've met."

"Not entirely," Papa Creola corrected. "But close. It's gotten way too close to you for comfort. Your parents, having learned that the entity wanted you—"

"Why did it...does it want me?" Paris asked.

"The Deathly Shadow is an evil entity that sold its soul long ago, and through many transgressions, lost its body," Papa Creola explained. "In its current form it is powerful, as you've witnessed."

Paris shivered while thinking of the howling wind cutting through Santa Monica and stealing her protective charm.

"However," he continued, "if it ever got a body again, the

Deathly Shadow would be a force that could challenge me in the worst ways. I fear I might not survive that battle."

"And if something happened to you?" Paris asked.

"Night-night for you and all the world, sweetie," Subner stated.

"Thanks." Paris didn't mean it. "So the Deathly Shadow needs its body back."

"Not only that," Papa Creola corrected. "It needs someone who can give it back its body and better, which requires a halfling such as yourself. Not just any halfling, but half-magician and half-fairy. Two magical types that are part of two wholes. Then it will have a body and mind more powerful than ever before."

"Okay…" Paris didn't know what to say. She knew that she needed to protect herself from what was after her but never had any idea that it was on a scale this size.

"Your parents," Papa Creola continued. "After learning of this prophecy, the consequences, and knowing you were in danger, hid you away from the beginning. No one knew what you were. However, it soon became apparent that wasn't enough, so they decided to create a plan to go after the Deathly Shadow and destroy it once and for all. That was the only way to protect you since a life of hiding wasn't what they wanted for you."

"Wow." Paris' heart suddenly ached. "So that's how they died? They went after the Deathly Shadow…"

"She's an awful listener," Subner interjected, not reading his book at all anymore.

"I'm great at giving black eyes," she retorted.

"Your parents did go after the Deathly Shadow," Papa Creola confirmed. "When you were five years old, they left you with a family friend who often watched you, deciding this was a mission that would require both of them. I reviewed the plan myself and thought it was a good one. However, the Deathly Shadow was one step ahead of all of us."

"This is the part of the story I can't stand the most," Subner grumbled.

"Good, let's care what that guy doesn't like," Paris complained.

"Your parents followed the Deathly Shadow, thinking they were about to trap the monster," Papa Creola explained. "They jumped through what looked like a portal to chase after the creature. Even then, we didn't know much about the thing—which is hardly a man anymore. We didn't know that it was as formless as it was. You see, the Deathly Shadow didn't go through the portal, which wasn't a portal. It only appeared to. Instead, it stayed in this realm."

"If it wasn't a portal, what was it?" Paris asked.

"It was a vortex," Papa Creola said heavily. "To another parallel dimension, usually unreachable from this one."

CHAPTER SEVENTY

"Wait, my parents jumped through a vortex?" Paris was surprised by the words coming from her mouth.

"They thought they were chasing the Deathly Shadow," Papa Creola added. "But he never went through since he couldn't without a body. With his remaining power, he closed the vortex behind them."

"Trapping my parents in another dimension," Paris added, then exclaimed, "Oh my gosh! My parents are alive!"

"Your parents are in another dimension," Subner stated, always the bearer of bad news.

"Wait, but we can get them back, right?" Paris looking between Papa Creola and Subner.

Father Time gave her a less than reassuring look. "Opening a vortex to another dimension isn't something even I will try. The Deathly Shadow was powerful and risked a lot to attempt such a thing. We've tried to duplicate it. To bring back Liv and Stefan. It simply isn't possible. Only the Deathly Shadow can open the vortex to that specific dimension."

"So what does that mean?" Paris felt lost and confused.

"It means that we've been waiting a very long time for you to mature, Paris," Papa Creola explained. "Your parents kept you safe and protected because the Deathly Shadow wanted you. It still wants you. Ironically, the only one who could ever defeat it is you. Now that you've matured, you're the only one who can get rid of it and open the right vortex, retrieving your parents from where they hopefully still are."

"Bu-But-But," Paris stuttered, having a hard time putting everything together.

"Oh good, she's not making sense," Subner stated blandly.

"I have to defeat the Deathly Shadow? I have to open the vortex that gets my parents back?"

"Yes," Papa Creola answered. "I'll warn you. I suspect wherever they are, time has moved differently than here."

"Differently how?"

"Differently," he simply said.

"There's the Papa we all know and love." Subner sounded happy for the first time.

Paris shook her head. "Can we back up a bit? How did I become Paris Westbridge instead of Guinevere Paris Beaufont?"

"That's the cleanup we had to do after Liv and Stefan disappeared," Papa Creola explained. "You see, we didn't know how long they'd be stuck in the other dimension. One, two, three days, weeks, or years."

"I was voting for decades," Subner added.

"You're a very unhappy person, aren't you?" Paris needled.

He nodded.

"Anyway, the vortex was new to us then, so we simply made a contingency plan," Papa Creola stated. "We had a child that the Deathly Shadow wanted, and it had taken two Warriors from the House of Fourteen to protect it. We had a family and set of friends who would do anything to help, but the whole lot were blabbermouths. So I did the only thing I could—"

"You silenced them with a spell," Paris guessed.

THE MYSTERIOUS LOST CHILD

"I had to," he answered. "Otherwise, they could have let a ton of things accidentally slip. Or they could have looked you up, checked up on you, done anything to ruin the witness protection program I put you into."

"Tell me more about that," Paris urged.

"Well, I knew that the Deathly Shadow was looking for a child who was born to two Warriors for the House of Fourteen and was both magician and fairy," Papa Creola stated. "That had been your parents' problem all along. They didn't deviate from the prophecy."

Seeing the look of offense on her face, Papa Creola waved Paris off. "Oh, come on. I can criticize."

"It's why I like him," Subner stated.

"Shocking," Paris remarked.

"Anyway, if your parents would have changed from the prophecy, I think the Deathly Shadow might not have been able to find you, but that's not entirely supported," he explained. "You see, I had to orchestrate a lot to keep you protected all this time, and as soon as it broke down, the entire house of cards fell at once, making you vulnerable, so I'm not sure there was anything your parents could have done differently."

"Why did I live with Uncle John?" Paris asked.

"Well, he was your mother's closest living non-blood relative," Papa Creola answered. "I knew that I needed to hide you, but not with a House of Fourteen family where the Deathly Shadow would expect to look for you. And not with another Beaufont like Sophia."

"So that took care of two of my only blood relatives on the Beaufont side," Paris stated.

"Yes," Papa Creola affirmed. "John was a Mortal Seven for the House of Fourteen, and in being one, he was powerful and just. He had certain advantages that protected you that even a member of your father's family, the Ludwigs couldn't offer. Finally, he was the person your mother had left you with last when she and Stefan went after the Deathly Shadow, thinking they were taking it down for a final time, so I felt that was who she wanted you with."

For the very first time, something occurred to Paris. "You cared about my mom?"

"He didn't," Subner stated.

"Very much so," Papa Creola said at the same time. "I never told her, and I'm not sure I would ever, but she was unlike anyone I've ever met, and I've met them all."

"So you put me with Uncle John because my mom liked him," Paris mused on the notion. "A family friend..."

"Her first employer," Papa Creola corrected. "You've already guessed it. He owned the electronics repair shop below Clark's place, which was actually Liv's place."

Paris' eyes widened with satisfaction at the idea that she guessed that one right. "It makes sense that Uncle John repaired electronics because he's always tinkering with stuff around the place. But wait, you said that Uncle John was a Mortal Seven. He's a fairy."

Papa Creola shook his head. "I've had to do a lot more work on this than others to make it work. It was crucial that the Deathly Shadow not find you and to do that, we needed to hide you. So you became a full fairy. Not associated with a Beaufont or Ludwig or the House or anything connected to your old life. We moved you and John to Roya Lane, and he became the detective for the Fairy Law Enforcement Agency, which didn't exist before that. It was to police magic on Roya Lane, and from that moment forward, no House members could step foot there."

"So I'd never meet Clark or Sophia," Paris guessed.

Papa Creola nodded. "I didn't do it to be cruel. I did it because I needed you not to know who you were. The spell is very simple and very complex. The moment you knew who you were, the Deathly Shadow would as well. Until then, you could waltz right in front of him, and he wouldn't know the difference."

"But one hint of my real life..."

"And it would all come rushing back to you." Papa Creola finished her sentence. "Which is why I spelled you not to wonder who you were, where you came from, want to read, care about your heritage, or a whole host of other things."

"Wow, I think it's my turn to say you really freaked up my life," Paris remarked.

"Waah! Give the baby her bottle," Subner said with no inflection.

Ignoring him, which was getting easier, Paris focused on Father Time. "Again, Uncle John isn't a fairy. So how did he get this new job on Roya Lane?"

"He's a mortal," Papa Creola stated. "This next part I have to tell you is a little harder because it illustrates how everyone reconstructed their lives for you. For me. For the world. For your parents. To make things better. To stop the Deathly Shadow. To bring Liv and Stefan back. It's all a part of the same mission, believe it or not. You and your parents and me and even fairy godmother college all share a common thread in this."

"I don't know about you all, but I'm bored," Subner stated. "Anyone up for takeout?"

"Go on," Paris urged.

"Chinese, maybe?" Subner offered. "Maybe Greek. I don't know...."

"Shut your face," she scolded, then refocused on Papa Creola. "Tell me what happened."

"Uncle John was the right person to raise you. As a Mortal Seven he could get onto Roya Lane," Papa Creola stated. "Also he was with Alicia, a magitech scientist and magician. She helped to construct his fairy wings, which are magitech when and if you ever see them."

"Wait, but she's married to Uncle Clark," Paris stated.

"Because when Liv disappeared there were no more Beaufonts left to fill her spot," Papa Creola explained. "So it was either have the Beaufont name leave the House of Fourteen or have Clark marry someone. We didn't know how long Liv and Stefan would be gone. We hoped that it would be a few days, then a few weeks, maybe a few years…"

"Spoiler alert," Subner cut in. "Fifteen years later…"

"So Alicia, Uncle John's girlfriend, married my real uncle to keep the Beaufonts in the House of Fourteen," Paris filled.

Papa Creola nodded. "Similar concessions happened to fill your father's role as Warrior with Fane Popa-Ludwig. That's what we had to do."

"Then none of them could talk to each other or tell me anything because then I'd know the truth," Paris stated, but it all felt like a lie at this point.

Papa Creola nodded though. "Paris, it was complex magic, meant to keep you safe, but please know this has never been about you."

"How can I think such a thing?" she retorted.

He shook her off. "If the Deathly Shadow absorbs your unique essence, it will be powerful enough to overpower me and this world. Your parents sacrificed everything to protect you and in doing so, protect our planet. I only hope you're as careful since you know the truth. *And* know what's at stake, now that you know the entire truth, as only I could tell you."

"I only want to know one thing at this point," she said with determination.

"What kind of side sauces they serve with the fries?" Subner cut in.

Paris shook her head. "How do we go about taking down the Deathly Shadow and getting my parents back? You say it relies on me, and I'm ready. Let's do this."

Papa Creola nodded, looking pleased although calm. "I'm glad to hear that. Now that you know the truth, we can start to lay the groundwork, but I'll warn you it takes time."

She sighed. "Why? Why can't we just kill him and be done?"

"Because it's not a video game," Subner retorted.

"Because the Deathly Shadow will take precision and strategy to take it down," Papa Creola answered. "Your parents thought they had the answer and he deceived them. This time, we have to be even farther ahead of him or pay the price."

"Then," Paris began, excitement building in her voice although she hadn't allowed it. "Then we can bring back my parents?"

"We will see," he cautioned. "They're in a different place. I can't assure you that they've aged the same as us. I know nothing of it. But yes, if we can do this right, we can defeat the Deathly Shadow and bring Liv and Stefan back."

Paris smiled and looked up at Subner for the first time. "Order some nachos. We're celebrating an inevitable win."

CHAPTER SEVENTY-ONE

Nothing made sense to Paris anymore. Yet, everything suddenly did. She knew who she was and why she was a halfling—because of a genie. That was stupid, but she'd deal with that part later. She also knew why an uncle she wasn't related to had raised her, why her blood family couldn't talk to her, and why Alicia asked strange questions.

Still, none of it answered the question she really wanted to know. How was she like Liv Beaufont? Everyone kept saying that, but Paris couldn't understand it. Not until she met this mother of hers, and that wouldn't happen until she brought her and her father back. All of that would happen, but not until she figured out how to defeat a baddie who scared Father Time, who she'd met— none of that was computing quite yet, but it would. Or it wouldn't, and she'd go and live in the Serenity Garden as a deranged AI. That was an option, right?

Paris' world had turned upside down again, but she wasn't giving up. Not even close. She was going all-in. Not only would she sign on to defeat this Deathly Shadow and bring back her parents, but she would also fix this love problem at Happily Ever After College because as far as she was concerned, it was the same.

Love was always the problem. Not enough of it and you got this black hole of evil. Too much of it and you got a bunch of Beaufonts. *Oh, what a problem to have,* she mused as she stepped through the portal that Papa Creola had created back to Happily Ever After College.

She'd expected to find Faraday there or somewhere nearby but he wasn't, and Paris worried for him. She knew he didn't belong at fairy godmother college, yet she missed him already.

Shrugging this off, she made her way to the headmistress' office, remembering that Willow wanted a meeting with her to review the Rose and McGregor case.

To her surprise, Mae Ling was there and looking like her old self. So was Christine, looking like her usual self, which meant no red hair since she was wearing the blue gown.

"Oh, Mae Ling, how are you—"

"Recovering from that stomach bug?" Mae Ling supplied. "I'm fine."

The look on the fairy godmother's face told Paris to shush her face quickly, and that word shouldn't spread that she'd been injured.

Paris simply nodded. "Well, I'm glad, and thanks for your efforts in the fight."

"Against deadly stomach bugs." Christine held up a victorious fist. "Anyway, shall we discuss the Amelia Rose and Grayson McGregor case?"

"Yes." Paris finally felt confident.

"After doing the investigation," Christine began, "I have absolutely, positively, no idea how to get these two together. They're completely at odds. Engaged to other people. Going in opposite directions."

Paris held up her hand and offered her friend a polite smile that she hoped said, "Shut up."

THE MYSTERIOUS LOST CHILD

"I think what Christine is saying is that things look bad," Paris began. "We wouldn't know where to begin, but the investigation told us three important things."

"It did?" Willow said.

"It did?" Mae Ling repeated.

"It did?" Christine echoed.

Paris nodded. "We know how to do everything critical to get those two together, which we all agree is crucial."

"Definitely," Willow agreed. "So what is it?"

"We have to," Paris began, "take down both their corporations, ruin their engagements, and lock them up together."

Christine laughed as if this was brand-new information to her. "How hard can that be?"

"Not hard at all," Paris stated with confidence. "I have a full plan and have detailed it here, but it will take time."

She passed out a report to the three, and as they reviewed it, she reveled in the way they nodded and smiled, seeming to enjoy the convoluted strategy she'd put together. It required many moving parts, but Paris thought that was necessary because Amelia and Grayson were past the stage of being thrown together at a train station. They needed something that made them stick together.

Willow lowered her report first. "I think this is edgy and different and something we've never attempted."

"I think we should do it," Mae Ling stated on the heels of that.

"Does that mean I get to participate?" Christine asked.

"Absolutely." Willow smiled, making Paris' plan a real one that would see the light of day...as soon as she got some real sleep.

CHAPTER SEVENTY-TWO

Paris tucked into bed, feeling satisfied, full of answers, and also really lonely. Lying in her canopy bed, she threw her arms down at her sides and sighed.

"If it makes you feel any better, I'll share my cheese sandwich with you," a squeaky voice said from her sock drawer.

Paris bolted upright in disbelief. "Faraday, is that you?"

The squirrel poked his head from the drawer, his familiar brown eyes blinking at her. "Of course. Who else would it be?"

"How did you get there?" she asked. "I left you in Santa Monica."

"Honestly, I don't remember. An hour ago, I was rummaging through a museum's exhibits, and this guy with stringy hair materialized and was like, 'you need to be there when she goes to sleep.' Then I showed up here."

Paris snuggled more into her blankets. "That was Father Time."

"Oh?" Faraday mused. "I always pictured him taller and with a beard and probably not wearing a graphic t-shirt."

"His assistant is the worst," Paris offered.

"The best always have the worst assistants," Faraday agreed.

"So you're back?" She grew excited.

"And ready to help," he confirmed. "What all have you learned?"

"You have no idea," Paris replied. "It's a lot. It changes everything. It means we have a lot of work to do on multiple fronts. Are you up for it?"

"Is that even a question?" He sounded sincere. "Can I get a nap first though? I had a big day running from that wind thing in Santa Monica."

Paris giggled. "Yeah, I could use a nap too."

"Oh good, did you have a fun adventure too?"

"I'd say." Paris felt giddy about the prospects of rescuing her parents and fixing love and helping Father Time and finally having a life when all the adventures were over—if they were ever over. First, she would sleep and rest up for the experiences to surely come.

"Good night Faraday. Thanks for going along with me and telling me to run."

"You're welcome, and thanks for running and surviving," he stated. "The world is a better place with you in it."

Paris smiled, feeling like she needed to make sure that statement was forever true. Her parents had sacrificed everything for that one idea, believing the world was better with her in it. Now she needed to prove it and bring them back. Then bring love back. But first, she needed to sleep.

Tomorrow she'd save the world...quite literally.

SARAH'S AUTHOR NOTES
APRIL 5, 2021

Thank you a ton for reading! Your support means more than I can ever say. Ever. However, you know that I'll try and put it into words. Your support is the axis to my Earth. Your support is the wind carrying seeds, spreading them across lands. Your support is like a sturdy branch and I'm a sloth napping upon it. Told you'd I'd try and put it into words, you just didn't know they'd be really bad metaphors. Anyway, thank you!

So we all know from the last author notes that Mike doesn't know what the square root of pie is, according to me. I hope you all had a nice laugh at his expense. I often do. It's all fair. He had a big laugh at my expense recently (and often too) when we went to lunch. I know! I finally got an Anderle lunch. He didn't make me pizza, but we will get there, once he improves his skillz.

So we're at lunch and I'm telling MA's lovely wife about how I wouldn't drive to West Hollywood for a date but will now fly across the globe for the Scotsman and Mike is crying with laughter, pointing at me across the table and saying, "This is not the girl from a couple of years ago."

That's true.

And then Judith is like, "I don't blame you. West Hollywood is far." She's right…

That wasn't the only time that Mike laughed at me during lunch. He and Judith bought a Cookie Monster milkshake and shared it with Lydia. It was huuuuge with donuts and cupcakes and syrup. I've played that trick before on people, buying their children indulgent treats and then waving goodbye as I hightailed it away before the sugar rush hit. In all seriousness, it was really fun and it's always nice when we can get together. Usually it's in Bali or London, so Las Vegas seemed so normal.

Let me tell you about the hilarity that was me, writing this book. You get to laugh. I might still be crying but in time, I'll laugh…surely. So on the current release schedule I have four weeks to write these books . Sounds easy, right? Well, despite what you all think, I have a life, sort of. My daughter is homeschooled through next August. It's March currently. She's 9 and common core math is stupid. I'm pretty certain educators got together (keep in mind my original profession was in education and curriculum) and they were like, how can we really make hard working parents stress the freak out? Let's teach math in alien ways. Cool.

Thanks jerks…

And to further support the idea of me having a life, I have the Scotsman in Scotland and then friends and then a hobby or two. Just kidding. I don't have a hobby. That's cute that you think I could have one. I do Pilates but that's more like a bad relationship where I keep coming back for punishment and abuse.

Anyway, my point is that I usually slack and take care of stuff/people I've neglected for two weeks on my deadline, giving me two more weeks to write a book. I only need two weeks to write a book, I've found.

I had over two weeks to write this book, and therefore took Lydia, my daughter, on a hike. We are walking down a steep slope and I'm like, "be careful and don't slip." Can you guess who actually slipped? Me... And even though I know better, as I was falling on my butt, I put my hand down to save my backside. And I didn't know until later that I tore the tendons in my wrist. So I go to Urgent Care and the doc says, "you can't type for two weeks..."

I had to inform this deranged doc that I had only two weeks to write a book. And so I did. Wine might have helped. I couldn't wear my brace when writing, so I had to muster through the pain. And that's what I do for you all. And also for me.

I love this book more than the first. That never happens. But the evolution and the characters were really fun. And I guess, my own experiences of overcoming challenges played into it. I wasn't late turning in this book. I was one day early. And as I write these notes I'm headed to the airport to fly to see the Scotsman who I haven't seen in five months. My friends are great. But if one more person says, "Have fun on your trip" as I set off to collect a piece of my heart, I might come unglued.

This isn't me on a campaign, but love isn't tourism. It's essential. Yes, we will have fun, but that's never been what it was about. When you realize that someone owns a part of your heart, every day without them is torture. Being reunited isn't fun. It's healing.

I guess it felt like I was going to the hospital to have my heart repaired after five months, and well-meaning people are like, "Have fun." I'm not going to Disney World. I have to take three COVID tests, while having a vaccine, fill out a boat load of forms and take three flights to get there and quarantine the entire time. This isn't a vacation. So if anything, this is my attempts to educate people who think love is tourism, that it's not. My friends mean well and I get it. But that's the tough part that we've dealt with. My friends can go to Costco to buy bean dip, but I can't see the guy who makes me feel whole.

I'll stop now but not before saying that the Anderles have been more than supportive in this all, knowing how tough this was for us. And because of that, I'll make no final tease about Bird Killer. Oh, I guess I just did. But that's it. Promise.

Much peace and love,
Tiny Ninja

MICHAEL'S AUTHOR NOTES
APRIL 7, 2021

Thank you for reading both this story and our author notes!

Tiny Ninja is my totem at times. There, I've said it.

I've always had admiration for those who can say stuff with no filter (or little filter), and whatever they said, it's fun.

Sara is like that. She has a way of metaphoring. It's a word; I just penciled it into my version of the dictionary. Now, I have to figure out a way to erase that @#@# off my screen.

Anyway, her comment about her relationship with Pilates cracks me up. Let's connect a healthy effort with a painful relationship situation. Oh, and it works because I know ALL healthy exercise should be connected to a painful relationship.

I hate physical exercise.

I have an unhealthy relationship with Coca-Cola. I love it, regardless of how round it is making my body. Now, if someone would make the dopamine receptors in my mind fire like the 4th of July whenever I exercise, I'd be Mr. Universe.

Well, perhaps not him because that means all clothes would have to be replaced, and I hate shopping.

...Ok, I can't keep writing like Sarah. My brain hurts, just trying to keep up with her Ping-Pong ball back-and-forth staccato flashes of inspiration and musings.

I admit, the sugar milkshake Judith and I had was a dirty rotten trick to play on Sarah that day. We allowed Lydia to grab whatever sugary delights were on the mug or plate with full knowledge of what it might set off.

Or at least I hoped it would set off.

I admire everything Tiny Ninja™ does for her daughter and the amazing efforts she accomplishes, including finishing a book with torn metacarpal tenda-ligaments. Or whatever it was.

Just for the record, I told her we could adjust some stuff to help her, and she told me to stuff it. She wouldn't listen to her doctor.

I make that statement so that in the future, I have a written record I can believe. Trust me, I can imagine Sarah giving me a line of...something...that would have me believe I was a ruthless publisher.

I'm a sucker that way.

Here is a snippet of how that conversation would go:

Sarah: Actually, you told me on my second book of Paris Beaufont you didn't care if I had hurt all of my torn metacarpal tenda-ligaments. I had to get the book finished.

Mike: Really? I don't think that's what I would have done.

Sarah: Yes, I was there. It was hurtful, Anderle. You were a real jerk about the whole thing.

Mike: But... That just doesn't seem like me. I'm really sorry. I can't believe what an @#@%# I was to you! How could you even keep working with me when I was a jerk like that?

Sarah: Do you feel bad?

Mike: Of course!

Sarah: Good. Because you didn't say it, and you had better *never* give Lydia sugar for lunch again, or I'll make you feel worse. <<POOF!>> Tiny Ninja™ disappears in a cloud of smoke.

Mike: *Dammit, Noffke!*
Have a fantastic week.

Ad Aeternitatem,

Michael

ACKNOWLEDGMENTS

SARAH NOFFKE

I have so many people to thank who make this all possible. Firstly, thanks to Mike, who really pushes me to be a better writer, coming up with the best ideas, not just the really good ones. We work together pretty well, I'd say. I wonder what he'd say... Anyway, MA gave me the opportunity to write with LBMPN a few years ago and it's been life changing. He's very supportive and really cares. Thanks Bird Killer.

A huge thank you to the LBMPN team who work tirelessly so that I have less stress. Thanks to Steve and Kelly for making my life easier and being on top of everything. Thanks to Tracey and Lynne for fixing all my editing mistakes. A big thank you to the JIT team whose feedback at the 11th hour before publishing is invaluable. Thank you to my alpha readers Juergen and Martin. Thank you to everyone who makes getting the books to the reader possible. I really can't do this without you. And you make it so much more fun.

Thank you to my daughter, Lydia, who inspires my stories over and over again. She's my muse and we are always discussing story. She's an avid reader and listens to the Liv Beaufont series at night and reads the Sophia Beaufont books with me before bed. She also reads other authors, which I guess is okay. But my point is that she's supportive of me in so many ways. I need to stay immersed in this universe and remember all the details. There are 12 book in each series so there's a lot to remember. And Lydia loves my stories and then also supports me by listening and reading them so I can keep crafting. But also, she puts up with me when I go all psycho pants during a big crunch of a deadline. I will be the first to admit that I'm pretty intense a day or two before a book is due. And she always just smiles and says, "Mommy, you can do it."

Thank you to my family, the Scotsman and all my friends. You all are always so supportive of me and for that, I'm infinitely grateful. I really couldn't do this without the encouragement of those I love. On the really tough writing days, the Scotsman points out all the things that I don't see, like my dedication to the craft or how much readers are enjoying the books. I don't know what I did to have the most loving and thoughtful people in the world in my corner, but I'm going to do everything to keep them and hopefully keep making them proud.

And finally, thank you to you the reader. Without you I wouldn't be able to do what I love. Your support means so much to me and my family. Thank you from the bottom of my heart.

Love,
Tiny Ninja

BOOKS BY SARAH NOFFKE

Sarah Noffke writes YA and NA science fiction, fantasy, paranormal and urban fantasy. In addition to being an author, she is a mother, podcaster and professor. Noffke holds a Masters of Management and teaches college business/writing courses. Most of her students have no idea that she toils away her hours crafting fictional characters. www.sarahnoffke.com

Check out other work by Sarah author here.

Ghost Squadron:

Formation #1:
   Kill the bad guys. Save the Galaxy. All in a hard day's work.
   After ten years of wandering the outer rim of the galaxy, Eddie Teach is a man without a purpose. He was one of the toughest pilots in the Federation, but now he's just a regular guy, getting into bar fights and making a difference wherever he can. It's not the same as flying a ship and saving colonies, but it'll have to do.

That is, until General Lance Reynolds tracks Eddie down and offers him a job. There are bad people out there, plotting terrible things, killing innocent people, and destroying entire colonies. **Someone has to stop them.**

Eddie, along with the genetically-enhanced combat pilot Julianna Fregin and her trusty E.I. named Pip, must recruit a diverse team of specialists, both human and alien. They'll need to master their new Q-Ship, one of the most powerful strike ships ever constructed. And finally, they'll have to stop a faceless enemy so powerful, it threatens to destroy the entire Federation.

All in a day's work, right?

Experience this exciting military sci-fi saga and the latest addition to the expanded Kurtherian Gambit Universe. If you're a fan of Mass Effect, Firefly, or Star Wars, you'll love this riveting new space opera.

NOTE: If cursing is a problem, then this might not be for you.

Check out the entire series here.

The Precious Galaxy Series:

Corruption #1

A new evil lurks in the darkness.

After an explosion, the crew of a battlecruiser mysteriously disappears.

Bailey and Lewis, complete strangers, find themselves suddenly onboard the damaged ship. Lewis hasn't worked a case in years, not since the final one broke his spirit and his bank account. The last thing Bailey remembers is preparing to take down a fugitive on Onyx Station.

Mysteries are harder to solve when there's no evidence left behind.

Bailey and Lewis don't know how they got onboard *Ricky Bobby* or why. However, they quickly learn that whatever was responsible for the explosion and disappearance of the crew is still on the ship.

Monsters are real and what this one can do changes everything.

The new team bands together to discover what happened and how to fight the monster lurking in the bottom of the battlecruiser.

Will they find the missing crew? Or will the monster end them all?

The Soul Stone Mage Series:

House of Enchanted #1:

The Kingdom of Virgo has lived in peace for thousands of years...until now.

The humans from Terran have always been real assholes to the witches of Virgo. Now a silent war is brewing, and the timing couldn't be worse. Princess Azure will soon be crowned queen of the Kingdom of Virgo.

In the Dark Forest a powerful potion-maker has been murdered.

Charmsgood was the only wizard who could stop a deadly virus plaguing Virgo. He also knew about the devastation the people from Terran had done to the forest.

Azure must protect her people. Mend the Dark Forest. Create alliances with savage beasts. No biggie, right?

But on coronation day everything changes. Princess Azure isn't who she thought she was and that's a big freaking problem.

Welcome to The Revelations of Oriceran. Check out the entire series here.

The Lucidites Series:

Awoken, #1:

Around the world humans are hallucinating after sleepless nights.

In a sterile, underground institute the forecasters keep reporting the same events.

And in the backwoods of Texas, a sixteen-year-old girl is about to be caught up in a fierce, ethereal battle.

Meet Roya Stark. She drowns every night in her dreams, spends her hours reading classic literature to avoid her family's ridicule, and is prone to premonitions—which are becoming more frequent. And now her dreams are filled with strangers offering to reveal what she has always wanted to know: Who is she? That's the question that haunts her, and she's about to find out. But will Roya live to regret learning the truth?

Stunned, #2

Revived, #3

The Reverians Series:

Defects, #1:

In the happy, clean community of Austin Valley, everything appears to be perfect. Seventeen-year-old Em Fuller, however, fears something is askew. Em is one of the new generation of Dream Travelers. For some reason, the gods have not seen fit to gift all of them with their expected special abilities. Em is a Defect —one of the unfortunate Dream Travelers not gifted with a psychic power. Desperate to do whatever it takes to earn her gift, she endures painful daily injections along with commands from her overbearing, loveless father. One of the few bright spots in her life is the return of a friend she had thought dead—but with his return comes the knowledge of a shocking, unforgivable truth. The society Em thought was protecting her has actually been betraying her, but she has no idea how to break away from its authority without hurting everyone she loves.

Rebels, #2

Warriors, #3

Vagabond Circus Series:

Suspended, #1:
When a stranger joins the cast of Vagabond Circus—a circus that is run by Dream Travelers and features real magic—mysterious events start happening. The once orderly grounds of the circus become riddled with hidden threats. And the ringmaster realizes not only are his circus and its magic at risk, but also his very life.

Vagabond Circus caters to the skeptics. Without skeptics, it would close its doors. This is because Vagabond Circus runs for two reasons and only two reasons: first and foremost to provide the lost and lonely Dream Travelers a place to be illustrious. And secondly, to show the nonbelievers that there's still magic in the world. If they believe, then they care, and if they care, then they don't destroy. They stop the small abuse that day-by-day breaks down humanity's spirit. If Vagabond Circus makes one skeptic believe in magic, then they halt the cycle, just a little bit. They allow a little more love into this world. That's Dr. Dave Raydon's mission. And that's why this ringmaster recruits. That's why he directs. That's why he puts on a show that makes people question their beliefs. He wants the world to believe in magic once again.

Paralyzed, #2
Released, #3

Ren Series:

Ren: The Man Behind the Monster, #1:
Born with the power to control minds, hypnotize others, and read thoughts, Ren Lewis, is certain of one thing: God made a mistake. No one should be born with so much power. A monster awoke in him the same year he received his gifts. At ten years old.

A prepubescent boy with the ability to control others might merely abuse his powers, but Ren allowed it to corrupt him. And since he can have and do anything he wants, Ren should be happy. However, his journey teaches him that harboring so much power doesn't bring happiness, it steals it. Once this realization sets in, Ren makes up his mind to do the one thing that can bring his tortured soul some peace. He must kill the monster.

Note This book is NA and has strong language, violence and sexual references.

Ren: God's Little Monster, #2
Ren: The Monster Inside the Monster, #3
Ren: The Monster's Adventure, #3.5
Ren: The Monster's Death

Olento Research Series:

Alpha Wolf, #1:
Twelve men went missing.

Six months later they awake from drug-induced stupors to find themselves locked in a lab.

And on the night of a new moon, eleven of those men, possessed by new—and inhuman—powers, break out of their prison and race through the streets of Los Angeles until they disappear one by one into the night.

Olento Research wants its experiments back. Its CEO, Mika Lenna, will tear every city apart until he has his werewolves imprisoned once again. He didn't undertake a huge risk just to lose his would-be assassins.

However, the Lucidite Institute's main mission is to save the world from injustices. Now, it's Adelaide's job to find these mutated men and protect them and society, and fast. Already around the nation, wolflike men are being spotted. Attacks on innocent women are happening. And then, Adelaide realizes what her next step must be: She has to find the alpha wolf first. Only once she's located him can she stop whoever is behind this experiment to create wild beasts out of human beings.

Lone Wolf, #2
Rabid Wolf, #3
Bad Wolf, #4

BOOKS BY MICHAEL ANDERLE

For a complete list of books by Michael Anderle, please visit:

www.lmbpn.com/ma-books/

All LMBPN Audiobooks are Available at Audible.com and iTunes

To see all LMBPN audiobooks, including those written by Michael Anderle please visit:

www.lmbpn.com/audible

[illegible]

[illegible]

[illegible]/ebooks/

[illegible] Audible.com and iTunes

[illegible]

[illegible]/audible

CONNECT WITH THE AUTHORS

Connect with Sarah and sign up for her email list here:

http://www.sarahnoffke.com/connect/

Michael Anderle Social

Website: http://lmbpn.com

Email List: http://lmbpn.com/email/

Social Media:

https://www.facebook.com/LMBPNPublishing

https://twitter.com/MichaelAnderle

https://www.instagram.com/lmbpn_publishing/

https://www.bookbub.com/authors/michael-anderle

Made in United States
Troutdale, OR
06/28/2024

20887383R00196